Sugar Honey Iced Tea

A Novel

Kaya

ARCHWAY PUBLISHING

Archway Publishing books may be ordered
through booksellers or by contacting:

Archway Publishing
1663 Liberty Drive
Bloomington, IN 47403
www.archwaypublishing.com
1 (888) 242-5904

ISBN: 978-1-4808-4090-4 (sc)
ISBN: 978-1-4808-4091-1 (e)

Library of Congress Control Number: 2016920059

Print information available on the last page.

Archway Publishing rev. date: 06/26/2017

Contents

1
Story of Her Life

"*I* wonder if aliens are watching us right now."

Leilani giggled. "I'm sure we have a better chance of NASA versus *aliens,* Moon."

Her friend smirked. "Yeah, they're claiming to be up there researching space when they're really zooming in on us and getting off."

She laughed, "Girl, *wow.* You are silly."

Camille sighed, "Oh my God, why is this the highlight of our week? Being thirty *sucks*!" she groaned.

She chuckled at her friend and Camille scoffed, "Seriously, did you ever think you'd hate your life? We're supposed to be living it up, Lei! Tearing up Miami, Hot-Lanta, Jamaica... Not doing the same boring shit every day."

Leilani sipped the cocoa-flavored vodka martini and took in a deep breath, "I don't hate being in my thirties. I just hate certain parts of it."

Camille laughed. "Girl, please, you *hate* your life. I, on the other hand, just hate certain parts of it. And that's only cause' I have a well-paying job and no babies pulling on my wallet or my breasts."

"Implants, you mean?"

They both laughed and Camille jiggled her D plastics with a small arch in her back.

"Hey, if it wasn't for your referral to Dr. Magic, I'd still be getting mistaken for your little brother."

Leilani shook her head with a grin, taking another sip of the cocoa flavored nectar. She gazed at the sunset and relished in the cool breeze against her exposed skin. Nude sun bathing on the deck of her beach house probably wasn't the best idea since her childless and lesbian neighbors were less than one hundred feet away, but this was the perfect spot to keep her Brazilian golden complexion intact.

Her best friend, Camille, was as pale as they came. Her nickname, "Moon," perfectly aspired to match her milky white tone identical to that of the moonlight; completely resistant to the sun's beams no matter how long or often she lay out in its warmth. The soft jazz music playing from the surround sound speakers installed in Leilani's deck only made this feel more like a vacation getaway than her own home.

"I really don't hate my life, Moon," Leilani stopped for a moment, hearing footsteps edging their way towards them. "Man alert," she warned as her friend threw her robe across her nudity.

Darnell stepped into view, his eyes glancing down at Leilani's naked body, no change in his expression. He reached over and placed his hand atop Leilani's chaise, "I'm headed to the gym," he glanced over at Camille. "What time are you planning on cooking dinner?"

Why can't you cook dinner? I worked today too! Leilani swallowed down the sarcastic reply.

"In about an hour or so," she said instead.

"What are you cooking for dinner?" he asked.

Camille glanced over at her friend who was calm even though Camille knew Leilani was becoming irritated.

Leilani's gaze remained on the sunset. "I'm not sure; probably lamb chops and couscous with a veggie."

"Cool, I'll be back in about two hours. Dinner should be ready by then." And just as quickly as he entered, he was gone.

"Chef Boyardee to the rescue," Camille muttered, gulping down the rest of her martini. "Let me get out of your face so you can get to your *wifely duties*."

Leilani sighed, looking over at her friend. "As I was saying…I don't hate my life."

Camille looked at her. "I know you don't, Lei," she replied.

"I just hate being married to *him*."

Camille laughed and stood, throwing on her hot pink scrubs. "I don't disagree," she shrugged, "Maybe he won't make it back from the gym tonight—"

"Don't say that!" Leilani exclaimed.

Camille laughed. "I'm not saying I hope his ass *dies*. I'm just suggesting, that…well, maybe another unsuspecting and naïve woman will take him off your hands," she said innocently with another shrug.

Leilani sucked her teeth. "These women nowadays will spot that fake romantic, caring and loving routine a mile away – especially women *our* age."

Camille raised her eyebrows. "Yeah, true. You were younger…"

"And I was a silly rabbit," Leilani said softly, taking another sip of her drink. "Believing in fairytales."

Her best friend watched Leilani for a second. "Well, I'll see you tomorrow in the office?" she asked.

"Bright and early," Leilani replied cheerfully. "Just don't forget to have that new patient file on my desk first thing. I have to meet with that couple at nine. And we *both* know how you operate on CP time."

Camille smiled. "It's already on your desk, *smarty*. I dropped it there before you were driving out the parking lot," she slid her purse strap on her left shoulder, "Now, for that; I get an extra thirty minutes on my lunch break at your expense."

They both laughed. "Go home so you can be on time for work for once," Leilani said as she stood and finished her martini.

"At least playing the doting little house wife won't be on my agenda tonight," Camille teased.

Leilani tossed the remaining sprinkles of her drink at her friend. "Get out my *house* and go back to your *apartment*," she said with a smile.

"*Bye*," Camille sang with a grin, dodging the droplets as she strolled to her Camry.

Leilani sighed, reality sinking back into her pores as the sun disappeared behind the mountain range.

"Here we go," Leilani said, standing and making her way into the kitchen to start dinner.

Another day, another dollar. Leilani jotted notes on the notepad and glanced over at her clock.

9:15 AM. It was nearing time for the first appointment of the day. As stated, the patient profile was sitting on her desk as soon as she walked into her chilly office. Leilani reminded her receptionist to turn down the AC in the practice for what seemed to be the hundredth time this week. She didn't enjoy the cold and being a native of Brazil, she always wondered why so many enjoyed sitting in a room that's nearly forty degrees cooler than it is outside.

The humidity was quite a nuisance at times, but Leilani was born in the heat and always enjoyed being warm rather than needing to throw on long sleeves and sweaters while indoors if she could control it. She was warm-blooded by nature and her compassionate side always drove her to shut the vents in her office to accommodate the battle between her and her staff.

There was a soft tap on her door and Camille entered, looking nothing less than professional in the new tailored scrubs that Leilani purchased for her team.

"I have Mr. and Mrs. Worthington checked in for their 9:30. Do you want me to bring them in now?" Camille asked.

Their interactions at work were a complete 180° from "off the clock" buddy time and Leilani made sure that it always stayed that way. She did not partake in non-work related conversations with Camille and even though she was her best friend of ten plus years, the only personal time they had was if they took a lunch together. Of which, at most, it was off the premises and at a café or restaurant.

Leilani was a strict supervisor. As the successful owner of her fertility and OB-GYN practice, she could not afford to have ill commentary about how she ran her practice. Above all, with whom she chose to hire and she was quick to fire a friend as the next person she knew nothing more than what was in their job application and background check. Camille knew this and respected her role as Lead MA in the office.

"I will be ready for them in five. Just finishing up a few notes," Leilani replied, finishing up the last of her commentary.

> *Male, age 31. No history of infections or diseases.*
> *PP = 10+*
> *Female, age 34. Previous history of abnormal pap smears. Negative colp. PP = 13+*
> *TTC +2 years.*

There was another soft knock on her door as Camille entered.

"Dr. Mathews, here are Mr. and Mrs. Worthington," she said with a slight wink.

That was their classified signal if the male partner of the couples was attractive. Leilani smiled as she stood, walking towards the door.

"Thank you, Ms. Campbell," she said as her best friend stepped aside to allow the couple to enter.

Leilani took in a deep breath, composing herself for this couple's initial consultation. She smiled at the young, shorter woman with bright blond hair as she entered the room. Upon visual inspection, Dr. Leilani presumed she weighed no more than a buck five and was overly athletic. She could see from her stained bleached teeth that she was an avid coffee drinker and from her gums that she was an occasional smoker. Leilani shook her hand, greeting her.

Mr. Worthington stepped into view after his wife and Leilani took in a quick deep breath. He was a handsome man, quite attractive; his long legs drove him to stand a few inches above six feet and clearly equally if not more athletic than his counterpart. From the looks of his mouth, he was neither a smoker nor drinker – his teeth shiny and nearly as white as the paper of their patient profile. His eyes were a sapphire blue and his short hair a dark brown.

"Please, have a seat," Leilani said and walked over to her desk, picking up the manila folder and pen as she made her way back to the seating area in her office, facing the two of them.

Mr. Worthington looked uncomfortable, his eyes scanning Leilani from hair to toe as his wife sat next to him on the plush sofa with a huge grin on her face. Mrs. Worthington was excited, ready to burst to say the least. Leilani could see that her husband did not share the same sentiments, or, he was uncomfortable with having a non-Caucasian woman treat them. He did indeed appear shocked when he laid eyes on her brown skin. Neither of which, she could put her finger on at the time. But regardless, Leilani remained professional with all of her patients – racist or otherwise. Leilani crossed her lengthy legs.

"So, I've reviewed your profile and I believe that we should run some additional tests to rule out any other fertility issues that the two of you may be having."

Mrs. Worthington raised her hand with a nervous grin. "I-I have a question."

Her drawl was ever present in her tone. There was no doubt she was a southern girl.

Leilani smiled. "You don't have to raise your hand, Mrs. Worthington. You can speak freely with me," she replied.

The smaller woman laughed nervously. "What-what type of

fertility issues do you mean, Dr. Mathews? We've been to several other doctors and can't seem to find anything wrong. Now-now you're saying we have to do *more* tests?"

Mr. Worthington shifted in his seat.

"Sophie, we talked about this already..." he muttered, reaching over and touching his wife's thigh.

Leilani glanced at him and he immediately looked away from her. This gorgeous man was uneasy. For what reasons, Leilani had no clue. She gave the couple a reassuring smile.

"Mr. and Mrs. Worthington, I understand your concern. I've read your medical history and I'd just like to run some blood work with you on certain days of the month to confirm if you're ovulating and check your egg reserve. After those results come in, and if they turn out to be in the clear, I plan to prescribe follicle stimulating medication for the first round and put the two of you on a sex schedule."

Mr. Worthington laughed. "A sex schedule?" he asked. He never made eye contact with Leilani. He was looking at the bookcase behind Leilani's head. He looked at his wife. "We are already very active as it is," Mr. Worthington said to his wife.

Leilani looked at him. *Damn, he is fine,* she thought. She softly cleared her throat. *Get it together, girl. He's just attractive and he's married AND about to knock her up*, she silently scolded herself.

"I understand, Mr. Worthington. And yes, a sex schedule. Even though the two of you have a relatively frequent and healthy sex life according to your profile, with fertilization and conception and more specifically, while taking this medication, there are certain days of the month that are strongly encouraged for sexual activity to increase your chances of conception. More plainly said, the two of you just may not be engaging in sexual intercourse on the most needed days of the month to achieve pregnancy. Secondly, you may actually be having *too* much sex. I believe, if your wife's blood work comes back normal and her FSH reserve is good, that your wife will not need medical intervention and the two of you will just have to track for ovulation and have sex specifically on certain days of her cycle," she explained.

Mrs. Worthington quickly sat forward. "We would like to move forward with this. You're the first doctor to mention this treatment plan. Others just recommended in vitro and gave us a good luck pat on the back," she smiled ear to ear, showing off her slightly stained veneers and glanced at her counterpart. "Honey, I believe we are in the right place finally."

Mr. Worthington smirked and shook his head. Leilani took offense to his reaction and gulped, refusing to allow it to change her demeanor.

Leilani smiled and nodded. "I'm glad to hear that. If you would please sign the agreement to move forward with the receptionist, I will send your paperwork to the Charge Nurse. The receptionist will schedule what appointments work for you for the blood work and we will go from there."

Leilani stood and they followed suit.

"It was very nice to meet the two of you. I really look forward to helping you achieve your dreams of having a baby just as I've helped thousands of other couples just like you," she encouraged.

Mrs. Worthington surprisingly hugged Leilani and shook her hand again.

"I am so excited! I really have heard great things about you, Dr. Mathews!" she exclaimed.

"That's always encouraging to hear. I really do look forward to helping you, Mrs. Worthington," Leilani said with a warm smile.

Mr. Worthington rolled his eyes, glancing down at his TagHauer, seemingly annoyed with Leilani's presence. Mrs. Worthington stepped out of the office and waved back at Leilani with a huge grin. Her husband followed behind her, his hand on her lower back; no response, no acknowledgement of Leilani.

Leilani shook her head as she closed her door.

"It's sad that people can't see past complexion and are *still* so hung up on race in this day in age."

"Girl, money is green. Credit cards swipe and as long as you get paid and my paycheck isn't disturbed, I really don't give a shit who cares if I'm black, Cuban, Puerto Rican, Haitian or a zombie."

Leilani laughed, popping a cherry tomato in her mouth. "Moon, he wouldn't even look at me."

"*And*?" Camille shrugged. "Why is that a concern of yours?" she asked.

Leilani looked around at all the passersby and others eating at the restaurant. All were the same race in their groups. Separated. No mixing. She shook her head.

"It's just disappointing, is all. I'm a *damn* good doctor and I've worked my ass off to get through school – to open this practice and I'm *damn* good at what I do – even as a business owner."

Camilla nodded. "I don't disagree with any of that." She sat forward. "But, Lei, if he's a racist, *fuck him*. Besides, you're not married to him. You're treating them. Honestly, you're mostly just treating his wife. The only concern you should have about his tail is if his payments clear. Other than that, shit, he can kick rocks."

Leilani took in a deep breath. "You're right, girl." She smiled. "But, oh my God, was he fine or what?"

"You never lied about that. When I saw him walk in, I wanted to get on the speakerphone and announce that we had a fine ass white man in the building," Camille quickly replied.

They both laughed and Leilani sighed. "Girl, he screws her more than five times a week," Leilani stated, staring down at her salad. She looked up at Camille. "Moon, I'm lucky if I get it five times *a quarter* from Darnell."

She shook her head. "That's cause' he's a selfish bastard," she said, taking a colossal mouthful of her burger.

Leilani squinted. "I take care of so many couples and I watch how they interact. It's nothing like my marriage. Darnell and I are so…separate. Like robots. Plus, the sex isn't even that great when I do get it."

Camilla raised her eyebrows. "Lei, you've been married to Darnell for what? Close to ten years. And he's been distant and cold like this for what? About *twenty* of those years?"

Leilani scoffed. "That's what it feels like. But—"

"But, nothing. Lei, you've been singing this song now for so long, girl. You're beautiful. Amazing. Most would say you're fine as hell. But, with Darnell, it's like he doesn't even give a shit about you. You'd think he was married to a damn goat!"

They both laughed.

"I *do* have my ugmo days," Leilani said.

"Chile'! Save it! The only time I see you looking off is when you're having a bad day. Other than that, you're on point – even if you feel like you look like crap. You're a good ass catch physically and personally. A perfect package," she paused. "Scratch that. That sounded so lesbian. You're ugly."

Leilani laughed with her. "*Aw*, aren't you the sweetest?" Leilani said, "Thanks, Moon."

Camille raised her eyebrows. "I'm serious, Lei. If Darnell doesn't be careful, you're gonna be the one getting scooped up by someone else right from under his tired ass."

Leilani couldn't stop thinking about the dark brown haired and sapphire blue eyed 6'2 sex symbol that graced her office with his presence earlier. Even though she knew Mr. Worthington was obviously abhorred by her presence, she began to fantasize about him. Imagine his lips kissing her from head to toe, his groomed, big hands caressing her. Her mind sketched how his toned body looked beneath the dress shirt and slacks he wore into her office the other day. She knew he had to be good in bed and not lacking in the size department considering how happy go lucky and bouncy Mrs. Worthington's demeanor was.

"Why can't I have that?" she asked softly.

"What?" Camille asked.

Leilani looked at her best friend's dark green eyes. "Why can't I have romance, excitement, and shit...a man that will give it to me on a regular?"

"You get it on the regular, kinda—"

Leilani shook her head. "No, I mean the regular and with some romance. It doesn't hurt to want to feel sexy and attractive... and just *wanted* not just when he needs to get his jollies."

Her best friend stared at Leilani, seeing her demeanor sadden.

"You have sex, how often?" Leilani asked.

Camille grinned. "Counting by myself or actually with a man?"

"Moon, you're a fool," Leilani said and they both laughed. "You know what I mean."

Her best friend sighed. "Well, considering that I'm single and have been single for a few months now since Rasheed the jackass cheat...With him, it was about four to five times a week – even with him stepping out on me. Now? I get it in probably a few times a week."

"With who?!" Leilani exclaimed. "You're single, hoe!"

Camille laughed. "I have my side pieces. Don't sleep on me now. Single doesn't mean celibate."

"And is it good?" Leilani asked, curious.

Camille shrugged slightly. "Not *every* time. But, overall, the shit's good. The guy will be kissing me, talking sexy during it, flirting with me before we get to it," she paused, "*Chile'*, you about to have me speed dial one of my pieces with these questions."

Leilani laughed. "You kiss during sex?" she asked.

Camille looked at her as if Leilani confessed that she was a mass murderer.

"You don't?" she exclaimed.

"No. Darnell and I don't kiss. Never during sex and barely otherwise. We hardly touch each other," Leilani explained.

Camille furrowed her eyebrows in disbelief. "*Girl*, what the hell?" she said loudly, drawing the attention of other customers.

Leilani glanced around the room, embarrassed.

"You two..." Camille stopped and took a moment to compose her thoughts. "Wow. Let me be honest here. From your bestie to you, from the bottom of my heart, Lei, you *really* need to be with someone else," she said. "Darnell doesn't realize what he has and if he hasn't all these years, he never will."

Leilani stared at her. She sighed and placed her fork down on the plate. Brutal honesty typically was the first thing to make an appetite swiftly depart.

"I think we should take a vacation this year. How does Fiji sound?"

Darnell raised his eyebrows, laughing at her for a second as if she was making a joke. He continued to type away on his laptop, his eyes never leaving the screen.

"I'm serious, Darnell," she said in response to his silence.

He glanced her expression and cleared his throat. "Have you priced it out?" he finally asked.

Leilani watched him diligent at work. She was fresh out the shower and wearing a skimpy mini lace nightie, her brown areolas clearly seen through the intentionally wider spaced holes in the fabric. She smelled like warm brown sugar and her skin was freshly exfoliated. It was soft and supple to the touch. Her below-the-shoulder length curly hair was damp from air drying and her flawless skin cleared of all mascara and eye shadow she wore earlier that day.

Her exes having seen her like this would be jumping on her like wild rabid dogs on a cornered wounded rabbit. She wouldn't stand a chance in getting away from any of them looking the way that she looked right now. She always was told and knew that she was at her most beautiful when she was bare – no additives and makeup only served to make her light brown almond shaped eyes more dramatic and bold.

She stood in the doorway of his office, leaning against the wooden frame and watching her husband who had just gotten home from work around eight pm. He took ten minutes to be back on his laptop. This was his typical daily routine that she had grown accustomed to over their years together. It used to bother her in their earlier years together, but over time, Leilani stopped caring if her husband took a moment to greet her with a kiss or hug, or even acknowledged her presence.

Each day, he would come home and immediately run to the restroom, ask her what was for dinner, and disappear to the gym or to his office with his laptop being his main point of attention. She was lucky if he joined her on time for dinner. Most times, she spent them waiting for him as the food she'd taken her dear time to prepare grew cold as he worked on things that were seemingly more important than their bonding time.

Leilani admired her husband's work ethic. He was dedicated to his career as an entertainment attorney and even though he did not have to spend every moment of his free time doing work, he chose to do so. The "black tax" was what drove him to work harder, longer and be more of a workaholic than his non-minority counterparts.

She knew that he did this to prove himself – even though the firm was well aware of his talent and skills the moment they presented him with an offer of employment and the numerous raises, bonuses and promotions he had received during his years at the firm. She didn't push anymore, she just let him be. She found their relationship to be more peaceful that way.

"Our travel agent found a few just under eight grand for about seven days, including the flight, hotel, rental car—"

"Seven days?" he asked and for once in the whole evening, he looked at her.

Leilani nodded. "Yeah, seven days. Saturday through Friday."

He shook his head, his expression now of irritation.

"I'll think about it," he snapped.

"Okay," she replied, disappointed.

"*Don't* book anything," he said suddenly, his tone stern. "I have to check my schedule."

She took in a slow, deep breath. They had this discussion every year, but work always got in the way of them doing anything remotely close to what would be considered a real vacation. Even on the times that they took a day off to do something, his Blackberry was attached to his hip and was checked every hour on the hour.

"You have more than enough vacation, Darnell," she began.

He furrowed his eyebrows, still typing and his eyes never left the screen.

"I said I'll think about it, Leilani. Right now, I'm working on something for a case that I have to get out tonight. Just don't book anything until I let you know."

He was dismissing her and she knew that she had used up her visitation time with him for the evening. Leilani nodded and turned to exit the office to hear his voice.

"Is that new?" Darnell asked.

Her pulse skipped a beat and she grew slightly excited. He had noticed her recently purchased lingerie.

With a slight grin, she answered, "Yeah. I just got it from Fredericks."

His eyes remained on the laptop screen as he nodded. "Oh, okay. On sale?" Darnell questioned.

She closed her eyes, annoyed, keeping her back to him.

"Yes," she lied.

"Oh. Good. It's nice. You going to bed now?" he asked.

She pushed back her unruly hair. "In a little bit. I have patients tomorrow starting at eight thirty. It's already after ten."

Darnell nodded again and rubbed his low cut hair. "I'll see how long this takes. But, it shouldn't be all night."

A silent promise for potential sex. Even though their encounters weren't paparazzi eligible, Leilani was always excited to have her husband's attention. She went to their master bath and sprayed more Gucci perfume on her wrists, inner thighs and neck – double checking her pubic area and legs to make sure she didn't miss any hairs that needed to be plucked or shaved before their rendezvous. She wanted to be perfect for him when he came to bed.

She turned on the mounted flat screen. HBO would be her friend tonight to keep her awake for him. Real Sex typically was entertaining enough to keep her senses alive and functioning into the late hours of the night. In her favor, a new one hour episode had just started. She could feel herself growing anxious. It had been over two weeks since their last sexual encounter, so she knew her husband's sex tank was nearing time for a fill-up.

Tonight was their night to have sex and even though she wasn't entirely horny, she definitely needed some type of affection and wouldn't turn down a chance to get a piece since that temporarily filled the void. After all, they were married and sex was something they should be doing regularly – no matter the quality. All she had to do was stay awake for about an hour and Darnell should be coming to bed to join her.

2
Where Is the Love?

*C*amille walked into Leilani's office, quickly shutting the door and plopping down on the chair in front of Leilani's large Ikea desk, a huge grin on her face.

"What are you doing?" Leilani asked; her eyebrows raised high.

"Coming to ask did you get laid," she asked with a grin.

Leilani groaned and rolled her eyes as she closed the patient's folder and leaned back in the chair.

"Do I need to write you up?" she asked in a serious tone.

Camille's eyes widened. "For what, Lei?!" she exclaimed. "We don't open for twenty more minutes, so this technically isn't work time. We are *friends*, not colleagues right now."

Leilani laughed. "Colleagues? You mean I'm not your boss right now."

"Potatoes, po-tot-toes." Camille shrugged. "It's all the same," she said.

They both shared a short laugh.

"But, seriously, what ended up happening? I got your excited text. So, did you get some?" Camille asked.

Leilani sighed and opened up the manila folder, resuming her notations.

"Nope!"

Camille sucked her teeth. "What the hell happened or *didn't* happen?" she asked.

"Girl, the usual, I go to the bedroom and expect to wake up to him in the bed and, welp, he ends up sleeping on the sofa in his office." She shrugged slightly. "I give up. He apparently loves humping the sofa over his damn wife. I'm just gonna buy me a dildo the size of the Empire State Building and call it a day."

They both smirked.

"More like you might as well just get one stitched permanently inside your cooch," Camille suggested.

Leilani smirked. "Smart ass." She glanced at the clock. "You have ten minutes, lady before I do write you up!"

"Okay, okay, whatever… Anyway, did you have on something sexy like I told you to do next time to get his attention?"

Leilani rolled her eyes again. "Epic fail! I wore that nightie that we picked out from Freddy's and…all he said was *is that new—*"

"Nope."

"Asked *was it on sale—*"

"Nope," Camille said quickly.

"Then he told me it was nice."

Camille furrowed her eyebrows. "Nice? *It* was nice? Not you *in it*, but the nightie was nice? What is he a fucking cross dresser!?" she exclaimed, irritated. "This ain't Project Runway!"

Leilani groaned in frustration. "I don't know what to do anymore, Moon. I'm obviously not sexy to him."

She stood and opened her closet door, reaching for her crisply ironed lab coat, but pausing to look at her frame in the full length mirror.

Camille raised her eyebrows. "You need to stop smelling super glue. I know you looked like a hot momma in that outfit."

"I was cute – or at least I thought I was. I couldn't even bring myself to ask how I looked; couldn't bear to deal with his lack of complimenting." Leilani paused as she turned her back to the mirror, looking over her shoulder at her round perky bottom in her black slacks. "I think that maybe my ass isn't big enough for him." She turned to the side. "Y'know he's always been an ass man."

Camille sucked her teeth. "Girl, you got the boom doom, *all that* going on with your body. And that nightie was skimpy as hell. How could he *not* get an instant hard-on?"

Leilani shook her head. "No clue, girl."

"Did you have a damn twelve inch strap-on on underneath it or something? Shit." Camille exclaimed, bewildered.

They both laughed.

"I'm sayin', what is his error message? Cause we need to call the manufacturer and get that glitch fixed and *fast!*" Camille said.

Leilani decided against wearing her lab coat for the day. The blouse she wore was low cut enough that it showed a teasing amount of her C cup cleavage. If her own man didn't want to look at her, at least maybe she could get a few sneak peeks from some of the husbands that would come see her today with their wives. Any confirmation that she still "had it going on" would suffice at this point in her life. She closed the closet door and looked at their wedding photo. She snatched it up and held the frame towards her best friend. Camille looked at it and then at Leilani.

"What am I looking for?" Camille asked.

"He's not smiling," Leilani pointed out.

"*Okay*, most men don't like taking photos, Lei. What's the point—?"

"No, look at his expression. He looks like--"

"Show me to the nearest exit," Camille finished. "You looked very pretty though. I told you that already though a thousand times."

Leilani opened her desk drawer and laid it inside, face down. Her best friend watched her, wishing she could read Leilani's thoughts at this moment. Camille shifted in her seat, knowing that the wrong words could cause more hurt than intended.

"Lei," she started, "I remember your wedding day. It was beautiful and *so were you*."

"Yeah, it was beautiful. But, we weren't as a couple. He

wasn't happy. He wasn't into it. For crying out loud, we argued before the wedding!" she explained.

Camille was silent for a moment.

"I," Camille paused, "I think that you need to do some real soul searching, Lei. You're obviously not happy. You're obviously not satisfied and I think you need to just take some time and do you – find out what makes you happy."

"I know what makes me happy, Moon," she replied, "I *love* Darnell. God knows I do. But, he's just…" Leilani groaned. "He's so difficult. Besides, I'm in my thirties. If I ain't figured that shit out by now, we've got a major problem."

"Lei, its women walking around here ninety three that don't know what makes them happy," she held her hands up as Leilani opened her mouth to interject, "*All* I'm saying is, as far as you and Darnell are concerned; not what makes you routinely happy. I know you know that part or at least a majority of it. But, what you are willing to deal with and how much longer you're able to go along with this half-assed," she paused and rephrased, "with your marriage."

Leilani glanced at her desk clock. "Your time's up. So, who am I seeing today?" she asked.

Camille glared at her. "Slick ass! Change the conversation and avoid the obvious—,"

"Moon, I don't have time to think about this. I have patients to consult and take care of. Now, who's on my agenda for the day since the receptionist should have given you my report already."

Camille looked at her iPad, "You have…three colps, five consults, three follow-ups, a couple of refill scrips and," she paused, "Mr. Worthington?" she asked, confused.

Leilani furrowed her eyebrows. "What about Mrs. Worthington?"

"It's a notation here saying that Mrs. Worthington's out of town, but wanted to keep the appointment, so he's still coming in for their follow-up," she explained.

Leilani rolled her eyes and sighed. "Just great. I get to deal with the racist one on one," she muttered.

"He's your last appointment for the day. Other than that, it's busy but spaced enough for you to get decent breathers in between. Then you're done at four thirty instead of five, like usual," Camille said.

Leilani nibbled her bottom lip and her friend watched her.

"I can keep him occupied, if you like," Camille said with a grin and a wink.

She glared at her. "*No thanks*, I don't need any sexual harassment suits coming my way."

Camille giggled. "I'm just offering..." she muttered with a grin.

"*Mmm-hmm.* You sure are *offering.*" Leilani smirked. "Any way we can reschedule the Worthington's? I'd rather have the both of them together. He wasn't friendly the first day and I really don't expect him to be any different this time around – especially with his wife not here to run the show."

Camille flipped through the schedule on the iPad. "You wouldn't be able to fit them in for another month, Lei. You're completely booked. So," she looked at her, "You gotta take on the fine ass racist."

Leilani sighed. "Alright then. Let me anoint myself and baptize this room before he gets here."

"I rebuke you racist demon! I rebuke you out of that fine specimen!" Camille exclaimed and they both laughed as she headed to the door.

"You are so silly. Now get to work before I *do* write you up," Leilani said, laughing and shaking her head.

Camille turned and looked at her best friend with a grin. "It's good to see you still smiling, Lei. You always keep your head up regardless. That's how I know things are gonna work out. You will get to happy. You deserve it."

Leilani smiled. "Thanks, Moon."

Leilani's day blew past her and before she knew it, she was reviewing the test results for Yoga Instructor, Mrs. Sophie Piper Worthington, wife of CEO, Mr. Evan Chase Worthington. Her other patients were a breeze. All were friendly, appreciative of Leilani's skill set and confident in her ability to take good care of them. Overall, it was a great day, so great that she hadn't even thought about having to deal with Mr. Worthington solo... until now. She could feel herself growing nervous, anxious at the thought of being alone with this man.

During lunch, she took a fifteen minute nap on her chaise and had a dream about *him*. They were on the beach and she walked by in a bathing suit, waving at him and his wife who was showing off her glorious five month baby bump, all smiles. Mr. Worthington looked at her and spit in her direction, mouthing epithets at her that would offend even the most profane individual. She was then being carted off by police officers claiming she had assaulted the lovely couple. The dream did not leave her feeling warm and fuzzy as it came back to her memory at that moment. Neither did it make her follow-up with Mr. Worthington one to be welcoming and enjoyable as her others.

She scribbled down a few final notes, biting her bottom lip and was interrupted by a soft knock on her office door. She knew it was Camille before she walked into the room. This time, Camille shut the door and walked to Leilani's desk, her iPad in her hand – another gift from Leilani to her staff – to use for work, of course.

"You had a reschedule. So, you could push the Worthington's to next week Tuesday if you still preferred to see the both of them together," she said in her professional tone, omitting any additional sidebar of Mr. Worthington's seeming disdain for Leilani.

Leilani glanced at her Breitling wristwatch. "Is Mr. Worthington here already?" she asked.

Camille nodded. "Yeah, he's actually about fifteen minutes early. He's on his Bluetooth, so I guess he's working while he waits." She raised an eyebrow with a grin. "And *chile'*, he's looking *deliciously good.*"

"Ms. Campbell!" Leilani snapped. "Work time," she reminded sternly.

Camille covered her mouth. "Oops! I didn't even realize I said that!" she exclaimed with a laugh. "My bad."

Leilani raised a threatening brow. Camille cleared her throat, composing herself. "Yes, Dr. Mathews, Mr. Worthington is here already."

Leilani sat back in her chair and let out a deep breath, closing her eyes.

"After having such a good day, I hate to end it with him," Leilani muttered, tapping her fingers on the desk in contemplation.

Camille watched her. "You can reschedule him, Lei," she reminded, "See the both of them together."

She closed her eyes for a moment and shook her head. "No, just," she paused, "just send him in. How bad could it be? It's not like he's walking in here ready to burn a cross in the reception area."

Camille laughed; she never reminded Leilani of the same "work time" etiquette as Leilani did because she enjoyed their friend moments.

"Not yet at least," Camille muttered as she headed towards the door. "I'll bring him to your office in about ten. I'll stay nearby in case you need a 9-1-1 rescue."

Leilani smirked. "Yeah, thanks," she said.

As the door clicked, Leilani closed her eyes and leaned her head back against her chair – taking a moment to relieve the tension building in her shoulders.

She snatched her smartphone, hoping for a text or missed call from someone, anyone just wanting to talk to her. Because she kept her friendship with Camille off the books at work, she had no one else who was as close as she and Camille to distract her during the day even if for a short moment. She never heard from her husband during the day unless he needed something from her. Other couples that she knew spoke sporadically throughout the day to check on one another or just to say hello because they missed each other. Not Leilani and Darnell.

They were total strangers when apart or at least that is how Darnell treated their relationship to be. She learned the hard way when she called him a few times throughout their first year of marriage and he'd blatantly be annoyed with her - claiming that she was interrupting him if she didn't need anything and he had more important things to do and would see her when he got home. She tossed her smartphone back into her Louis Vuitton handbag. She stared at her notes from Mrs. Worthington's test results and closed her eyes. She was exhausted from today and really did not have the interest in facing Mr. Worthington's rude behavior.

Leilani thought that the earlier nap would give her a shot of energy due to her back to back patients, but with the remembrance of Mr. Worthington's behavior during their first consult, she wasn't too sure if she had enough energy to deal with him. Surely, she had dealt with racism before, but it was typically outright. She always would rather know upfront that someone was racist than to see it in their actions – subtle yet plain. It was then that she felt it to be more draining, especially when dealing with a patient or fellow colleague because it forced her to work harder than she needed to in order to prove her competency as a M.D.

There was another soft knock on her door and Leilani glanced at her desk clock: **3:35.** She took in a deep breath and stood as the door opened, preparing herself mentally for Mr. Evan Worthington's entrance.

He entered the room and her eyes slid down his sleek appearance. He was GQ in his style, primped and pressed from head to toe. He was a well-groomed and appearing approachable man. Leilani smiled at her own thought that he must have grown up around some *soul* because of the Denzel Washington swag in his walk. It was a confident stroll; one that demanded respect.

He definitely was not a preppy boy even though he clearly made Wall Street money. He didn't make eye contact as he entered and Leilani shared a glance of encouragement from Camille before she shut her office door, following Mr. Worthington to her sitting area – he and his wife's patient folder in her hand. She sat down in her chair as he relaxed on the other single chair opposite, yet to the side of her.

Leilani cleared her throat at the realization that he was placing more distance between the two of them and assuring that he did not sit directly across from her on the sofa as before. It was a clear sign that he could not bear the sight of her brown skin.

"Good afternoon, Mr. Worthington. It's nice to see you again," Leilqni began in her professionally courteous tone with which she greeted all of her patients.

He shifted in his seat, adjusting his Ted Baker tie. Despite his confidence, she could see he was uncomfortable in her presence, but Leilani ignored his discomfort as best as she could. This was business. Point blank.

"Good afternoon, Dr. Mathews," he replied.

The bass in his voice caused Leilani to imagine what he sounded like during intimate moments. Its quality was just as attractive as he and she knew that his moans had to be sexy as hell. She felt her body growing warm and she crossed her legs, softly clearing her throat to clear the thought from her mind. Now was not the time to wander. She looked at him and for a split second, their eyes made contact and he looked away quickly. Leilani opened their file and began to explain her findings and treatment plan.

"Well, after reviewing your wife's results, her FSH is fairly high considered to what is normal and it appears that she is not ovulating regularly." She didn't look up. "I am recommending at this point in time that we begin a round of injections with Follistim. The goal of the Follistim is to stimulate ovulation. I've marked on this sheet the expected days of her cycle, with one being when she starts menstruation," she stood and walked over to him to sit on the sofa, holding the paper in her hand atop of their folder, "If you take a look at the numbers marked below, this—"

Mr. Worthington shifted suddenly, leaning his torso towards the opposite side of the leather lounge chair, her now close proximity to him appearing to make him even more at unease. Leilani released a short, nervous laugh. She was amazed at how this grown man was not able to handle a person near him simply because of the difference in their complexion and grade of hair. She was always taken aback at how racism towards another human could even exist. She sat the paper on the armrest nearest to him and moved away, going back to her seat.

"How about I let you look that over and I'll explain it? You can follow me on the sheet. I have my own copy right here," she tapped the folder with a forced grin. He still did not look at her, his eyes remained glued to the instruction form.

"That would be ideal," he replied, his eyes skimming over the sheet she left for him.

Leilani laughed nervously again. This was beyond ridiculous and she could not fathom how or why people could be racist. She stroked her eyebrow and began to further explain to him the sheet as he regularly interrupted her with clarification questions.

She let out a final smile. "My last recommendation is that your wife slows down on her exercise. It appears that she does quite a bit of high intensity training which, I believe to be the cause of her irregular ovulation. If she minimizes her training to just her instructing of yoga in conjunction with the round of fertility shots of Follistim and tracking, the two of you will be parents in no time."

"Did the results show that Sophie isn't ovulating regularly or is that simply *your own* presumption?"

Leilani stared at him for a moment, offended. She softly cleared her throat and swallowed her pride; forcing a friendly smile.

"It's a bit of both. Quite a few studies have shown that highly active women typically have irregular cycles and if the woman is having regular cycles, they are not always accompanied by a release of a viable egg for fertilization."

He nodded and she continued, "Mr. Worthington, the two of you are very active people. This does not drastically affect you – as you stated that you take multivitamins, wear the proper undergarments, eat a fairly clean diet and do not smoke or drink regularly. However, your wife listed that she smokes and drinks approximately three to six plus cups of coffee daily. Her BMI is also very low for her height and age. These are other factors that can majorly affect fertilization in women. I'd strongly recommend that she reduces her coffee to one or two cups a day and tries to gain some weight if the two of you are really set on having children within the next few years. The smoking," she paused, "I'd like to see her quit that entirely, but that's not always as easy as pie. And we all love a good piece of pie," she said with a smile.

There was an awkward silence in the room, not a peep out of Mr. Worthington –not even a slight indication of a smirk which caused Leilani to become a bit self-conscious. She cleared her throat and adjusted the papers on her lap.

"I really would have liked for your wife to be here so that she could hear this firsthand. But, if you are not aware, after age thirty-five, pregnancy rates drop dramatically and with your wife's lifestyle, it will continue to make the road to conception quite a bit more difficult than the average non-smoking, average caffeine consuming and relatively active female in her age group."

He raised his eyebrows.

"Like yourself," he muttered.

Leilani laughed nervously again. "Excuse me?"

She wasn't sure if he was insulting her or making a general observation. Mr. Worthington still did not make eye contact. He folded the paper and stood, preparing to leave.

"Thank you, Dr. Mathews, I will meet with your receptionist to schedule another follow-up. I concur that it would be more beneficial for my wife to hear this from you as this was," he paused, "To speak candidly, I find this to have been a futile meeting that had absolutely nothing to do with me. I am not sure why my wife sent me instead of rescheduling."

She laughed nervously at his raw commentary. "In my opinion, this has everything to do with you, Mr. Worthington. Your wife *surely* can't have a baby without your participation. I believe this follow-up was very beneficial to you as well as you can be a reminder to your wife of what it takes to be on the right track towards the two of you conceiving."

He smirked. "I would prefer that we stick to your *professional* recommendations," he bit.

"Vous n'êtes pas un psychologue agréé," she heard him mutter.

His French vernacular caused a chill to sprint down Leilani's spine. However, the insult of her not possessing a license in psychology resonated louder than his accent's erotic tone. Leilani cleared her throat, embarrassed as she raised her hand to show him out. But, he immediately had helped himself and was swiftly making his way down the hall.

She stood in the doorway, watching his 6'2 physique confidently stroll its way to the receptionist's station.

Leilani let out a deep breath.

"Unbelievable," she said softly and shut her office door.

❖

"What an ass hat," she scoffed, sipping on her merlot.

Camille laughed. "You seriously just called him ass hat." She scanned her friend's tense demeanor. "He must've really showed his ass in there. Cause' you're *way* uptight."

Leilani scoffed again. "Moon, I have never been so pissed over a client! He was insulting me. But, not outright insulting. It was *subtle shit*. I was telling him my treatment proposal about his, what I think to believe, is a fucking anorexic wife!"

Camille laughed.

"And he was asking was that simply *my* assumption?" Leilani finished.

"Oh no he didn't--"

"*Oh, yes he did!*" Leilani exclaimed, her eyes wide with emotion. "He just—" Leilani paused and fanned the air. "He's an asshole."

"He's a piece of *fine* ass," Camille muttered and Leilani tilted her head to the side, looking at her disappointingly.

"*Really*, Moon? You're still focused on the fact that he's attractive despite his rude and—and clearly racist behavior?"

Leilani was getting riled up and Camille knew it was time to cut off her tab of merlot. She reached over and slid Leilani's wine glass away, her hand cupping the top.

"All I'm saying is, he's fine. I mean, yeah, he sounds to be rude as hell. But, our receptionist has nothing but high remarks about him—"

"*She's white*, Moon." Leilani interjected.

Camille sat back, crossing her arms over her. "Oh yeah," she smirked. "I keep forgetting cause she comes up in there wearing those nineties finger waves and French rolls."

They both laughed.

Camille sat forward, resting her forearms on the table, "Well," she shrugged. "What can you do about it, Lei? Like I said before and like he even said, he's going to be sending his wife because it had nothing to do with him. As long as he keeps the checks comin', forget him."

Leilani squint her eyes. "See what I mean, who says that type of shit? He's her husband. This has got everything to do with him."

Camille stared at her best friend for a moment and took a sip of her martini.

"Darnell would say that," she stated.

"That was a rhetorical question," Leilani snapped back, snatching her glass of merlot and finishing it off as she looked around the restaurant for their waiter to request another refill.

"How long have you guys been trying now?" Camille asked.

Leilani sighed. "I've stopped counting." She shrugged. "I'm about to buy a damn dog or cat…a horse—something!"

Camille laughed. "Lei, *please* don't be one of those ladies kissing their dogs and dressing them up in little outfits with all the baby talk. That shit is disgusting."

"*Girl*, please. I'm not talking about a lap dog. I'm thinking more like a big ass wolf beast of a dog."

"Why? So you can train it to eat Darnell for you?" Camille teased with a grin.

They both laughed.

"Smart ass," Leilani commented, picking up her vibrating iPhone.

Leilani rolled her eyes. "Are you kidding me," she muttered, irritated.

"What is it?" Camille asked.

Leilani groaned in frustration, replying to the text.

"It's Darnell. He's asking me when I'm planning on getting home so he can eat."

Camille sucked her teeth. "I'm *so glad* I'm not married." She signaled their waiter, pointing to their glasses for refills. "You two make me not wanna get married."

Leilani sat her smartphone back on the table and glanced at her Breitling.

"C'mon, Lei. We *just* got here. Seriously, why can't he cook – hell, order out! You work long hours just like him," Camille whined.

Leilani closed her eyes. "Don't go there…"

"Man, I *so* don't plan on getting hitched. It's not like you sit at home on your ass all day while he brings home the bank. Why are you playing Betty Crocker housemaid – simply cause' you don't have a dick?"

Leilani rubbed her hands together, trying to relieve the tension in her muscles that shot into them once she started thinking about Darnell.

She closed her eyes. "Moon, let's just pay the check and get outta here."

Camille groaned in disappointment. "Here you go again," she muttered. "Running off to cater to him."

"I just don't want to hear his mouth," Leilani explained, "He only does this when—"

"When *he* wants something, but whenever his tail is out and about, you're not even in his mind. You can barely get a hold of him." Camille shook her head; "He's such a douche bag."

Leilani looked up and her eyes grew slightly wide in shock. Camille turned her head slightly to see Mrs. Worthington headed towards them, smiling cheerfully as always. Her husband was behind her.

"Dr. Mathews!" she exclaimed, shaking her hand excitedly. "It's so good to see you again! Don't you look beautiful! What is that? Chanel?"

Leilani laughed and shook her head.

"No." *Spoiled bitch,* she thought in her head. Her outfit was purchased at Macy's.

"We're really looking forward to how this first round goes! Maybe we will be having a celebration dinner next month!" Mrs. Worthington continued.

Leilani glanced at Mr. Worthington who was looking down at his LG. Her mind went back to Darnell and the moments that if he wasn't on his laptop, he too was glued to the screen of his smartphone – barely talking to her. She smiled at Mrs. Worthington and nodded.

"Thank you. I look forward to it as well, Mrs. Worthington. You two have a lovely evening."

"Honey," Mrs. Worthington said, turning to her husband and grabbing his hand. He followed her to their table and Camille looked at her best friend.

"He *is* rude," Camille said, "What the hell did you do to him?"

Leilani raised her eyebrows. "Racist, I told you."

Camille watched the couple walking to their booth in the

back corner, secluded and romantic. Mrs. Worthington was peppy like a cheerleader and her husband was cool, calm and collective. Camille caught him glancing over at their table.

She furrowed her eyebrows. "He keeps looking over here."

"Probably trying to figure out how long his KKK brothers are gonna be to knock us off in the parking lot," Leilani replied.

Camille laughed and they stood to exit.

"You are *so* dramatic," Camille said as she peeked at Mr. Worthington, taking note of him surveying Leilani again. "I think he might have a taste for some chocolate mousse."

Leilani scoffed. "Yeah and I'm the Pope."

———————————— ✤ ————————————

She watched her husband type away on his HP, patiently waiting for him to join her at their dining room table. He was in the den, surprisingly not in his office as Leilani usually found him after work. Tonight, he only waited in the open area near the door timing her on her arrival home to make dinner. Darnell did not care entirely for Camille.

Even though he knew that she and his wife were nearly sisters in their bond, he didn't care for Camille's ability to allow his wife to have fun. She was married. In his mind, it was okay to have a life, but not when it came between her taking care of home.

Leilani rushed home and cooked baked sesame coated chicken, broccoli, homemade cornbread and asparagus. Dinner was speedily ready and as usual, she was not greeted at all by Darnell besides his typical, *"How was your day? What are we eating for dinner?"* And now, she waited for him for the past ten minutes as the food grew colder. She knew he'd complain about his meal not being hot, even though it was entirely his fault. But, she'd be blamed.

She sighed and said her own quick grace, she wasn't going to starve herself any longer especially on a meal she had prepared and knew it was delicious. She was always waiting on him and

Darnell never rushed to minimize the time. However, when the shoe was on the other foot, she had to march to the beat of his drum and Darnell had zero patience for her.

Many times, Leilani wished that she could be inconsiderate as her husband, but it wasn't in her nature. She struggled being rude, uncompassionate, uncaring and arrogant as her husband. But, it took too much effort and she always believed you treat others how you want to be treated.

Darnell joined her at the table as Leilani was midway through her meal. He looked around at the food.

"Eating without me?" he asked.

"You were taking forever and I was hungry," she glanced at him as he touched the chicken, feeling the temperature.

He furrowed his eyebrows. "This is cold," he complained, grapping his plate and heading towards the kitchen.

Leilani rolled her eyes; she was annoyed. She never understood how Darnell could be so self-absorbed that he never linked his actions to the results that came from them. It was always someone else's fault; never his own. It was almost as if he was too prideful to admit being anything less than perfect. She finished her food and took her plate into the kitchen, seeing him waiting at the microwave as he tip tapped on his Blackberry. She shook her head and washed her plate.

"You shouldn't overheat that or you're going to dry out the chicken," she recommended.

No response. She glanced over at him. He was in his own world and as usual, she was unimportant to him. Leilani scanned her husband as he stood in his slacks and tee. He had taken off his dress shirt, his Kenneth Cole's at the door as he placed them each day to not track any marks on their hardwood floors.

Darnell was a relatively handsome man, reminding her of Idris Elba and often was mistaken for being a relative of his. Even though Darnell wasn't an athlete, he wasn't a slob in her eyes. He kept himself active and well-groomed. He stood a few inches taller than her, around 6'0 even though he took credit for an additional inch that his shoes typically granted him.

She reminisced to the day she first laid eyes on him. She was at a barbecue on campus – a small shindig she and her sorority hosted to bring in more potential recruits and to mingle with their frat brothers. She remembered seeing him walk into the room with his buddy – both of them all smiles and laughs as they looked around at all the fresh meat.

She felt excitement, anxiety, nervousness—all of the above and she felt a connection with him that at the time could not be measured. But, as the years went by, she soon realized that her "connection" was nothing more than her own feelings of what she desired her relationship to be. He just filled the most needed asset – the man.

The reality was masked over by her own fantasies of her ideal companion. She didn't feel a spark between the two of them and the more the distant professional behavior Darnell alluded to in their relationship continued on, the more Leilani found it harder to feel any love and attraction towards him. She felt as if they were just floating through each day in their own little worlds.

They were in a dull routine of interaction and she no longer felt excitement or anxiousness—she no longer missed Darnell when he was not around. She enjoyed him being gone more times than not and Leilani knew this was not a good sign. But, she was stubborn to admitting failure – especially when it came to marriage.

The microwave beep snapped her back into reality to see Darnell had made his way towards her. He had the all too familiar goofy, playful look on his face that Leilani no longer found cute or seductive. It outright annoyed her because she had grown to learn it was just his way of getting something from her. She took in a deep breath, trying not to openly show her disdain.

"So," he started, his finger stroking her forearm.

Darnell hadn't touched her in weeks unless it was an accidental bump while they were in bed or their hands brushed while moving about the house. She didn't understand how he could be robotic. Even the coldest person appreciated some type of physical interaction and even though Leilani didn't particularly want a man hanging from her teat, one who showed her regular affection would be enjoyable for a change.

"What is it, Darnell?" she asked, continuing with her motion of washing dishes

He edged closer, this time, his hand reaching to stroke the small of her back.

"I was thinking about that trip to Fiji."

"What about it?" she muttered.

She wasn't interested to hear the rest, but she figured she'd oblige anyway.

"*How about* you pay for it and," he paused, "I'll give you some of this chocolate-frosted banana in return," he said with a grin as he pressed his groin against her thigh. "We both how much you like bananas."

Leilani didn't look at him. She had grown tired of his antics. She was fed up with fitting the bill with his offerings of penis in return for her funding – whether it be monetary or through actions. She smirked, shaking her head. She didn't feel like entertaining his childishness, not after dealing with Mr. Worthington's rude behavior.

"How about no," she replied, her tone flat, one eyebrow raised high. "We can split it."

Darnell sucked his teeth and walked away, opening the microwave and snatching out his plate. "Guess you won't be getting any tonight," he said as what appeared to be a joke, exiting out the kitchen.

Leilani didn't watch his departure, she shook her head.

"Don't do me any favors," she muttered.

She finished loading the dishes into the washer, headed to the deck and eyeballed her sound system. She decided she didn't want to listen to any music, so she walked out the glass door, stepping onto the deck that led to the sandy beach. She closed her eyes to the cool breeze that greeted her, the salty smell of the ocean and the sounds of the crashing waves. It was silent. Peaceful.

She sighed and walked to the wine chest, grabbing a glass and pouring herself a half a cup of Dom Perignon. She lit one of the lavender scented candles next to her chaise and covered herself with the fleece throw, feeling her body ease into the plush fabric beneath. She looked at the clear sky, at the waning moon and the views of the distant landscape of lights. For a moment, she closed her eyes and took it all in.

Her life was good – what others would consider awesome. She was blessed more than the average person; thanks to the head start from her parents. She lived in a European, French Country design house on the beachfront, paid in full. She owned a BMW and a Land Rover. The only debt she had was a few thousand on an AMEX credit card. Otherwise, Leilani owed nothing more than her bills to maintain her thriving clinic. She was worth over six figures out of all of that, she was only in her early thirties. She owned her own doctor's office and contributed to charities yearly. She invested wisely and all things considered, it all worked in her favor.

The only thing missing in her life was love. Even though Leilani was married at twenty-three to a successful black man, who didn't cheat or abuse her, she didn't have *real* love. Others would praise her on the fact that she was lucky to be married – especially being a female minority in this day in age when divorce rates were sky high. But, Leilani wasn't proud of her marriage. She felt that if Darnell walked out of her life tomorrow, she'd be just fine.

She believed without a doubt that he would not fight if she chose to leave him. The only thing he'd miss would be being married to a well-off woman. Darnell didn't love her. He loved the idea of her. She knew that. She felt it every day when he didn't touch her, kiss her, and tell her he loved her. She could see it in his eyes when she'd interrupt him while he was working or if she didn't move fast enough to finish something that he wanted her to do.

The same lack of excitement she felt, she knew it was mutual. Only she was the only one out of the two of them that would admit it. He was comfortable in this place that others called a "great marriage". But, she wanted more, needed more; the only problem being, she was married to a man that was content with the way things were, yet she strongly desired for things to change.

Leilani sipped again from her wine glass and a distant noise distracted her. She turned to look in the direction it came to see her neighbors on their deck. She knew they hadn't noticed her relaxing all by her lonesome. By her God-given exceptional vision, Leilani could see them kissing, caressing each other – both in their nightgowns.

After living next to them for the past few years, Leilani still couldn't figure out which one was the male or female in the courtship. Both stood around 5'6, slender and fit. She guessed them to be in their early forties. One was Hispanic and the other Caucasian. This was the first interracial couple that Leilani had the chance to observe up close.

She could hear their laments between the soft crashing of the waves coming from the both of them. Even though she wasn't into girl on girl action, Leilani was spellbound by the passion between them. It emanated from their bodies so thick that you could slice it with a knife. Leilani felt herself longing for that type of emotion; wishing that she and Darnell had an ounce of their desire for each other.

She felt the sting of tears begin to fill her eyes and Leilani looked away, wiping them away before they slid down her cheeks. She couldn't be weak. She had to stay solid during this time. The good in her life far outweighed everything else – especially compared to what others were or had endured in their own lives.

After all, it was *just* a lousy marriage.

3
Occupy Your Time

8:15AM

"*I*'ll have a cinnamon hot chocolate. Tall. And your egg white omelet, please."

Breakfast was on the go today as she had overslept and was now rushing to the office. No patients scheduled until after nine. But, there were patient charts to be reviewed and follow-ups to prepare for that would take up quite a bit of her morning in the office. She occasionally found herself making her way to Starbucks for the usual order and did not feel bad to indulge in the extra calories from their specialty hot chocolate. It was her favorite, but she knew she couldn't make a regular routine of it or else her waistline would pay the price.

A familiar voice filtered through her ears, but she did not turn to confirm who it was. Her mind was on other things, like the discussion she had with her husband a few nights before. They barely had deep, if any, conversations, but this one was triggered by a discussion he had with his mother. It was about finances. To which, Darnell jokingly stated that he married her under the plan that she'd become rich and he could live off of her success and wealth.

To Leilani, it was no joke and even though Darnell would never admit it, she truly believed that he married her for his own personal reasons that had nothing to do with love. His comment didn't rest well with her and she found herself researching on matters of financials in the circumstance of divorce in the state of California. She needed to know how much she stood to pay him if she and Darnell's marriage did not last. Two calls in to her attorney friend and long term CPA was expecting a response within the next few days to hopefully ease her concerns.

"Thank you," she said as she picked up her order from the cashier.

The cashier gave her an extra-long smile and slight wink as she retrieved her bag. Leilani smiled back, but quickly turned to avoid any additional commentary from the man obviously fresh out of high school. *I'd snap your young self in two,* she thought with a smirk.

She jaggedly hit into a solid body, watching her heated beverage splash onto a crisp white dress shirt. Leilani's mouth dropped open and she gasped.

"Oh my God, I'm *so, so* sorry!" she exclaimed with a loud gasp, turning to the nearest table to sit down her belongings and reach for napkins. She turned to wipe and her hand froze in midair when their eyes made contact. It was electric and she felt a tingle run down her spine.

"Um, hel-hello, Mr. Worthington," she stuttered, trying to compose herself.

He stared at her for what felt like eternity and Leilani grew nervous, stepping back a few inches to put more space between their bodies. This was the first time he looked at her and it was her turn to feel uncomfortable. His gaze was unrelenting and bold. His sapphire blue toned eyes were stunning. His pupils were dilated and she felt herself being drawn into them. She broke their gaze and held the wad of napkins out towards him; mortified.

"I really am sorry, Mr. Worthington. Here. Take these," she offered.

He didn't speak; he scoffed and looked down at his stained shirt. His eyebrows raised high. Leilani knew he was upset and she braced herself for his angry tone. She knew he already could not stand the sight of her, but now she had started his morning off with a nice, hot splash of a mess.

He didn't take the napkins and Leilani tossed them into the trash can nearby, coming back to the table and snatching up her belongings. Mr. Worthington was wiping his shirt with a wet cloth from the cashier. She watched him, expecting some type of response, but she received none. He turned his back to her and continued to wait for his order; treating her as if she barely existed. Leilani looked around in embarrassment and quickly retreated from the restaurant.

What a great start to her day.

"All over his shirt?"

"Yes, *all over* his shirt." Leilani held her hands up, fingers extended. "*All over it*. Like pladow!" she explained.

Camille giggled. "That's hilarious! What did he say?"

"Nothing."

"What did *you* say then," she asked.

Leilani licked her lips. "I apologized. I offered him napkins. He didn't take them. He was using some towel to wipe his shirt that the *white* cahier gave him."

"*Damn,*" Camille said, surprised. "That's pretty messed up, chick."

"I was so embarrassed, Moon. I rushed the hell up outta there as fast as I could."

"I know you did!" she exclaimed.

"I didn't know if he was gonna spit on me or call me a black bitch," Leilani continued as she reached for her Amex to pay for their lunch.

"I just know he better not had used the N word," Camille said with a raised brow. "Or else it'd been smoke in the city."

Leilani laughed. "*Girl,* you're right about that."

Camille furrowed her eyebrows. "What the hell was his rich ass doin' in the 'Bucks *any*way? I'm sure he has a personal assistant with his rich ass," she muttered to herself and scoffed. "You too with your cinnamon chocolate addiction."

Leilani sucked her teeth and grinned. "Leave me and my hot chocolate alone!"

Camille smirked. "So what's new with you and Mr. Darnell?" her best friend inquired with a raised inquisitive brow.

Leilani shook her head and gave a slight shrug. "Nothing. Same ole'. Same ole'."

"Russell told me that he overheard you talking to your attorney at their firm. He said you were asking about divorce and your prenup."

Leilani's eyes opened wide in shock. "What?" she exclaimed.

Camille nodded. "Yeah, he was over at my pl—" she abruptly stopped. "I saw him and he asked me what was going on with you and Darnell."

"Whoa, whoa, whoa. Wait a second. Rewind, hussy. He was over *where*?" Leilani drilled.

Camille gave off an innocent expression. "I didn't say anything of the sort."

"Yes you did, you little hussy," she scoffed. "I can't believe you're doing Russell!"

Camille's mouth opened in shock. "*I am not,*" she paused at Leilani's expression of disbelief. "Okay, so I mess around with him a few times a month. But, it's nothing serious."

Leilani laughed, shaking her head. "You're unbelievable, Moon."

"*What*?" she raised her palms up, "It's the bomb! What was I supposed to do? Send him packing? He's a grown man."

Leilani leaned in. "He's a grown *married* man, need I remind you?" she scolded, her eyebrows were raised high.

Camille shrugged. "He's not married when he's with me."

Leilani's thoughts went to Russell. She didn't blame Camille for having an eye for him as he was indeed an attractive man, standing over six feet tall with a body of a god. He was African-American, Cuban mixed; curly hair and dark grey eyes that'd make any woman's skin melt. On top of that, he had enough sense in his head to be a successful divorce attorney and was a well-spoken man – in his professional settings. But, in all of his perks, Leilani never considered him anything more than a friend because he was close pals with her mate, Darnell.

Leilani shook her head. "I can*not* believe you! We've known him for nearly ten years *and* his wife and you're running around with him?" she scolded. "You know better than that."

"First off, I don't know his wife. *We* know Russell. He just got married to that broad two years ago. That doesn't automatically make her our friend too," she defended.

Leilani sucked her teeth. "You're a piece of work," she said as she sorted through her wallet to slide the credit card back inside.

Camille watched her. "Don't be jealous of me just because I'm getting some good dick."

She smirked and raised a brow. "Under those circumstances, I'm not."

"Yes you are. You're jealous cause your husband is a lame duck and you're walking around here spilling hot chocolate on white men to get attention," Camille teased with a laugh.

Leilani laughed, tossing her napkin at her. "Floozy," she said.

Camille adjusted her plastic breasts in her low cut top. "Trust me, all you need is one *real* fuck and you won't be concerned about who the guy's going home to after he's done with you."

Leilani stared at her best friend, her mind drifting back to the electricity she felt when she looked into Mr. Worthington's eyes earlier that day. She couldn't deny the attraction she felt with him. However, she knew it was one-sided. But, it was indeed running through her veins.

She had a desire towards Evan that couldn't be denied. That's why his acknowledgement or lack thereof of her bothered her to the core. She wanted him to want her. But, he was out of her reach. It was a fantasy that would forever remain chained in her imagination.

If Darnell would just fuck me more, I would be fine, Leilani thought with a deep sigh.

"You used to be so much fun. But, you've become this dull person afraid to live," Camille stated. "It's like your marriage has sucked the life out of you."

"I do live," she said. "I just have a lot of responsibilities, Moon."

Camille sucked her teeth. "Yeah, I know. You're always working, *cooking*, rushing to do this and that for *Darnell.* You constantly do for others. But, you rarely do anything for yourself, Lei."

Leilani stood and glanced at her Breitling. "I do treat myself from time to time."

Camille looked up at her; she opened her mouth to speak, but decided to hold her tongue.

"Okay," she smiled. "You're right, Lei. Let's go back to work. You have patients to see."

"We still need to talk more about this Russell thing, young lady," Leilani said as they strolled to her Land Rover.

"What? You wanna know how big he is?" she asked, "And what he does to me in the bedroom—well, not always the bedroom," she said with a giggle.

They both laughed and Leilani shook her head.

"Cause you know I'd tell you," Camille offered, still smiling.

"Lord *knows* you would. That's the scary part, Moon."

"I have a question for you," she said softly.

Darnell raised his eyebrows and inhaled sharply. Leilani closed her eyes, turning her head away from him. His expression spoke volumes. She hated trying to have serious conversations with her husband.

"What is it, Lei?" he asked, his tone annoyed.

She watched him, nibbling on her bottom lip, unsure if her next step was a wise one. They had been here numerous times before; sitting in a small space together, tense, feeling the desire for him to get as far away from her as possible.

She scanned his frame. He was focused in on whatever he was typing on his laptop. Leilani was lonely. She craved for Darnell to just give her the same unwavering attention he gave everything else; even if just for a brief moment. She licked her lips and shifted.

"Are you still in love with me?" she blurted out.

He took in a deep breath and stopped typing for a short moment.

"What is this about?"

Leilani stared at him. "It's just a question, Darnell. A simple question that shouldn't take another question to postpone the answer."

Darnell began typing, faster, his fingers pounding on the keyboard.

He smirked. "Nothing with you is ever a simple question," he said angrily.

"What is that supposed to mean?" she asked, offended.

Darnell shoved the screen of his HP back further to get better lighting. He was irritated with Leilani. He knew that every question that she asked him would be forever engrained in her memory with his response. Only to be used on him at a later date. He always felt like he was married to a detective – needing to hide things, unable to tell her the truth.

He had gotten to a point in his marriage that he felt it was pointless to even talk to her about his life or his feelings because he felt that she always used it against him later on. His wife had no clue to what type of man he really was because he chose to hide it all from her. It was better that she didn't know about him, his past or at least what he felt she didn't need to know. Leilani was never a simple person.

He sighed. "Bae, I have work to do. I don't feel like going through this tonight," he said, avoiding eye contact.

She scoffed, shaking her head. "You're unbelievable," she said softly, standing to exit the room. "I'm sure if your mom called and asked you, you wouldn't drill her," she snapped.

"My mom wouldn't ask me something she already knew the answer to," he replied.

Leilani turned to look at him. "You treat her different. You actually *show* your love towards her. So she already doesn't have a doubt about it."

Darnell laughed and she shook her head. "What's so funny?"

"She's my goddamn mother!" he yelled looking at her. "There is no comparison!"

They stared at one another in silence. Leilani rolled her eyes.

"Forget it, Darnell," she said.

"You always do this!" he yelled, "Every few months you find something to bitch and moan about, Leilani! I don't feel like dealing with it! I don't feel like having to spoil you so that you're okay with your own insecurities."

She felt a stab in her heart from his cruel response and tears stung her eyes, but she swallowed them down. Tears didn't work anymore on Darnell. Over the years, it only caused him to become angrier and more annoyed with her. She looked away, her eyes scanning around their great room.

"Just forget I asked. Excuse me from wanting to improve things," she retreated.

Darnell looked at her in disbelief.

"Nothing is wrong with us! *You're* the one always looking for something to be wrong. Then you jab at it and jab at it until you kill it. *You're* killing this marriage, not me! You're the one always searching for something I'm not doing right or that I'm not doing enough!" He yelled.

She didn't respond. This was the typical response she received from him. He was unable to accept being anything less than perfect and Leilani knew this was his way of forcing her to keep from shining the light on the obvious fact that he did not love her.

She stood there, staring ahead at the fireplace. She couldn't bear to look at him, knowing his expression was one of arrogance and annoyance mixed in one.

"I just wanted to hear you say you love me. You haven't said it in a while, Darnell," she said softly, fighting the tears. "It is nice to hear once in a while."

He laughed again. "It's nice to not be bothered with stupid questions too!" he yelled.

She looked at him. Darnell's expression was tense, heated.

"Why does that question make you angry?" she asked.

Darnell shook his head, not replying. His eyes were glued intensely to the screen of his HP; the tapping of his fingers becoming harder onto the keys.

"Why are you even mad at me? It was just a question, Darnell," Leilani pressed.

"It's never just a question! My job isn't to give you self-esteem," he paused. "I swear, I think with you being mixed, you are completely on the deep end with your insecurities! You need help to get over whatever *new* issues you have rolling around in that head of yours."

Her eyes opened wide in offense. "*I* need help!" She scoffed. "*I* need help for asking my own husband if he loved me! No, this relationship needs help!"

"You know what, maybe when you end up alone or married to a fucking asshole, then you'll see how good you had it with me! Maybe that's what you need, Leilani! Someone to treat you like total shit for you to feel love!" he yelled. "Cause I'm tired of having to listen to what's wrong in our marriage!"

Leilani was silent. She took in a deep breath and exhaled slowly.

"All of this attitude just from me asking if you loved me."

Darnell raised his eyebrows. "That's not all you were asking."

She nodded. "You're absolutely right, Darnell, *as always*."

Darnell continued to type. He was done with the conversation and wanted Leilani to get out of his hair. He was frustrated with her for approaching him about this meaningless of an issue. He already had enough stress with work and listening to her be needy was the last thing he felt like catering to.

She gulped, trying to calm her nerves. "I just won't ask anything from now on. I won't bother you anymore with my *stupid* questions."

He laughed and shook his head. "We'll see how long that lasts."

She turned and Darnell watched her exit the room.

He shook his head. "She needs to see a shrink," he muttered.

Darnell heard the French doors click softly as it closed.

"*Fucking women,*" he groaned. "Finally, peace and quiet," he said with a sigh of relief.

9:15 P.M.

She checked her smartphone for about the fifth time, still no response. Leilani rolled her eyes, sending off a quick text and turning off her smartphone.

"She's probably messing around," she muttered and signaled the bartender for a refill of the cheap merlot she was drinking.

After she left the room, Leilani felt as if she was suffocating. She needed to get out of the house; away from Darnell. She needed to be away from her reality of being in an empty marriage – even if it was for a few minutes. She had sent a few texts to Camille.

She needed to vent. But, this late at night, and knowing her best friend, she was probably laid up with one of her pieces, as she called them. Even though Leilani knew the odds of her husband trying to find out where she had gone was slim to none, she still shut off her phone. She wanted quiet. No interruptions of weather alerts or new emails. She needed silence.

Leilani looked around the trendy restaurant. It was a quaint café in town that was quietly crowded at night with couples and many on first or second dates. She spotted all of the ones meeting each other for the first time and watched their mannerisms. Happy, excited, anxious and nervous all in one mix.

She looked around at her menu and felt a grumble in her stomach. She realized that she hadn't eaten dinner because she was rushing from the gym after work and was preparing to cook dinner until she and Darnell passed words. She didn't give a care if he was hungry, he had hands just like she.

"Excuse me, is this seat taken?" she heard a voice ask and her pulse skipped about a thousand beats.

Leilani turned and looked up to see Mr. Worthington standing next to her.

Her eyes widened and she laughed, looking around. "I'm-I'm sorry, are you talking to me?"

Mr. Worthington raised his eyebrows and nodded. "Yes, are you waiting for someone? Or may I have a seat?" he asked.

She sat back and held out her hand. "Be my guest."

He slid off his blazer and hung it on the back of the chair across from the two-seater before taking a seat. Leilani's eyes skimmed over his body. He was wearing dark jeans and a casual button down shirt. No tie this time around. She saw the shimmer of the diamonds in his white gold Rolex; immediately acknowledging their similar taste in fine jewelry. Her eyes scanned to his wedding band. It was simple, titanium, no diamonds. He looked handsome as always. Except, this time, Leilani noted, he was more relaxed and not his usual guarded self.

Mr. Worthington was crisp from head to toe in his appearance. His dark hair was perfectly in a rustled look that somehow he pulled off to still appear as kempt. He reached for the drink menu and skimmed through it. Leilani sat there in silence, watching him. It was awkward tension between the two of them and she was not sure why Mr. Worthington was sitting at her table at this very moment.

"I'm sorry, but," she paused, perplexed, "Is there something that you need, Mr. Worthington?" she asked.

He looked up from the menu and they made eye contact. Leilani felt the shiver skid down her spine from the electricity between them and shifted in her seat. Mr. Worthington's gaze made her uneasy, but not in a bad way.

He didn't smile. "No. I just came here for a light dinner and I happened to look over and see you here all by your lonesome."

She was silent, not sure how to respond. Mr. Worthington sat down the menu and ordered once the waiter approached.

He looked at her and smiled. "I ordered you a refill. I hope that is alright."

Leilani was stunned. She softly cleared her throat and leaned forward, resting her forearms on the table.

"Mr. Worthington, I'm sorry…I'm really at a loss at what's going on right now."

"What do you mean?" he asked. He was relaxed. Not as uncomfortable as he typically was while in her close vicinity.

Leilani tried to find the right words. "I…I'm not sure…" She paused and smirked, shaking her head. "This is completely off the record. But, why are you sitting here? I only do meetings in my office with my patients." She blurted out.

Mr. Worthington slightly furrowed his eyebrows. "If this is off the record, please, call me Evan."

"*Okay*," she said, still perplexed. "*Mr. Worthington*," she emphasized, "why are you sitting here?"

He smiled, introducing her to his pearly whites. His teeth were a perfect result of childhood orthodontics and regular dental visits. Her eyes observed him. He was indeed good-looking. His hypnotic sapphire eyes were striking, his features hinting a faint possibility of mixed blood coursing through his veins. She found him quite intriguing to say the least.

"This isn't a house call," he answered finally, watching her. "I just came over to talk with you."

He extended his hand.

"Allow me to officially introduce myself. I am Evan Worthington, it is nice to meet you."

Leilani laughed and crossed her arms as he put his hand down.

"Leilani Mathews," she answered with a stiff smile.

This must be a fucking joke, she thought. She looked around for any familiar faces, but saw none.

"It is very nice to finally meet you, Leilani Mathews," he said with a smile.

The way Mr. Worthington's eyes slid over her frame made her feel more chills up and down her spine. Leilani shifted again, straightening her low cut blouse and glancing down to ensure that she was not flashing him her C cup goodies.

She laughed, louder this time. "I really am sorry. But, is this some type of joke?" she asked. "Is Ashton Kutcher going to jump out any second?"

Evan's confused expression increased her own. "What do you mean?"

Leilani shook her finger between the two of them.

"Voulez-vous ma réponse professionnelle?" she asked smoothly in French with a croon of her neck.

Evan chuckled and scratched his brow. Leilani made note of his astonishment by her fluent French. *Yeah, chew on that asshole. I speak three languages. I'm not a higher education handout*, Leilani thought with a raised brow.

"Touché. But, I would more accurately fancy your frank response this time," he replied, "In English."

"Fine!" she snapped. "This is what I'm talking about—you sitting here right now, talking to me. Mr. Worthin—Evan, you don't even acknowledge me at your appointments. So, are we waiting for Mrs. Worthington to arrive or-or is this some ploy for me to be holding the table for the two of you?"

Evan nodded, realization striking his expression.

"Ah. I see." He licked his lips. "I do want to apologize for that, Ms. Mathews. It is nothing specifically towards you. I just," he paused for a moment and looked away. "I just have been going through an..." He raised a brow, searching for the correct term. "*Ordeal* with Sophie. We've been to about twenty doctors and I am really just at a point that I have no interest in seeing anymore. I only came to the appointments because she begged me. I was at my breaking point. It was in no way a slight at you or your abilities as a doctor. I just did not want to be there. Sophie knew that. But," he shrugged slightly. "I have to be a supportive spouse."

Leilani sighed, relieved and closed her eyes. "I feel so stupid," she muttered to herself, looking down at her hands.

Evan watched her. "Excuse me?" he asked.

She laughed and shook her head. "It's nothing. Just me being...me." She shook her head. "Really, it's nothing."

He smiled slightly. "What did you think?" he asked, curious.

She looked into his eyes again and felt another chill, looking away immediately. This man was dangerous. Even though she now knew that his seeming abhorrence was not directly related to her, she also now felt her attraction beginning to build as she was in closer proximity to Evan and had the opportunity to take all of him in.

She knew nothing of him besides his elaborate patient history and her assumptions based off of his previous behavior. Her attraction was purely physical. But, she knew that if he indeed turned out to be a charming man, mixing it with his looks would be a battle to conquer.

Leilani took a sip of her merlot and licked her lips.

"I thought you were racist," she bluntly answered, not breaking eye contact. She wanted to see his full reaction – did not want to miss a second.

Evan's eyebrows rose and she could see his slightly tanned smooth complexion turning a soft shade of pink. He was blushing from embarrassment. He cleared his throat and looked down for a second to compose himself. She had caught him by total surprise again.

"And all this time I just thought you would have considered me an uptight and arrogant asshole," he replied.

She laughed even though it wasn't a joke. She raised one of her perfectly threaded brows.

"Oh, believe me, I considered that too," she stated flatly and he laughed this time.

Mr. Worthington nodded. "I can grasp how I gave off that impression. I let my emotions get the best of me and I was in rare form. But," he looked into her eyes, his gaze unrelenting. "I can guarantee that is the *last* thing you have to be concerned about my character. I am far from racist."

They stared at one another for a short moment in silence and Leilani could feel her heart pounding through her chest. She had never really *looked* at a man of his race and had one look back at her in return on a head on gaze in an unprofessional setting. Typically, it was quick looks, not what they were sharing at this moment. She didn't know if it was just the color of his eyes or the seriousness of his expression. Either way, it was intense.

She broke their gaze and let out a deep breath, not realizing that she wasn't breathing for that small amount of time. She shifted in her seat, aiming to shake her emotions. She was just upset from her argument with Darnell earlier that night and her loneliness was being transferred to the attention she was now getting from Mr. Evan Worthington. This was nothing more than a patient wanting to clear the stale air between them. He was not interested in her.

She couldn't fathom why he would either way. He had a beautiful blond-haired, blue-eyed, ex-cheerleader wanna-be Barbie toothpick thin and fit wife. Here she was just a Brazilian and black woman with a splash of Creole in her blood from her grandfather's side as far as she had learned from Ancestry.com.

She had rare interactions with her relatives over the past ten years after learning that she was adopted. Even though Leilani knew she too was a very attractive woman, her typical advances were made mainly from fellow minorities – very rarely, if any being men of the Caucasian persuasion. Mr. Worthington was simply being polite and she needed not to get ahead of herself.

Evan continued to watch her. He was intrigued by Leilani and she was someone that he wanted to get to know. He saw an opportunity to speak with her when he spotted her alone as he sat at the bar. Seeing as though she was his fertility specialist at the moment, it worked that this conversation would not fall on deaf ears.

He took a drink from his glass and licked his lips. "There is something that I want to speak with you about," he began. "It's about my wife's treatment plan."

Leilani's brain lit up and she immediately snapped into MD mode.

She nodded. "Sure, what is it?"

He took a moment to compose his thoughts and placed his forearms on the table.

"I do not want children," he blurted out shocking her.

She laughed. "Excuse me?" she asked.

Evan nodded. "I know you're probably wondering what the hell is going on. But, the truth is," he paused, "I know this may be a bit much to throw on you. But, I am planning on divorcing Sophie and…she has been trying to get pregnant for a few years now. It's not because she hasn't," he paused, "I am just not happy with her and I don't want her to be the mother of my children."

Leilani was speechless. She opened her mouth and then closed it, opened it and sat forward, closed it and sat back, she wasn't sure if her wanted response was appropriate at this time.

"Mr. Worthington, why are you going to fertility doctors with your wife then?" she asked instead.

She wanted to ask, "*What the fuck?*"

"Honestly? To keep her off my back. Sophie." he paused. "Sophie can really, *really* be a handful," he paused again, staring off as he thought about his wife, "She is very persistent. I do it to appease her. But," he looked at Leilani, "I don't want to get her pregnant."

"Well you've been doing a great job for the past three years, I must say."

Evan smirked. "Yes and it has been hell to pay. Sophie has had me go see *at least* ten doctors to make sure I wasn't the one with the limitation. I feel like I am a lab rat as much as I have been poked and prodded," he complained.

"So, how are you making sure you don't conceive? The two of you don't use birth control," she pointed out, fluently recalling their charts and questionnaires.

"It is all been about timing these past few years," he answered. "Sophie keeps a detailed calendar at home. I keep one as well. I know when to have sex and when to avoid her like the plague." He shrugged slightly. "I have gotten pretty inventive with business trip planning and other things that will get me out of the house for a few days when I need to."

Leilani thought about her situation and the fact that she and Darnell had been trying for the past two years with no success. She wondered if her husband did the same as what Mr. Worthington was now confessing as their sex life was sporadic and unpredictable, yet barely there. She felt sadness begin to loom over her and Leilani looked at Evan.

She leaned towards him, resting her forearms on the table. "Mr. Worthington, you *really* should be discussing this with your wife…and not me," she encouraged. "It's only fair that she knows so she can stop wasting time and *your* money with all the tests, prescriptions, visits…"

He stared at her. "Are you married, Ms. Mathews?" he interjected, glancing down at her bare finger.

Leilani had left her ring at the house. She never wore it to the gym in worry that it'd get lost or damaged.

"I know I have seen you wearing a ring, but I wasn't sure if it was just for show to build rapport with your patients," he stated.

"No. I am married," she replied.

Evan had been far more observant of her than she originally thought.

"And have you ever at any point in your marriage felt like things *were not* there? That there wasn't a connection with your husband?"

Leilani gulped uncomfortably. "Um, there have been rough patches, but, all marriages have ebbs and flows—"

"That, I understand. But, I do not love my wife anymore," he interjected. "I stopped loving her a long time ago."

"Then you need to be man enough and leave," Leilani snapped before she could catch the words. She closed her eyes for a second. "I'm-I'm sorry. Excuse my rudeness."

Mr. Worthington smiled. "It is okay. This really is not your problem. I felt that you would be someone who could understand. You seem…" His eyes scanned over her. "You seem like you have a broad perspective on life. Especially when you gave me your candid input about impregnating my wife at our last appointment together," he replied.

Leilani watched him and he continued. She realized that he needed to vent and obviously, like her; she was the next best thing.

"I don't know how to talk to her anymore. She becomes so defensive, especially when it comes to me being hesitant to starting a family. I want children. I want to build a legacy. But," he shook his head. "Not with her and she is trying to force me into a corner thinking that I won't be able to leave if she gets pregnant."

"Would you stay?" she asked, curious.

His explanation hit home to her situation with Darnell. She knew what he was saying all too well, but chose not to share with him about her personal life. She didn't really know this man nor did she know who he knew.

Evan contemplated, taking in a deep breath and leaning back in the chair, raising his toned torso slightly before exhaling.

"It would be very difficult to leave. I am a family man with a strong conviction in being committed and loyal to one's family. Sophie doesn't have a dependable job. She used to be a Cowboys cheerleader until we relocated and since we've been married, she's just been a yoga instructor. I make a substantial living, so she never took it upon herself to really establish a career of her own. She dropped out of college. Her parents left her with a trust fund and she blew through that when I began really earning large sums of money. Now she's looking into instructing Zumba."

He scoffed. "For Christ's sake, those come a dime a dozen in today's market. She wouldn't be able to care for a child without me providing," he shook his head, "I couldn't abandon her."

"There are plenty of companies hiring people without degrees," Leilani stated, considering that Camille used to be one of those people.

He smirked. "You don't follow me, Mrs. Mathews. Sophie literally has zero job experience. Her yoga is damn near volunteer work considering her wages."

She wanted to reach over and touch his hand, to be of some comfort to him, but she fought the urge. This was a grown man – pretty much a stranger who was confiding in her about personal issues in his life. Leilani would not cross the line. He was her patient's husband. She found Evan watching her and snapped out of her private thoughts.

"What are you thinking?" he asked.

She raised her eyebrows. "This is a lot to take in. I'm not sure what to do with it. I'm…processing," she replied.

Evan smiled and grabbed the menu the waiter brought over to him earlier.

"I tell you what," he glanced at his Rolex. "While you are *processing*, the kitchen will be closing soon. So, why don't we order something before we starve," he suggested.

She smiled, feeling her stomach growling again. "That's not a bad idea," she replied, checking out the menu in front of her. "I think I'll have the lamb. I've been eyeballing that since I got here. A sistah' is hungry," she said and immediately closed her eyes in regret. "I'm sorry."

She was embarrassed beyond measure.

He looked at her. "Don't apologize."

She dreadfully looked at him. "I actually like it," he said with a grin.

Leilani stared into his eyes and smiled. "You really have surprised me today all around, Mr. Worthington."

"Call me Evan," he corrected as he signaled for the waiter.

12:45 A.M.

Leilani quietly unlocked the deck of their house. It was always quieter to enter from the back entrance instead due to the heavy wooden doors in the front that tended to slam behind her. Even though their home was fairly large, she knew her husband would awaken to the slightest sound other than his own breathing.

She figured Darnell was awake, possibly doing work. He hadn't called her; neither did he send a text to check on her after she had left their home shortly after 9pm that evening. Here it was, almost 1am and she was just getting in from her unplanned evening with Mr. Evan Worthington.

They ate dinner around 10:15 and continued their conversation of his relationship or lack thereof with his wife, Sophie. Evan was a well-rounded guy. She could definitely see them being friends, but she knew that considering her relationship with he and his wife, it was better if they remained simply friendly acquaintances. Leilani had never held a long conversation with one of her patients. It was her first time ever and she thoroughly enjoyed his input and insights about life, love and all the in between.

She silently wished that she had never met him the way she had – needing to be his fertility specialist, well; his wife's to say the least. She knew too much of their private life—even down to their blood types and number of sexual partners. She knew that it was only a matter of time before one of two things would happen: either Sophie would end up pregnant or Evan would leave her.

Either way, Leilani's services would no longer be needed and whatever potential she and Evan had at being friends would be smashed to oblivion. She knew there wasn't even a chance that Evan and Darnell could be friends. Now that she knew a little bit more about Evan's personality, Leilani gathered that Darnell's arrogant tendencies and lack of compassion would be the crux to Evan having any interest in spending time with him beyond a hello or goodbye.

Leilani reminisced to the last few minutes of their dinner together when Evan walked her to her car.

"You don't have to walk me. I'll be fine," she said as they headed to the front of the restaurant. Onlookers watched them with surprise of this white man with this black woman, or so that's how Leilani interpreted their glances and stares.

"No, ma'am. A gentleman never lets a woman walk to her car alone – especially at night."

Leilani laughed. "I thought you were just my patient?" she asked as she reached for the door.

He laughed. "That I am. But, I deem we have become a bit more acquainted now."

Evan moved ahead of her, opening the door.

She looked at him with surprise. "Thanks," she said.

"Women shouldn't open the door if a man is behind her. It's called common courtesy," he stated.

She laughed again. "What are you? The proper police?" she joked.

Evan shook his head and came to stand next to her once she stepped outside. "No, it's what men should do. I believe that women shouldn't carry things, open doors, or walk alone unless there is absolutely no man with her." He shrugged. "It's just how I was raised."

She watched him, forcing her eyes to not scan over his sexy, athletic physique but to remain focused on his gorgeous blue eyes. "That must be the good ole' Texas boy coming out in you," she said and he smiled widely.

"That good ole' country boy," he said with a wink.

He lacked a southern accent, but she equated that to him being a resident of California for quite some time now—far removed from his Texan roots.

Leilani began to stroll and he followed beside her. "It would be nice to have gentlemen around more often," she said, thinking as to how Darnell barely showed her common courtesy.

Evan looked at her. "Your husband isn't a gentleman?" he asked.

She smirked. "Let's just say that he was born far, far away from Texas."

He laughed and nodded. "I see. But, in case you didn't know, I am one of a kind. Not everyone from Texas is bred like me."

Leilani raised an eyebrow, her thoughts forbidden in response to his statement. They reached her luxury sedan and she reached to open the door, to only have Evan's hand interrupt and grab the handle. She laughed, shaking her head.

"You really don't have to be so nice, Mr. Worthington."

"You should let people do nice things for you more often, Ms. Mathews," Evan said as she climbed inside.

She reached to close her door and he pushed it, smiling at her as she laughed again. His courteous behavior made her uneasy. It wasn't too often that someone was this polite unless they wanted or needed something from her. They smiled at each other and Mr. Worthington slid his hands into his pockets.

"You have a nice rest of the evening, Ms. Mathews. Get home safe," he said as she cracked her window to bid adieu.

Leilani nodded. "Thank you for everything, Evan. This was cool."

He smiled again and there was a moment of silence between them. It was the infamously awkward moment at the end of date when the pair are topping off the evening in the living room with a nightcap.

She broke their gaze and asked, "Where are you parked?"

He slightly nudged his head to the left. "Valet."

"I can drive you over there," she offered and they both laughed.

"No. Thanks. I wanted to make sure you get on your way safe and sound," he said and tapped the roof of her car. "It has been a real pleasure, Ms. Mathews."

She reached for the gearshift and looked at him. "Oh yeah, I forgot to add. You'll be getting a bill for my services tonight."

They both laughed.

"You are worth every penny," he said and Leilani let out an awkward laugh. She wasn't sure if he was flirting or was it just her attraction to him hoping that he was.

Leilani put her Benz in reverse as Mr. Worthington stood there watching. He began to walk towards valet as she drove to the exit. Leilani glanced in her rearview mirror to see him handing over his ticket to the valet attendant. He turned to look in her direction and waved with a faint one sided grin. She gently honked her horn, turning the corner and heading home.

She smiled to herself as she turned on the foyer light to see her way to the staircase. Darnell had turned off all the lights on the first floor. She then realized that he was not awake, but must've gone to bed. As she made her way upstairs, using her smartphone's flashlight app so she would not trip, she entered their bedroom to see Darnell sound asleep, snoring and sprawled in the middle of their bed.

Leilani rolled her eyes in disgust of his inconsideration and turned to head to one of the extra bedrooms. She didn't feel like having to ask him to move over in their bed so she could lie down. She yanked off her clothes and lay under the fleece throw on the bed. She chose not to interrupt his sheer enjoyment of her not being in the bed with him.

"Un-freakin'-believable," she muttered.

Darnell had no concern for her safety or well-being until it directly affected him. He had no idea or interest in knowing if she had made it home after she left. Nor did he try to check on her at all that evening. She could've been lying in a ditch or better yet, had an unforeseen accident for all he knew.

She sighed, trying to rest, but all she could think about was Darnell's lack of care for his own wife and Evan – a man who wouldn't leave his wife, a wife that he didn't love simply out of concern for her well-being if she were to become pregnant.

They were two totally different men. Only the characteristics of her ideal, she unfortunately had not married.

4
The Grass is Greener

"*I* think I found the one," she said with a huge grin on her face.

Camille laughed. "You're insane, woman."

Leilani turned and looked at her. "What? You don't think it's worth it?" she asked and Camille raised a threatening brow.

"*What*?" she pressed, wanting an explanation from her best friend.

Camille raised her hands. "I'm just saying; that's a pretty hefty price tag for a pocketbook, Lei!"

Leilani looked down at the Prada bag and stroked the soft leather fabric. "But I'm *in love* with it," she pouted.

Camille snatched it out of her grasp. "I'll make you a damn bag that looks like this if you just wanna pay me six G's!" she exclaimed, examining the piece. "Look, it doesn't even have pockets inside!"

She snatched it back from her bestie. "So!"

"For an extra thousand, I can make the bag with as many pockets as you want. I'll even put some on the outside; instead of you throwing away money on an expensive ass bucket they're calling a handbag!"

They both laughed and Leilani sighed, handing the purse

back to the salesperson who was now glaring at Camille. She returned the look as they turned to exit the boutique.

"That's ridiculously priced, Lei. Don't waste your hard earned money just for a name."

"*Yeah, yeah, yeah.* You're just jealous because your pockets are deflated," she said jokingly.

Camille smirked. "No, I know that your dear ole' hubby would have a cow. He wouldn't even have to see the price tag. Just seeing it's a Prada is enough for him to get on you about spending money."

Leilani raised an eyebrow as she inventoried through the windows of the passing boutiques.

"Don't remind me."

"It's not even *his money*, but he wants to tell you how to spend it. That's what's fucked up about it the most. He treats it like you have your hand in his wallet," Camille complained.

Leilani rolled her eyes. "Again, don't remind me," she said, glancing down at her smartphone. "I have to get going. I have to catch up on reports."

Camille looked at her. "It's Sunday! You've been slacking off on your job, Dr. Mathews. What's been all up in your space? Cause it for sure hasn't been me!"

"Yeah, I know because you've been too busy playing home wrecker with Mr. Russell the *married man*," Leilani scolded, changing the subject immediately.

"Potato, po-tot-toe," Camille replied and they both laughed.

"Yeah, you won't be potato, po-tot-toe-ing if Cheryl gets a hold of your ass," Leilani said with a serious expression.

Her best friend shrugged. "She's not going to find out. Russell is on the low with his indiscretions. Y'know how good law-i-yers are."

Leilani laughed. "I hope his on the low is just with you and you don't mess around and be like Tiger Woods' mistresses; one outta' ten to twenty," she said as they walked to the valet booth.

Camille looked at her after handing the ticket to the attendant.

"I have a lot of fun with him. *A lot*," she shrugged. "Too bad he's married cause' we'd be good together."

"Moon," she started, "You're worth more than being someone's side piece. You know eventually he's just going to toss you to the side like none of this ever happened when he's ready to stop being a cheat."

They looked at each other.

"He may be our friend, but he's still just a man," Leilani reminded.

"Lei," she paused, becoming irritated. "Shit, don't rain on my parade just because your marriage is as exciting as a nursing home."

Leilani smirked, shaking her head. "I'll pass if it means I have to be sneaking around with somebody else's man."

Camille began to text on her phone.

"No regrets," she said.

Leilani looked at her, knowing her friend was probably scheduling a rendezvous with Russell.

"What?" Leilani asked.

Camille looked at her. "Life. You can't live it with regrets."

She raised a brow in disagreement and Camille turned to look at her.

"Lei, you have been living with your regret of getting hitched to Darnell for *years* now." She shook her head. "I refuse to do that shit. Especially if I know I could actually be happy with someone else. I have one of *this* here life. Not gonna waste it living with regrets especially not tied to someone who doesn't give me what I need emotionally *or* physically."

Leilani took in a deep breath, fighting her sadness from showing.

"Moon, I…I don't regret it. I just know it probably wasn't the best choice, but I loved him when I made that choice. For better or worse, remember?"

"Yeah, but you're not stuck with the decision. You can walk away," Camille replied.

"Marriage isn't that simple, Moon. I don't believe in hopping in and out of marriages. That's serious business to me. And it's not like one of your little *rendezvous* with whoever these men you're hooking up with," she jokingly insulted with a side grin.

"It's not death row either!" Camille exclaimed. "And if I have to be with some guy *til' death* and I am miserable, then his ass is gonna have some decades knocked off his life!"

They laughed.

"That's why your crazy self isn't married," Leilani said, handing the valet driver a fifty-dollar bill and walking to her Benz.

"It's time for you to start living, Lei. You're not Catwoman! You don't have nine lives!" Camille said loud enough for her best friend to hear through the rolled down faintly tinted windows. "Get out before you have children. That's my advice."

Leilani replied with an obvious sarcastic 'thumbs up' partnered with a fake cheer and waved before driving off. Camille laughed. She turned and grinned at the valet attendant handing her Camry keys over.

"Are you allowed to take phone numbers for tips?" she flirted.

The younger guy smiled, scanning her from head to foot in return. Camille grabbed the pen out of his breast pocket snagging her another potential.

7:33 PM

Leilani scribbled onto the patient records as she aimed to update the twenty files before she left out of the office. She glanced at her desk clock and sighed. This was taking longer than planned. She was to blame for the extra time because her thoughts of Evan continued to invade her focus. She changed the subject with Camille about why she had been behind on updating records because she had been on a few friendly after five dates with him over the past few weeks, shutting off her smartphone to block interruptions during their time together. She noticed that Evan did the same.

She didn't want to include Camille in her blossoming friendship with the man she once accused of being a pure racist simply because she knew her friend would not let her live it down. Plus, her friend would be all in her business and Leilani didn't want to taint the fun she had been having.

Their time together was innocent – nothing more and she did not want to hear encouragement from her bestie to add a little excitement to her life by making a pass and seeing what happens. She enjoyed her time with Evan and as long as her attraction to him stayed silent, the safer their growing friendship remained. She didn't want to complicate things with her own curiosity and lust towards someone she could never have.

Her office phone rang unexpectedly, jerking Leilani out of her private thoughts. She knew it wasn't Darnell calling unless he was checking on the status of dinner after returning from his secluded world away from his marriage. She figured that it would not be Camille as she was increasingly spending time with Mr. Russell, their attorney friend. She was pretty certain that it wasn't any other friends or relatives calling her at this hour. Leilani stared at the number and did not recognize it.

She typically gave her returning patients her office number to call in the case of any emergency needing to be made. During business hours, it was screened by the receptionist, but after hours, it automatically went directly to her office with the expectation that she would not be in. She picked up the ringer, assuming that whoever it was must desperately need her assistance. Her overnight voicemail was usually never full the next day from emergency calls.

"This is Dr. Mathews, how may I help you," she answered professionally.

"Dr. Mathews! This is Sophie – Sophie Worthington." She sounded exacerbated.

Leilani furrowed her eyebrows. "H-hi Mrs. Worthington, are you okay? You sound out of breath."

"No, I am *not* alright!" she nearly yelled into the phone.

For a moment, Leilani's pulse skipped a beat. She hoped that it was not about Evan and their friendship.

"If this is a dire emergency, Mrs. Worthington, please dial 9-1-1."

Sophie let out a peculiar noise. "No, I just really need someone to talk to. Do you have time?"

Leilani closed her eyes. "Mrs. Worthington…" she began.

She did not want to be Sophie's shoulder. Especially not being her fertility doctor. It didn't bother her to be with Evan, but she was directly interacting with Sophie in her treatment and wanted to keep things as neutral as possible between them.

"*Please*," Sophie begged. "I really need to talk to someone."

She paused for a moment and sighed. "Sure, Mrs. Worthington, let's meet at the Starbucks on third in about fifteen."

Leilani hung up the phone, letting out a groan. She did not want to even begin to imagine what this impromptu meeting request could possibly be about with Evan's wife.

———————————— ❖ ————————————

She slowly parked her Benz and looked in the large window of Starbucks, easily spotting Sophie Worthington's bright blond hair in the back booth. She could see her flushed complexion from where she was parked. Leilani let out a deep breath, preparing herself and walked into the restaurant. Sophie's eyes did not gleam nor did she show her optic white teeth like usual when they met. This was the first time that Leilani had ever seen Sophie in an unhappy mood. Doom and gloom hovered around her aura and she knew something was indeed going awry with her life. She cautiously took a seat across from the smaller framed woman, her eyes scanning her fake breasts in the form-fitting yoga attire she wore, her belly exposed in the sports bra; navel ring glistening. Sophie had a set of rock hard abs to kill for and Leilani swallowed her envy.

Leilani relaxed into the wooden bench and cautiously watched Sophie. She could not gauge just how hysterical this woman could become, but after hearing of her mannerisms from Evan and observing her bubbly demeanor in person, she knew it was potential for a scene if her mood was any opposite of happy.

Sophie began to sob and Leilani leaned forward, touching her hand. "Mrs. Worthington, do I need to call someone – your husband?"

She violently shook her hand, wiping her tears as more followed, smearing the mascara down her cheeks. "No, I don't-I don't want anyone that matters to see me like this."

Leilani raised a brow in offense. *What the hell am I, chopped liver?* She thought.

"Your husband could—"

"He told me he doesn't want to have children with me," she blurted out, causing Leilani to quickly lean her back against the seat in shock.

"*What*?" she asked.

Sophie continued to sob, forcing her words through each wrenching sound. Leilani did not glance around, she knew that others were now watching this bleach blond white woman crying her eyes out to this black one and they were all probably holding their fingers on speed dial for the police. Her blue eyes met Leilani's and she looked nothing less than desperate.

"He told me he doesn't want children. With me," she repeated her voice low.

Leilani stared at her; she was at a loss for words. Of course, she knew that Evan had confided in her with his true feelings towards his wife and her interest in having a family with him. But, she could not confess to knowing this. It would damage her professional relationship with Sophie and she could not risk a situation that would add a smear to her name in the community. She licked her lips and raised her brows, trying to think of some encouraging offering to the young woman.

"I want to have his baby," Sophie said.

She watched the bleach blonde's eyes begin to turn into angry slits, her tears subsiding and her emotion changing from sadness to fury.

"Mrs. Worthington, I understand. Give it time. A lot of couples choose not to have childre—"

"I *am going* to have his baby," she said sternly.

"How do you expect to do that, Mrs. Worthington?" she asked, perplexed. "If your husband is unwilling to participate then—"

"I can get his sperm. I just need you to artificially inseminate me," she interrupted.

Leilani's eyes widened. "Excuse me?" she asked.

Sophie sat forward, resting her forearms on the table, her three carat diamond sparkling.

"I refuse to lose Evan. He *will not* leave me. And I know that a baby will keep us together."

She stared at Sophie, speechless. All this time she thought that Evan was embellishing how vindictive, sneaky, persistent and over reactive his wife could be. But, she was now seeing the fruits of her labor firsthand. Leilani uncomfortably shifted in her seat.

"Mrs. Worthington," she began, ensuring that her voice was equally as confident as Sophie's. "It is illegal for me to inseminate a woman with sperm that has been unwillingly obtained."

She laughed. "It wouldn't be *unwillingly* obtained. Evan is my husband. And he has sex with me – quite frequently. I know how to collect it. Besides, he's willingly depositing his sperm into the condoms that *he's* chosen to start wearing," she rationalized. "Consider it an innocent side effect of consensual sex, if you will."

Leilani stared at her and Sophie returned the blank expression. "Sophie," she began, shaking her head. "You do know that I could lose my license?"

"And I could lose my husband," she stated flatly. "And excuse my rudeness, but I honestly don't give a damn about your license if it means I lose Evan."

Leilani let out a deep breath, shaking her head as she began to open her mouth. "Sophie, I don't think you're thinking rationally about what you're asking me to—"

"Dr. Mathews, Evan doesn't have to know – no one has to know. He could very well be easily led to believe that this was a simple accident. I've been taking the fertility medication that you prescribed. And," she shrugged with a grin, "We both know that condoms break all the time."

Leilani watched her; Sophie's demeanor was a complete opposite of what she had first witnessed when she entered Starbucks. She then realized that it was all a show in hopes that she'd hear Sophie's plea and be willing to partake in her underhanded plan to chain down Evan.

"Mrs. Worthington, I'm sorry, but I can't help you," she said, "Not this way."

"Five hundred thousand," Sophie said quickly.

Leilani raised her eyebrows. "Ex-excuse me?" she asked.

"That's what I'll pay you," she answered.

She did not need the money, but that was an offer that not many would turn down especially when it involved something simple to do. This was a procedure that Leilani had done a dime a dozen. She could do it in her sleep and her success rates were highly ranked. She thought of Evan. He was a wonderful man and listening to the desperation in Sophie's voice and insane talk only confirmed how great of a guy he was.

"Mrs. Worthington," she said softly and closed her eyes. Leilani couldn't understand how Sophie could have access to that much money and her husband not notice it disappearing. She was playing with fire.

"One million," she offered.

Leilani took in a deep breath and exhaled, looking down at the tabletop. Sophie watched her.

"Everyone has a price and I'm willing to go as far as I need to keep you quiet."

"Please," Leilani paused. "I can't do this." *To Evan above all*, she thought.

Sophie sat back. "Then I will make you do it," she said angrily.

She smirked. "*Make me*? Let's not get ahead of ourselves here."

Sophie raised an eyebrow. "I have my ways of persuasion, Dr. Mathews. Everyone has a price."

"I'm not for sale," she stated.

"I know you are the best of the best and I am *not* willing to sit back and lose my husband. I know you think I sound crazy, but," she laughed, "If you had what I have, you would understand why I will go to great lengths to keep him."

"And I'd hope that you'd understand how valuable my ability to practice medicine is, Sophie," Leilani replied.

Sophie laughed, stood and slid a thick yellow envelope on the table towards Leilani.

"Consider that an incentive to your value," she paused with a grin as Leilani opened it and looked inside, her eyes growing wide. "I will be calling your office to schedule that appointment," she said and walked away.

Leilani stared at the envelope sitting on the table in front of her as if it was infected with a virus. She knew that if she took it, it'd be the end of her moral character as a doctor. She would be accepting a bribe to do something illegal. Above all, she could not swallow the guilt of trapping a man that wanted so desperately to leave a situation that he was unhappy in. She sighed and picked up her smartphone, sending a quick text message.

RAIN CHECK FOR TONIGHT. UNEXPECTED PATIENT ENCOUNTER.

She couldn't face Evan tonight after this unpredicted chain of events.

❈

Weeks Later - 5:34 PM

"When is this little medical conference of yours over?" Darnell asked.

Leilani smiled, thinking that her husband was going to admit that he missed her being home. She stopped undressing out of her two-piece Vera Wang suit and walked to the window, looking at the view of the Vegas strip.

"Why? You miss me already after only one day?" she inquired.

The sun felt amazing against her skin. She always enjoyed being on high levels of hotels because it gave the best view and the most exposure to the sunlight's beautiful rays.

He laughed. "It's only so much pizza I can order," he replied.

She rolled her eyes. "You're such the romantic," she said and he laughed again.

It wasn't a joke.

Leilani heard his fingers typing in the background. "Duty calls," she replied.

She was disappointed in her husband for his lack of being a husband. She paused, listening to him talk to himself for a few minutes and she grew impatient. Again, work had taken precedence over bonding with his wife who was out of town and alone for five days in Sin City.

"What did you say?" he asked.

She sighed, commencing the removal of her clothes. "Nothing."

She didn't feel like talking to him any longer, especially when he was obviously distracted by what he considered to be more important than her.

"Well, I'm going to go get something to eat before it gets too crowded. Call me later?"

"Uh, yeah—what? Yeah. Okay, talk to you later," he replied, barely paying attention to their conversation.

"Love you," she said to only hear a dial tone in response.

Leilani groaned and tapped her forehead on the cool glass of the window.

"Why am I still with you?" she muttered.

She turned and scanned around the living room of the suite. It was luxurious and she would have enjoyed Darnell being here with her to enjoy it. But, as expected, he made every excuse in the book why he could not afford to take off three days and the weekend to come with her to Vegas – all expenses paid.

He could have very well worked from the hotel suite, but Leilani knew that the gentlemen's clubs would be too much of a temptation to her husband. Besides, her being gone was vacation enough for him. She didn't expect him to willingly volunteer to go away with the person he enjoyed not having to be around if he could control it. He could enjoy his world without the interruption of his wife. She walked into the spa bathroom and eyeballed the jacuzzi.

"Looks like it's just you and me tonight," she said, unsnapping her bra and tossing it to the floor.

* * *

Day Two, Friday - 10:54 PM

Leilani leaned against the wall, sipping from her Ketel One martini as she observed the dancers and those looking to find their next one night stand. She had grown bored watching television in her suite and decided to use her VIP pass to Club Mix. She didn't think that Darnell would call her back, seeing as though he was barely interested in the short conversation they had earlier that evening.

A handful of guys had made their advances on her, their eyes raking her curvy physique in the pencil skirt and perky breasts peeking out of the low cut sleeveless lace top she wore. Her Louboutin stilettos made her derriere switch harder as she walked and demanded attention when at rest. As usual, she turned them down with a polite smile and sent the persistent ones on about their business by flashing her dazzling wedding set in their line of sight.

"*Ahhh*, so this is where you go hiding when you're not screening the calls to your suite," she heard a voice say that drew her to roll her eyes.

She turned to see Dr. Grizwold's furry facial hair and his dark brown eyes looking down at her through the bifocal lenses, his crooked bottom teeth looking freshly sharpened. He was a cardiologist with a specialty in neuro and Leilani was avoiding him like he had H1N1.

She had to spend an hour presentation listening to him banter in her ear with advances the minute he sat down next to her the day before. She had been successful in dodging him, but she knew that eventually and as persistent as he was, he'd find her like the needle in the haystack that she was trying to be.

"Dr. Grizwold," she greeted without a smile, turning to go back to her voyeurism of the crowd.

The older, darker man was easily pushing fifty and the scale had to tip him well past two hundred on his six foot even stocky frame. Leilani couldn't even imagine if he possibly possessed a past in which he was actually attractive. From what she had seen thus far from his unkempt facial hair, neglect on his exercise and nutrition and dental upkeep, she had concluded that he had to have been divorced if ever married at all.

He moved closer and she could smell his slight sweatiness mixed with Cool Water. It was hot in the club, but not enough to make someone's cologne begin to renege on their agreement. She eased her body away from him and he followed her like black on a leopard's skin. She felt his hand bump and linger against her rear and Leilani took in a sharp breath, calming the urge to knee him in his crotch.

"And where is this lovely evening ending?" he asked.

She smiled stiffly, angry that the crowd was now bumping her back into the older man; his hand continuing to accidentally grope against her buttocks. She turned, facing him to stop the assault and sat her finished drink on the passing waitress' tray. She was a little buzzed, but not enough to lose sight of Dr. Grizwold's unwanted advances.

"I'm going to bed. *Alone*," she replied.

He grinned and Leilani attempted to back away from him to only feel his clammy hands reaching for hers, pulling her back towards him. She grimaced, attempting to back away again. This time, his grip became tighter on her wrists as he pulled her against his belly.

"Dr. Grizwold," she said angrily. "Let go of me."

He grinned. "A beautiful woman like you shouldn't be alone in a place like this," he said, leaning closer to her face as she backed away.

Leilani gulped, smelling the vodka on his breath. She put her hand on his chest, attempting to push him back, but his body was much larger than her own.

"I think you've had one too many, Doctor." she said.

Moments like this, she wished that she did not have to travel alone. She never had men do more than flirt and follow her a few feet, but she knew that Dr. Grizwold was far from a gentleman – not the way that he was man handling her.

"Where's your husband, Dr. Mathews?"

She stared into his eyes, seeing the hostility raging in them. She tried to pull herself away from his grip, but he held her tighter.

"Where is your husband?" he demanded.

"Leilani." They both heard a voice interrupt.

Dr. Grizwold loosened his grip on her. She pulled away immediately and turned, both of them seeing Mr. Evan Worthington standing there. Her eyes widened in shock and she gulped. She looked at Evan as if she'd seen a ghost. He smiled, covering the space between them and reaching behind her to place his hand on the small of her back. Her body jerked in surprise of Evan's touch; a chill running up her spine.

"I've been looking all over for you, angel," he said and looked at the older man, extending his hand.

"Darnell Mathews, and you are?" Evan questioned, his height and athletic frame towering over them.

Dr. Grizwold's eyes were as wide as an 8-ball. He began to stutter.

"Dr. Lawrence Grizwold," he shook his hand in return. "I didn't," he glanced at Leilani. "I didn't realize that her husband was…" he stopped.

"White?" Evan answered for him with a raised brow.

He shook his head and laughed loudly. "No! Not at all!" he exclaimed. "That you were—that you were *here* with her on the conference," Dr. Grizwold finished.

Evan smiled and looked down at Leilani, seeing her face flushed with embarrassment. He wrapped his fingers around her waist and pulled her closer to him. She gasped quietly, his intoxicating aroma and solid body causing her pulse to quicken.

"She wasn't expecting me," Evan gave her a gentle squeeze on the waist. "She's speechless from her surprise."

Evan looked at the older man. "It was nice meeting you," he said to Dr. Grizwold. "Now if you will excuse us, my wife and I have the rest of our evening to enjoy."

Dr. Grizwold grinned nervously at the two of them, glancing down at Leilani who remained hushed.

"I uh, I be—better get going. I have a presentation to attend first thing in the morning."

The doctor looked at Leilani and extended his hand. "It was lovely seeing you again, Mrs. Mathews. I look forward to the rest of our conference together."

She didn't shake his hand. Evan had intercepted it with his own rigid handshake.

"Goodnight, Dr. Grizwold," he said, firmly dismissing him.

They both watched him retreat quickly through the crowd. Evan looked down, turning to face her.

"Are you okay?" he asked, concerned at her apprehensive appearance.

Leilani raised her eyebrows. "Um…yeah-yeah. I think so. Thank you, Evan."

He smiled. "It's no problem. I saw that you needed an intervention, so I am glad to help out when I can."

She furrowed her eyebrows. "Wait—why—why are you here in Vegas?"

Evan laughed. "You're the one getting harassed but you're concerned about me being here?"

She laughed with him. "No, I mean you—you just *swooped* in here like Superman. I'm not sure what help beacon I sent out for you to see."

He laughed again and licked his lips. "I attend some of the medical conferences that the companies I invest heavily in are participating. I flew in this afternoon on the company jet and decided to pop up here just to unwind before the craziness starts for me." He held up a laminated badge with a sideways grin. "How could I resist VIP?"

She nodded, her mood not lightening.

"At least I know you're not stalking me," she said with a nervous laugh.

Evan smiled. "Don't flatter yourself, *friend*," he teased with a quick wink, hearing her nervously laugh again.

Leilani closed her eyes and took in a deep breath, attempting to calm her nerves. She was on edge with how Dr. Grizwold behaved. She licked her lips and shook her head, exhaling.

"I can't believe he acted like that. He's usually very polite," she said.

He raised his brows. "Intoxication has a way of bringing out the Dr. Jekyll in all of us," he replied.

She nodded and snatched two Jell-O shots from the passing tray, swiftly swallowing them.

"No kidding. It sure took me by surprise because I had a lot of trust for him," she paused. "I can only imagine if you weren't here…" her voice trailed off as she stared into the distance; her mind gone.

Evan continued to watch her. Leilani began to appear increasingly aggravated.

"Let's get you out of here," he suggested and she nodded, allowing him to grab her hand and escort her through the socializing crowd of the VIP lounge.

Evan walked with Leilani to her suite and they stood in the doorway. He watched her fumbling with her key. She was still out of all sorts from her encounter with the doctor. He reached over and touched her hand to steady it and insert the key for her. Leilani laughed at herself as he pushed open the door.

"I'm sorry," she said, "My mind is just all over the place. That…incident has me beside myself."

"It's okay. Don't apologize," he replied and held her room key out to her; remaining outside.

Leilani leaned on the door and they looked into each other's eyes in silence. She smiled.

"I really appreciate you helping me, Evan," she said, feeling more at ease now that she was in her suite.

He shrugged slightly.

"What can I say? Superman to the rescue – although I have always been a big fan of Spiderman," he said and they laughed.

She straightened her posture with a deep sigh and his eyes skimmed her frame, his expression relaxed. Leilani wondered what went through his mind whenever he looked at her. He had a poker face and she could never read into what he was feeling unless it was during conversation about his wife.

Evan shifted, beginning to turn and her eyes admired his body, catching a glimpse of his toned ass in the Dolce slacks that perfectly fell against his Berluti Rapieces shoes. She admired his taste in fine clothes even though it was a bit pricey in her opinion just for a night in a Vegas club.

"Well, I guess I will be heading back to my suite now," he

said. "The club is about to close in a few, so I missed my chance to cut a rug," he ended with a smile.

She giggled. "I'd never peg you for a dancer."

Evan grinned as he adjusted his cuffs. "I'm not always Mr. Businessman. I do know how to have fun. You're also talking to lead stepper of his fraternity."

"*Ah*, look at you," Leilani said with a grin.

She was genuinely surprised at this news of Evan.

"Don't get too cocky. You happen to be in the presence of three year reigning cheer captain and dance troupe choreographer. I'm sure I still have a dance-off or two in me," she challenged.

They laughed and Leilani glanced down at her Breitling.

"I'll let you go. I'm sure your husband has probably been waiting up for your call," he said.

She smirked. "Yeah, you definitely don't know the real Mr. Darnell Mathews."

Evan shook his head. "Although I did enjoy being someone else for approximately ten minutes though."

"Yes, you did a good deed to save a friend," she replied with a smile.

He scanned her body again as he nodded.

"Yes," he raised a brow. "A friend."

They stared at each other for a moment and Leilani licked her lips, watching his sapphire blue eyes glance at the motion. His expression was still unchanging.

"Can I borrow you for a bit?" she inquired and he raised his eyebrows. "I'd like to discuss something with you," she said.

Leilani wasn't ready to bid adieu to her handsome friend just yet...

"So how are things with you and the misses?" he asked, gulping down the rest of his Corona.

Darnell shrugged. "Things are going, I guess."

Russell looked at him. "You guess?"

"Yeah, I mean, we're not arguing and fighting. So, things are fine."

Russell laughed. "*Man*, we been friends for *years* and this is the first time I've ever heard you say some shit like that to describe ya'll relationship."

"What you want me to say? We're doing alright." Darnell asked, irritated.

Russell nodded. "Alright, I'll leave you alone. I'm just sayin'. That sounds like you biding time for the grand escape, man," he replied.

Darnell shrugged, drinking from his Budweiser as he eyeballed a group of black women at the bar.

Russell followed his gaze and laughed. "*Way* too young for you, my man," he said, "They look fresh out of high school."

Darnell grinned at him. "Grown is grown," he said with a chuckle.

Russell leaned back in his chair and began to sip from the new Corona bottle the bartender dropped off.

"I got me a little bitty on the side," he said with a smile.

"Yeah right. You're bullshitting," Darnell said with a laugh.

"How much you wanna bet?" he asked, pulling out a wad of cash.

"I'll put five on it that that's all in your dreams," Darnell said, reaching for the green and tossing it on the table.

Russell nodded, grabbing for his cell.

"Alright," he nodded again. "Get ready to pay up," he said with a huge grin as he tossed his smartphone across to his friend.

Darnell's eyes widened as he looked at the photo. "Whose ass is this?" he asked, shocked.

His friend laughed loudly. "It *ain't* my wife's. So, don't worry about it," he said. "Just let me collect my dough."

He stared at the photo and Russell leaned forward, snatching it.

"I'll take that back now," Russell said.

Darnell shook his head in awe. "*Man*, that's all you?" His friend nodded. "You're for real?" he asked.

Russell nodded.

"How long have you been smashing that?" Darnell excitedly inquired.

Russell licked his lips, still grinning. "A few months now."

"And Cheryl doesn't have a clue you're stepping out on her?" Darnell asked, glancing back at the women at the bar.

"Let's just say that I work a lot of *odd* hours on this new case I'm handling," he said with a wink.

Darnell laughed and shook his head.

"You one lucky bastard. Leilani would catch my ass before I could even finish the fantasy in my head. She's on me like a damn detective."

Russell smirked.

"That's where we're different. Cheryl may snoop, but I know how to use her paranoia against her. She doesn't know where I am or who I'm with. It's none of her business, really. I'm a grown man and it took some time, but she knows who wears the pants. She stopped questioning me."

Darnell raised his eyebrows in envy. "If only," he said; his thoughts wandering.

Russell watched Darnell. He refused to tell what he knew about Leilani inquiring about divorce settlements between her and Darnell. He had been friends with them since undergrad and valued their relationship. They were good people and he would never put himself in the middle or be the cause of any drama between them.

"You ever step out on Lei?" he asked.

Darnell looked at him and glanced down at his Budweiser, twirling it in circles. Russell laughed.

"When'd you do it?" Russell asked.

Darnell licked his lips, shrugging one shoulder as he glanced back at the women at the bar.

"It's no big deal. I got close, but nothing happened beyond head," Darnel impassively replied.

"*What?* The Mr. Darnell Mathews actually sniffed him some poon tang other than Leilani!?" Russell exclaimed, elbowing his friend's shoulder.

They both laughed.

"What happened? Why didn't you dive in?" Russell questioned.

Darnell sucked his teeth. "Her sitter called."

He scoffed. "*Damn.* When was this?" Russell asked.

Darnell raised his eyebrows as he reminisced.

"Last year. It was this chick I worked with for a few months. We were the only two black people in the office and went out to lunch a few times, and then she invited me over her place and we kicked it there a couple nights." Darnell shrugged slightly. "No big deal. We were just kickin' it. She was a cool broad and I liked her company." He looked at Russell. "You remember when I was out of town doing that pro bono work?"

Russell nodded. "Yeah."

"It was then. She was a little bitty in the office." Darnell shrugged. "Wasn't much to look at. But, if you put a man and a woman together long enough…"

"Shit tends to pop off," his friend finished for him.

"*Exactly* and," Darnell shrugged again. "Lei's beautiful. Fine as hell if you ask me or *any* man."

Russell nodded in agreement.

"But, she can really stress me out. I don't get how she can be so insecure. Confidence makes a woman more attractive. Not the shit she's got going on," Darnell vented.

Russell raised his eyebrows and shook his head.

"Your lady *is* fine," Russell said and shrugged, taking another sip of his Corona. "But you know how females can be. One wrong comment and you can fuck up their whole image of themselves for life."

Darnell raised his eyebrows. "Well, that's not my problem. I didn't make Lei feel the way she does. I shouldn't have to pay the price for all the cats before her and whatever issues she developed when she found out she was adopted."

His friend nodded. "I feel you on that one. I'm glad I don't have to deal with that with Cheryl. She's as confident as they come. She has that I don't give a damn attitude. I love that about her."

Darnell looked at him. "Lucky you cause Lei can be a trip and a half. I promise, I think she really needs to go see someone."

Russell laughed. "You calling your wife crazy?" he asked.

Darnell smirked. "No. But, she's got some issues. I don't have the time nor interest to help her with it. She's always trying to drag me to the counselor. Talking about, *we* have issues. No, *you* have issues. I'm fine."

His friend laughed again, shaking his head. "Man, that pretty of a woman and—"

"And she can't even be confident with me around other women or when I go on road trips. She loses her damn mind. That's why I don't pick up the phone when I'm out. I call her when I get good and ready—I don't have time to deal with the nonsense." Russell smirked. "I got more important shit to do than to listen to her complain about what I *don't* do for her."

Darnell glanced at the women at the bar again. "I haven't *really* cheated, I don't go upside her head and I'm home every night. If I'm not home, I'm working or with you. That's more than what most brothers do."

Russell raised his eyebrows. "You got a point there, bruh. She's lucky to have you."

"Exactly what I tell her. These women nowadays want sensitive brothers. *Hold me, kiss me*, tell me you love me every single minute of the day." Darnell sucked his teeth. "I am a man. *Men* don't do all that foolishness," he said. "Shut up and put this dick in your mouth. Put it to good use instead of always being open complaining. Do us both a fucking favor."

Russell laughed and Darnell scoffed, taking another sip from his beer.

"Cheers to that," Russell said and they clinked their beer bottles together.

Darnell continued to look around the bar, eyeballing the different shades, shapes and sizes of the women. He thought of Leilani and remembered how attractive she was the first day he laid eyes on her. He felt like he had won a grand prize to have that beautiful of a woman on his arm. The perfect package. There were things she did every once in a while that drove him mad. But, he loved her nonetheless. Russell watched him scour the room.

"You regret it?" Russell asked.

Darnell looked at him. "Regret what?"

"Not tagging the ole' bitty when you had the chance?"

Darnell exhaled deeply. "It'd been nice to try something new. I've been with Lei for a while. But," he shrugged. "I don't think I'm missing out on much. I've got a good lady at home. She's faithful and," he paused with a laugh. "I'm not even gonna front. She can suck a mean one and she got that cocaine."

Russell laughed. "Cocaine is a helluva drug!"

They both laughed.

"I'm serious, man. The pussy is *on point*," Darnell said. "I have to ration it out so I don't get addicted."

Russell raised his eyebrows and nodded. "Yeah, then she's a keeper. I see why you put it on lock."

"So what would you say if Cheryl found out about your side bitty?" Darnell asked.

"It is what it is. I can't rewind time. I did it. I'm honestly at the point of move on or divorce me."

"Damn," Darnell said. "If it's been going on for a few months, how are you holding it down with your lady?"

Russell laughed. "I leave her satisfied so she won't be suspicious."

Darnell sucked his teeth. "See, that's the thing. I just don't wanna be bothered. One woman is enough and Lei is a handful all by herself. I already gotta lie or not tell her anything just to keep her off my back. She can be *so* damn judgmental."

Russell watched him. "What would you do if she left you?" he asked.

Darnell paused for a moment before answering, one woman in particular catching his eye that made her way over to one of the pool tables. His gaze slid down to look at the roundness of her ass – just the way he liked it.

Darnell licked his lips. "I'm not gonna fight to keep someone who wants to leave. That's just the way it is."

He looked at Russell and tipped his beer in the direction of the woman he was admiring, "As they say, on to the next one."

5
The Last Straw

"*So,* do you have any good news?"

Leilani came out of the restroom and tossed the white contraption in the trash bin, walking past Camille and into the living room of her friend's modest two bedroom condo. Camille followed behind Leilani and glanced in the bin.

"No?" she asked.

"No is correct. Another big fail," Leilani replied disappointingly and went into Camille's fridge, pulling out the bottle of Tropicana orange juice.

"Maybe it's all that damn OJ you're drinking that's diluting your urine," Camille said with a laugh.

Leilani looked at her and rolled her eyes as she poured herself a glass.

"Ha-ha, very funny," Leilani replied.

Camille sat down on the bar stool. "Maybe it's just too early to test," she encouraged.

Leilani looked at her. "I'm so done with this." She shook her head, looking down at the counter. "I give up on ever getting pregnant."

"Don't say that!" Camille exclaimed. "You gotta have at least one. You're too pretty to let all that beauty go to waste."

Leilani smirked. "Tell my husband that," she said.

"How long has it been?" Camille asked.

"Um," Leilani looked forward, placing the glass on the countertop and thinking. "We're at about three weeks."

"With no sex?" Camille yelled. "What the hell is wrong with ya'll?"

Leilani walked into the living room and sat down on her sofa.

"It's just how it's been for the past few years. I'm so used to it now, I don't even notice unless you ask me," she replied, grabbing the remote.

Camille sat down on the sofa next to Leilani and pat Leilani's thigh in reassurance. "You'll get knocked up in no time, Lei." She paused and shrugged with a laugh. "And if you don't, I say just rape his ass."

Leilani looked at her, narrowing her eyes.

"*Oh please,*" she said and sucked her teeth. "I've tried that before and Darnell has mastered the art of keeping it flaccid. I've even put in porn and tried to manually stimulate him."

"Nothing?" Camille asked, bewildered.

"Nada, zilch, not even a flinch of some life in his little pee wee." Leilani replied.

Her bestie giggled, "Little?" Camille inquired.

Leilani rolled her eyes. "Don't *even* get me started on that. With his ego, you'd thought his was dragging the floor. It barely surpasses his balls."

Her friend giggled at the unexpected confession.

"*Well,* I don't have that problem with Russell..." Camille bragged with a click of her tongue.

Leilani groaned in frustration. "His size doesn't bother me. It's fine," she replied.

Camille chuckled. "Better you than me," she muttered.

Leilani ignored her and continued. "I'm near my mid-thirties. Adoption is tempting at this point."

Camille laughed. "Its women in their forties and fifties having babies. All isn't lost for you, Lei."

She raised a brow. "Do I look like I wanna have a baby in my forties?"

"I mean, look at Mrs. Worthington, she's going on thirty-four and she's been blowing up the office trying to schedule appointments with you to get knocked up and it's been what – only a couples months for her with no success?" Camille said.

Leilani swallowed, her thoughts reminiscing to Mrs. Worthington's bold proposition.

"Some people just don't need to have babies," she finally replied.

Camille raised a brow. "I hope you're not talking about yourself," she said.

Leilani shook her head, thinking of Sophie Worthington and her incessant attempts to track Leilani down. Leilani had been screening her calls since she mailed back the envelope offered to her that day in Starbucks. She refused to partake in any piece of Sophie's scheme to hoodwink her husband.

She never told Evan of his wife's proposition. Yet, during their unexpected run in at the Vegas conference, she strongly encouraged him to check his condoms before having sex with his wife – called it a *woman's intuition*. She wasn't sure if he paid her any mind, but she had faith that he was keeping a watchful eye on his wife from then on out.

"It's been two years for me—"

"Yeah, but you and Darnell don't bone! That's the bottom line, Lei. There's nothing wrong with you or him. You two just are acting like a frigid old couple," her friend interjected.

Leilani looked at her. "That's not entirely me."

"*No,* but you don't push for it enough with Darnell. I'm sure if you approached him for it more, he'd be responsive. But, you've just kinda sat back and decided to deal with it, *as is*. I'd be yanking on that motherfucker's dick."

Leilani groaned loudly and rolled her eyes. "I'm *so* done with this conversation," she said softly, "Can we please move on?"

Camille shifted, grabbing her smartphone off the coffee table.

"*All* I'm saying is, desperate times call for desperate measures," she paused, "Shit, you can have mine if you really want a baby *that* bad."

Leilani looked at her. "What do you mean *yours*?" she asked with a raised brow. "Moon?"

The short-haired mulatto continued to stare at her phone, pressing onto the touch screen.

"*Moon*?" Leilani pressed, nudging her.

Camille looked at Leilani and sat her smartphone down on her thigh.

"What you think I mean?" she asked with a twist of her neck.

Leilani's mouth dropped open, "*Girl*," she paused, "Russell?" she asked.

Camille shrugged and Leilani shifted in her seated position, turning to face her more.

"Why are you shrugging?" Leilani exclaimed, her voice louder, "You're pregnant!"

Camille sprung to her feet, pacing.

"*Damn*, don't tell the whole Nation of Islam! Lower your voice, Lei! I *do* have neighbors!"

Leilani stared at her best friend, her eyes scanning over her petite frame. Her mind began to race as she attempted to calculate how far along in her pregnancy she was. Camille hadn't gained a pound – let alone did she look like she had another person growing inside of her.

Camille hadn't taken sick days nor was she suffering from morning sickness—none that she had witnessed at least. Leilani's eyes skimmed over her flat abdomen in the tan tank – ruffles from extra material moving along with her stride. The fabric hadn't begun to stretch from a growing womb.

Leilani swallowed. "Moon, how long have you known about it?"

Camille stopped walking and began to calculate. "The last time I had a period was like two months ago. So, I don't know, I guess I'm about three months or so."

Leilani raised her eyebrows. "You haven't been to a doctor?"

She sucked her teeth, attitude flowing from her pores. "I don't have time to be bothered with it. I figured it was just my birth control going haywire. I missed it a few days and, well," she shrugged. "I didn't think nothing of it until I missed one period—"

"Then another one," Leilani interjected.

"Thank you, Dr. Mathews," she replied with attitude, "Besides, Russell has a wife. He ain't got time for the drama either," Camille explained.

Leilani watched her best friend, she was calm, unmoved by her state of events. Leilani wondered how she could be so at ease with her situation. She was carrying a married man's child – she'd be a single parent all the way through. They both knew that Russell would deny it to the ends of the earth. He would not risk losing anything that he had worked so hard to earn – especially not his money if this came to the light.

"So, is it confirmed then?" Leilani asked.

Camille furrowed her eyebrows. "Is what confirmed?"

"Did you take a test of *any* sort?"

"Yeah," Camille nodded. "Of course. When I missed the second period, I took one."

"And?" Leilani pressed.

"*And* what?" Camille replied, "It came back positive. Then I took like three more and they *all* came back with the little fucking smiley face like the shit is good news," she said. She was irritated.

Leilani leaned back against the sofa and inhaled a deep breath. She was wrestling with her rising envy of Camille being pregnant—with the ease with which she had gotten pregnant without trying. To add fuel to the fire, she had become with child while on birth control. She closed her eyes, forcing down her envy and reminding herself that this was not about her. She needed to be a friend first.

"So what are you going to do about it?" Leilani asked her voice soft, her focus on her freshly manicured French tipped nails.

Camille sat down beside her and sighed. "I'm getting rid of it. I already have an appointment scheduled."

"So you thought jokingly telling me I could have your baby was a good way to break the news to your BFF?" Leilani asked with a raised eyebrow.

They both laughed and Camille shrugged slightly.

"I wasn't planning on telling *any*body. I just wanted it over and done with. But," she looked into her eyes, "You really want to be a mother. So, why not give you the option—even if it is your best friend's illegitimate baby?"

Leilani looked at her and there was awkward silence between them. She licked her lips and took in a deep breath. "Well," she began, "let me talk to Darnell about—"

"Lei, no," Camille closed her eyes. "No, don't talk to him." She shook her head. "Shit, I don't feel like dealing with that asshole."

"*Excuse you*," Leilani said, offended.

"I'm just saying. I don't—" She shook her head. "Plus, he and Russell are all buddy-buddy. I don't need," she paused again. "No. It's just simpler if I get rid of it."

Leilani watched her. "He's my husband, Moon. I can't bring a random baby home like it's a bag of groceries."

"I know that. But this is *my* personal business. Darnell isn't gonna raise a kid without knowing the whole story. That just ain't gonna happen. You and I both know how he is."

"Yeah, but Moon, he's also very giving—"

Camille scoffed. "Yeah to *charity*. And I'm not charity. I could raise this baby on my own if I wanted it. I don't need him holding this over me." She shook her head, "Besides, he hasn't even gotten *you* knocked up. So what makes you think he really even wants kids in the first place?"

Leilani felt the stab of harsh reality. She gulped, feeling her emotions of disappointment begin to well up inside of her. She would not take it out on her best friend. Camille meant no harm in her words.

Two Days Later

"You busy tonight?"

"Yeah, unfortunately, I have to catch up before my boss notices. I've been bs-ing on my j.o.b., thanks to *someone* texting me all day during work," she said with a grin.

His deep laugh reverberated, causing her smile to widen. He was charming and he knew she couldn't resist it.

"You like those sexts," he replied, *"That's why you should let me come over tonight."*

She giggled. "I told you I have to catch up—"

"And I need to catch up on them draws. You've been dodging this D for a week now. You starting to make me think I'm old news."

She laughed. "No, you're far from old news."

"A-ight, then let me come by and show you how CNN special I am then," he flirted and they both laughed.

She waited, considering the offer.

"Come on girl, you know you miss this special edition I break off in you. And I'm tellin' you; tonight will be front page headlines."

She smiled and looked down at her stomach, rolling her eyes as she ignored his seed growing inside of her.

"You won't regret it," he cooed.

Camille nibbled on her bottom lip and the soft fluttering was replaced with anticipation. She wanted him; couldn't avoid his specialties no longer than she could any other great opportunity. She licked her lips, her body growing excited as he continued to whisper sweet nothings in her ear through the Bluetooth.

"So, you gonna let me come by or no?" he finally asked.

She raised a brow. "Yeah, bring that D on over. I'm headed home now."

He grinned widely and hung up, sending a quick text, OPERATION DL.

Dinner Table

"What are you grinning about?" Leilani asked, watching her husband smiling childishly at his smartphone screen. She wanted in on the fun.

He did not reply to her question as they ate dinner that she had prepared. She knew he was intentionally ignoring her and as usual practice. He enjoyed the distraction of other things than attempting to have a conversation with his wife.

Darnell sat down his fork and began to text back, OPERATION NOSEY WIFE. ENJOY THE FREEDOM! He laughed as he placed his smartphone face down on the table – opposite the side of Leilani so it was out of her reach. He did not allow her to peruse through his phone. After all, it was HIS property and none of her business what was inside of it even if she was his wife.

Leilani watched him, growing envious of his happiness of interacting with others. She did not understand why Darnell was married to her for all these years. It had become apparent that he sought pleasure through his relationships with others and she was not on his A-list. He barely conversed with her, and she constantly found him rudely on his phone with others during what could be an opportune time for them to bond; case and point, while eating dinner together in the privacy of their home.

However, Darnell always found a way to bring other disturbances to their lives. She didn't understand how they could manage having children if a mere pet was a deal breaker in maintaining their livelihood. She attempted to not allow his disregard change her mood. Her mind had been on Camille and the possibility of being a mother – even if it wasn't her own child. She licked her lips and swallowed the bite of food in her mouth.

"Would you ever entertain adopting?" she began.

Darnell furrowed his eyebrows, not making eye contact. She was interrupting his peacefulness and Leilani could see his body growing tense, his smile fading at the sound of her voice breaking the silence. It seemed as though her talking to him was uncalled for unless he initiated the conversation.

"Did you hear me?" she asked, watching him.

He raised an eyebrow in acknowledgement, but continued to eat. Leilani was not going to let him dodge another serious conversation with her. She had grown irritated with him and would not be hushed like she was "the help".

"Would you entertain it?" she pressed.

Darnell took a slow drink from his glass, moving slowly as he sliced into the tender steak. He was intentionally drawing out the response as long as he could. He did not want to know where this conversation would be headed if he participated in it. Leilani continued to watch him, waiting for an answer as he avoided eye contact with her.

"Darnell," she said, "I asked you something."

He looked at her. "And I heard the question."

"Aren't you going to answer?" she asked.

"I don't have to answer you just because you start talking to me," he snapped.

"What kind of shitty comment is that?" she was growing upset.

Darnell broke eye contact. "If I don't feel like talking, Lei. I don't have to."

She scoffed. He continued.

"When I come home, I just want peace and quiet. I talk to people *all* day long."

"Yet you're texting on your phone like a stupid teenager," she muttered. "You have time for that, but not me."

He laughed, shaking his head. "Actually, I don't have time for *this* shit tonight," he said.

She stood, taking her plate with her as she made her way towards the kitchen.

"Excuse me for bothering you, *asshole*," she snapped.

Darnell watched her bounteous, perky ass switch against the floor length-sleeveless nightgown she wore and felt a twitch in his pants. He still found Leilani tremendously attractive. She was a damn good looking woman and he knew that he was lucky to have her. But, he had grown tired of the responsibility of being with her. She was draining and no matter how much her beauty made him want to bend her over and take her right then and there, the frustration of her emotional baggage superseded the desire. He chose to just be left alone.

Leilani returned and he glanced at the plenteous cleavage temptingly poking out from the V-neck of the gown. She was still infuriated and began to coarsely wipe her section of the table.

"You're unbelievable, Darnell. I really don't know why you got married because you aren't involved in this marriage one bit. You're just as bad as Russell's two-timing ass."

He looked at her, taken aback by her knowledge of his friend's infidelity. Darnell furrowed his eyebrows.

"Don't bring Russell into this," he retorted.

She looked back at him and raised an eyebrow. "*Don't*? Why shouldn't I? You hang with him like he's the next best thing since sliced bread."

"He's my boy—"

Leilani nodded. "Yeah, he *sure* is. That's what concerns me. That you enjoy being around a cheat."

Darnell laughed.

"So, let me get this straight. You trying to say that I'm a cheater just cause he is?" he asked.

Leilani stopped cleaning, equally taken aback as he.

"So *you know* about him cheating on Cheryl?" she asked.

He panicked, but did not let it show in his expression. It was an honor code, he couldn't betray his friend. Darnell shifted, breaking eye contact with Leilani.

"I don't know what he's doing and honestly, it's none of my *or your* business," he barked.

Leilani walked next to him, snatching up his smartphone and going through his texts. She swiftly moved away from the table to create distance between them. Darnell jumped from his seat and chased her, forcibly snatching his phone from her grasp.

"Have you lost your mind?" he yelled.

"Oh, so I can't look at your cell? Why, Darnell? I am your wife after all."

He scanned his screen, setting his security lock and sliding it into his holster. He stomped towards the table.

"Don't start something you can't finish, Leilani," he warned, yanking the dining chair backward and taking a seat.

Leilani watched him, pacing back to the dining room table.

"What is that supposed to mean?" she challenged.

Darnell raised his eyebrows. "Don't go through my shit."

"*Your* shit? The last time I checked, we're married. There shouldn't be secrets between us!" she yelled.

"That doesn't mean you have to know every fucking little thing!" he shouted.

Her offended expression stunned him.

"I have nothing to hide," Darnell quickly added.

Leilani laughed. "Then why do you lock your cell? Keep it with you all the damn time? Lock your laptop when you leave the room? I'm not the fucking CIA. I'm your wife," she argued.

"I don't give a damn who you are. My shit is my shit and it's not yours to go through."

"What's operation nosey wife? *Enjoy the freedom*, huh? What is that supposed to mean?"

Darnell took in a deep breath. He realized she had seen his texts to Russell. He licked his lips and continued to eat.

"Back off, Lei," he cautioned.

"You know what? Fuck you, Darnell! Fuck you and this shitty

marriage! I'm so tired of you treating me like I have to have approval to be with you! You're full of *so* much shit!" She was livid.

He refused to look at her. Darnell was attempting to contain his temper. He had grown tired of Leilani and her emotional breakdowns.

"You need to go see someone to get your head straight," he said. "Cause' I'm tired of dealing with this bullshit Lei—"

"No, you need to be a goddamn husband! Cause' what I'm getting is a second hand version!" she yelled, "That's the bullshit *I'm* tired of!"

Darnell smirked. "You know what? If you don't like the model you got, then trade me in. Obviously, you're not happy. So, why are you with me, Lei?" He looked at her. "Huh? Why are you with someone that doesn't do anything right?"

She stared into his eyes and Darnell stood, facing her.

"Just leave me. There's the fucking door. It's locked from the inside. I'm not making you stay and don't think for a second that I'm going to fight your decision."

Leilani stared into his eyes. His expression was emotionless and her heart sank at the harsh truth that her leaving him meant nothing to him. He'd easily move on without her.

She nodded, swallowing tears. "Thank you," she began, "Thank you for letting me know how much you don't care about me *or* this relationship."

Darnell scoffed and turned to walk away. "Woman, you're certified crazy."

"Crazy? *I'm* crazy!" she yelled. "You're sitting up here knowing that your boy is cheating and you think it's justifiable! And your response to that is, *leave me*? That's bullshit, Darnell!"

He quickly turned. "You know what? Consider yourself lucky cause' I've had plenty of opportunities to step out on you! But, if you think that I should cause' I'm hanging with a guy and mind you, one of *both* of our friends, who's chosen to do so, then maybe I should!"

"Yeah, I'm sure that'd be right up your alley," she stated. "Don't do me any fucking favors. Let Russell keep that in his court. God knows he's already done enough for Camille."

Darnell's face twisted in disgust. "*Camille*?" he scoffed. "She wishes! Russell ain't got shit to do with her ole' raggedy ass!"

Leilani raised her eyebrows, offended.

"Oh really? Is that what he told you? Maybe you should ask him how he's gonna break it to his wife that he's gonna be a daddy with her *ole' raggedy ass*!"

They stared at one another in deadened silence. Both of their hearts were pounding, their breathing heavy, and their emotions torn.

Leilani shook her head and exhaled as she broke their contact.

"You know what? I just need to leave," she said calmly. "I can't be here. I need to think."

He watched her for a moment before responding.

"You need to think about what?" he snapped.

She quickly looked at him. "Why does it matter Darnell? You don't give a shit and you won't have to deal with your *wife.* Consider that a favor from me," she barked and walked out of the room.

* * *

"Talk to me," he encouraged quietly.

She looked into his eyes and closed hers, letting out a heavy sigh as she looked away.

"It's nothing."

She didn't want to involve him in her personal life even though he had opened her to all of his.

"This is something I just need to figure out on my own," she added.

Evan shifted in his seat, moving closer to her and placing his hand atop of hers. He felt her tremble and snatch her hand away, looking at him with an expression of shock and fear mixed in one conglomerate. There was an awkward silence between them and he couldn't understand why she was so apprehensive with his closeness – especially at this point in their friendship. He watched her move her body away from him.

"Do I make you uneasy?" he inquired, his eyes scanning her slightly flushed face. "Even after all the time that we have known each other?"

She wouldn't look at him. His touch made her want to jump out of her skin; not for a bad reason, but for those that she chose not to entertain. He had become her friend, someone that allowed her mind to get off of all the bullshit intermingled in the greatness of her life.

Leilani shook her head. "No, Evan. You're great."

She closed her eyes for a brief moment and looked at him.

"You're such a great friend. Let's just talk about something else, okay?" she gently requested.

They were talking low because of the crowd in the restaurant. When she left her home after arguing with Darnell, Leilani received a text from Evan inviting her out for a nightcap to top off his late night at the office. She accepted and met him at a new spot on the other side of town.

It was a quaint little bar slash professional's club – not the place that any average person would go. No cell or cameras allowed. This was strictly for those who made six figures and above – a spiffy joint on the wealthier side of town. Leilani would never go to a place like this unless, like this, she was invited. This would be something out of her usual taste.

Evan looked scrumptious in his Gucci attire when she laid eyes on him as they met in the lobby. As the waitress greeted them, Leilani noticed the cut in her grey eyes at this ridiculously and obviously wealthy handsome white man with this black woman in *this* establishment. She knew that even though it was a laid back business, they didn't see too many of her kind venturing through their doors – especially not partnered up with someone of the majority of the nationality represented.

Leilani laughed to herself at the ignorance of others. After all, it was just a difference of the packaging, they all were human. But, deep inside, Leilani was self-conscious being with Evan one-on-one around a ton of *his kind*. She felt like she was walking naked with the stares and side glances that she was receiving.

She knew that many of them, even though she was beautiful, did not particularly care for her presence in their location with one of *their* kind. She was out of place, plain and simple. No matter how wealthy she may be. She was still black.

The club was dim, romantically lit with soft golden lights and various candle variations on each private booth and filler tables. She was appreciative of the fact that they would blend into the darkness, but Leilani still noticed the looks she received of passersby of their table.

She silently wished that she had turned down Evan's offer for her to meet him at the bar. She should have said no. This was not appropriate; both of them sporting their wedding bands, seeming a couple to those who saw them. But, they were far from being anything more than friends.

She looked at him, noticing the flickering of the candles dance against the striking sapphire blue shade of his eyes. Her gaze slid down to his narrow, pointed nose and slightly full lips. She took in a deep breath, her eyes moving further to admire his hands. They were much larger than hers, long fingers and his nails well groomed –manicured. She raised a brow at the realization that sexy hands were to be added to her lengthy list of attractive things about this man.

"So where would you like to begin?" his alluring voice snatched her out of her inventory and her eyes shot up to his gaze.

"Excuse me?" she asked.

He grinned slightly, flattered. He knew that she was admiring him. But, he would not embarrass her by stating the obvious. Evan licked his lips and leaned closer to her, noticing her body slightly move away, putting more distance between them. She looked away when he moved in and even though someone could easily sit between them, he sensed her agitation with the too close for comfort space.

"You asked to talk about something else," Evan began.

He paused, his eyes raking her exposed arm; the creamy cocoa butter complexion of her flesh enticing his curiosity to touch it. He resisted.

She smiled, laughing nervously.

"I did, didn't I?" she asked.

Evan's eyebrows furrowed slightly. "Are you sure you're okay?"

Leilani cleared her throat. She didn't know if it was the three glasses of wine she had guzzled or the dreamy ambiance in the room, but she needed to get away from Evan. Her senses were all over the place and she couldn't sit still due to the building moisture between her thighs. She was horny, deprived and frustrated. Mix those with costly wine and an attractive man and any woman runs into problems immediately.

She nibbled her bottom lip and looked away, her eyes scanning the club. She needed to clear her head from the fuzziness of sexual disturbance. They both were married and he was just a friend – a boundary that she never crossed and for sure was not going to start with him. Camille would never let her live that down.

"I, uh," she paused, taking in a quick breath. "I think I should be going," she said softly.

Evan watched her. "Is something the matter? Are you okay?"

She laughed aloud at herself as she searched the leather-lined booth for her Burberry purse and keys, "Yeah, I— I am. I just…" She shook her head. "It's not you. I just need some fresh air. I—I need to go home."

Leilani hadn't told him that she was actually headed to Camille's, not her humble abode. He knew nothing of her issues with Darnell. Leilani liked to keep it that way.

Evan began to stand. "Let me walk you out—"

"No!" she nearly shouted, causing him to freeze in motion.

Evan looked startled – obviously caught off guard. Leilani put her palm against her chest.

"Um," she tried to slow her breathing; the desire coursing through her body was fighting her and she needed to retreat with haste.

"You have...you've done enough. I'll see you around. I just can't do this tonight. Please don't be offended," she apologized.

Leilani bumped into a smaller frame upon turning and her eyes widened with shock.

"Sophie," she said softly, her voice barely audible. She felt the blood rush to her cheeks and her long legs froze in place.

The bleach blonde's eyes skid past her to place upon her husband sitting in the booth that Leilani was now leaving. The couple then made eye contact back with hers and she glared at the taller woman. Sophie was alone, thankfully. But, Leilani knew that did not minimize the threat of a full on scene in the club.

Sophie pushed past Leilani and faced her husband. "So this is what you have been doing when you're *working late*?" she seethed, her southern accent spewing from her bright red lips.

Evan stood and gently grabbed her forearm, attempting to escort her outside.

"Do not do this here, Sophie—."

She snatched herself away. "Don't you dare try to hush me! I will *not* be quiet!"

Her voice grew louder; drawing the attention of nearly the entire section near them.

Leilani was frozen in place. Her mind was telling her to leave, especially now that Sophie was no longer blocking her exit. But, she couldn't budge. She kept her back to them, her heart pounding against her ribs; the throbbing filling her ears. She could still hear them arguing.

"Sophie, I am not doing this with you. Not here. Not now. Let's take this outside and talk," Evan requested. His voice was calm, yet threatening.

"Is this what you're leaving *me* for?" Sophie yelled, looking up at him as if he had lost his mind. "You're leaving me to be with a *coon*?!"

Leilani quickly turned and her eyes met Evan's. She could see his desperation to apologize to her for his wife's hurtful words. She was more in shock from the information that Evan had told Sophie he was leaving her than the racist comment. Leilani gulped and turned, quickly leaving the restaurant.

Things had gotten way out of hand.

A Week Later

Leilani flipped through the pages of the real estate portfolio, turning to see Camille step into the room. Camille tossed her gym bag on the floor at the entrance of her apartment and let out a loud groan.

"*Girl,* I hate my damn trainer with a passion!" she exclaimed, stripping down to her undies and making her way to the bathroom. "Strike up the oven, we baking some brownies tonight, chile'!"

Leilani laughed at her best friend and closed the magazine, standing to grab a mixing bowl out of the cabinet.

"I'm on it!" she yelled.

Leilani turned to hear her smartphone vibrating against the countertop. She picked it up and pressed ignore. It was Evan. He called her daily since the incident with Sophie, but she was avoiding him at all costs. She was nervous as to the backfire that would happen to her from Sophie's vehement accusation that she was running around with her dear husband. Little did she know, Leilani hadn't so much as shook his hand since they had become friends.

She kept her distance – a safe one at that. Besides, Leilani concluded that she and Evan's interactions were strictly platonic. He didn't flirt; he was a gentleman – always polite and never going out of the way with her. Which is more than Leilani could say for any of her other male friends over the years. She didn't think Evan would ever try to test his boundaries with her; considering the facts that he was married, Sophie was her patient, she was black, and he was white. End of story.

Leilani hadn't heard from Darnell since she left their home a week prior. Of course, Camille kept her in the loop via her continued affair with Russell, but it was limited. It was apparent to Leilani that Darnell didn't miss her. At this point in her life, she was contemplating if he even loved her in the first place. She continued to make the brownie mix, her thoughts jumping from one thing to the next. What bothered her most was that as she learned from Darnell's lack of concern was that the past week, the only person she thought about was Evan.

Darnell was a passing flicker, but Evan lingered in her mind. Leilani wondered how he was doing, what happened with him and Sophie, was it really true that he told her he was leaving her or was she jumping to conclusions after seeing him with another woman in such an intimate setting. A part of her was slightly anxious of the confirmation of the possibility of him being a single man. Yet, it was smashed with the reminder that Darnell was still her husband.

"What you in here day dreaming about, Lei?"

Camille's chipper voice stole her thoughts from her mind. Leilani turned to glance at Camille licking the batter from the bowl, the small bump of her belly showing against the sleeveless top she wore. She had rescheduled her appointment about four times despite Leilani's threat that she was nearing the point that she'd miss her chance to get rid of the evidence. But, her friend paid her no mind even though her growing belly was beginning to slightly show.

Russell still had no clue about the child he would be a father to if Camille missed her deadline. Leilani was not surprised that Darnell didn't spill the beans to his buddy. Honor code. He couldn't and wouldn't let his boy know that his lady knew about his affair – especially if a baby was stemming from it. Leilani knew that her husband would refuse to be mixed up in such drama especially if he was the one to be considered the blabber mouth.

"Just thinking," Leilani replied as she scooped out the brownies onto a plate.

"M-m-m! Those look mighty delicious!" Camille exclaimed, snatching up one and biting into it.

Leilani laughed at her. "Eating like that, you won't be able to hide that belly from *any*body!"

She sucked her teeth. "Won't be a problem in a week."

"Girl, you said that two weeks ago. You need to stop playing around and get it done," Leilani said with raised brows. She grabbed the 2% out of the fridge and poured them a glass each.

Camille snatched the brownies and they made their way into the living room, plopping down on the plush sofa as Camille turned on Netflix. Leilani couldn't focus on their bonding time of sweets and movies. She needed to talk. She shifted and slightly faced her friend.

"Moon, can I ask you something?" she asked.

Camille looked at her and pressed mute on the remote. "Anything."

Leilani thought for a moment, trying to package her words.

"Could you," she paused. "Could you ever see me with a guy that's not black?"

Camille furrowed her eyebrows, "What? Like a Hispanic?"

Leilani shook her head.

"Cuban?" Camille asked.

"No." Leilani said.

Camille sat up suddenly. "You better not be going African on me!" she exclaimed.

Leilani laughed. "*No.* I mean," she shrugged slightly. "Could you see me with a white guy?"

Camille shrugged. "Why not? You don't really fit with Darnell." She noticed Leilani's despondent expression. "I'm sorry. I didn't mean that," she apologized.

Leilani stared at her in silence and Camille sat forward and touched her hand.

"Lei, I really, *really didn't* mean that."

Leilani fought the tears welling inside of her. She shook her head and forced out a smile.

"Don't worry about it, Moon. I know you mean well."

Camille watched her and sat back. "Damnit," she said softly. "I shouldn't have said that though. It was a shitty comment to make."

Leilani raised her eyebrows and shrugged one shoulder.

"It is what it is. Darnell isn't worried about me. You told me yourself that he's been chillin' with Russell like he's single. And you know Cheryl isn't gonna say a damn thing about it. She has her head so far up her *own* ass that she barely notices that Russell is spending nearly every night *not* at home."

Camille smirked. "Yeah, except for this week though."

"That's only cause' I've been here," Leilani said.

Camille laughed. "We make it work. I just wouldn't sit on the backseat of my or his car for a good month. Let that get good and cleaned about five times first."

Leilani grimaced. "Oh *yuck*!" she exclaimed.

Camille laughed, scratching her low cut curly hair.

"Hey, get in where you fit in," Camille replied with a huge smile.

"You are such a hooker," she said with another laugh.

Leilani grabbed a brownie, munching on it.

"That's how you got that bun in the oven now; being a hot ass."

Camille laughed. "At least I'm getting *some* ass," she teased with a laugh.

"*Anyway*, you ever have been with someone not black?" Leilani asked.

Camille chewed as she reminisced.

"A few. No white guys though. A Mexican, um, a Puerto Rican and," she paused. "Oh wait, I was with a white guy once. He reminded me of Eminem."

Leilani laughed. "Eminem?" she asked. "Now *that's* a black guy."

They both laughed.

Camille raised a brow. "He *did* put it down though."

Leilani felt her curiosity spike. "Is it weird being with a white guy?" she asked.

Camille looked at her.

"Why would it be? He has a dick just like the next one. They might come in all shades, but still gets the job done," she said. "*Especially* if they know how to work what they got. But, shit, that's *all* men. A guy can have a nice size one and not know how to screw worth a lick," she said and laughed. "I had one of those too. But, good old Eminem." She shook her head. "He was a good—no, a *great* fuck."

Leilani continued to listen, immersed in the firsthand experience confession coming from her dazed friend. She saw Camille's eyebrow arch as she reminisced.

"Hmm." Camille grinned slightly. "Yeah, he really put it down. That's one thing I have noticed about white guys compared to all the guys I've been with. He was the most affectionate – more in tune with pleasing the woman first." She paused and nodded, "Yeah, homeboy was *real good*. I wonder where he is now."

Camille shrugged and moved on past the thought.

"I'm sure he's married," she muttered.

Leilani's imagination painted her a picture of Evan in the nude. She wondered what his canvas looked like underneath all the pricey clothing that draped the physique. She could tell by his build that he was indeed in good shape. She caught a glimpse of the muscles in his back as he pulled on his suit jacket during their first dinner together. She recalled the male review that she and Camille had attended a few months prior.

It blew Leilani's mind just how attractive white men were. Never in her wildest dreams had she fathomed being with a white guy until one of them came to dance with her from the stage; his nearly nude body brushing against her. She remembered how she closed her eyes to hide her embarrassment, but above all to not allow her best friend to see how excited the white dancer was making her.

Her mind pictured Evan doing the same to her; only in the privacy of their own room. Leilani gulped down a swig of milk. She didn't doubt for a second that his body was any less than the muscular men she saw on stage. Camille began to grin.

"Who is tickling your fancy, *Ms. Leilani*?" she inquired.

Leilani snapped out of her fantasy and looked at Camille.

"No one. I'm just asking."

"Yeah, right!" Camille paused and watched her best friend's flushed skin begin to return to its normal shade, "This is about Mr. Worthington, isn't it?"

Leilani looked at her quickly and Camille noticed the flushed cheeks returning.

"*Oohhh!* What did you do?" Camille exclaimed.

"Nothing!" Leilani said loudly.

Camille sucked her teeth.

"You got down with the swirl?" she exclaimed.

Leilani jumped up from the sofa.

"Girl, you have gone bye-bye! *No*, I did not touch that man" Leilani said walking to the kitchen to refill her glass of milk.

Camille watched her, her eyes scanning over Leilani's curvy figure in the Victoria's Secret striped pajamas.

"I knew he wasn't a racist," she said, her mind recalling the moments she caught Evan's eyes watching Leilani when his wife wasn't looking.

"You *are* right about that," Leilani replied, sitting down and seeing Camille's mouth drop open.

"*But,* I haven't done anything with him besides go out to eat a few times, texting and phone convos about his marriage and life in general. So let me put that out there cause' I know how you get," Leilani quickly added.

Camille popped her neck backwards.

"How *I* get?" she asked, offended.

Leilani couldn't hold back her laugh.

"Yes, how you get. You start going off on tangents about what I *need* to do and how I *need* to have some excitement in my life. Evan is just a friend," Leilani replied.

Camille raised an inquisitive brow.

"*Oh*, it's *Evan* now?" she teased with a grin. "M-hm, you'll be screaming that name with your legs sky high in no time. How much you wanna bet?"

Leilani's mouth dropped open in shock, but she felt a tinge of excitement between her legs.

"You better stop!" she yelled and her best friend laughed.

"You like it!" Camille yelled. "Why not try the swirl?" she asked with a wink.

"Because I'm married," Leilani reminded with raised eyebrows.

"Shit," Camille said with a smirk. "Not for long."

Leilani flicked milk in Camille's direction.

"Ass," Leilani commented and began to grab the remote to turn the movie back on.

Camille hit pause. "What's the big deal?" she asked.

"The big deal about what?" Leilani asked.

"You and Evan? Why couldn't it happen?" Camille pressed.

Leilani took in a deep breath.

"Let's see, um, I'm black. He's not. And on top of that, he's a rich ass white guy. It's plenty of other Dallas Cowboys cheerleader lookalikes walking around here in Cali that he could have his pick at. His wife used to be one herself. Why would he want me?" she explained.

Camille tilted her head to the side.

"Lei," she started, "You really need to let that insecure shit go."

Leilani looked away at the television screen, "There are plenty of women that are his type out there," she said. "I'm not white."

"You don't even know *his type*. You're assuming." Camille encouraged.

Leilani sucked her teeth. "Duh, his wife…."

"Have you not looked in the mirror at yourself?" Camille interrupted. "You're beautiful, Lei"

Leilani rolled her eyes. "That's not what I mean, Moon."

"Girl, Darnell has really got you fucked up," Camille stated, "Seriously."

"Have you seen his wife?" Leilani asked.

Camille sucked her teeth. "Fake boobs, fake hair, fake teeth, fake, fake, fake. Just *all around* fake. She's like a damn walking Barbie. I can see why his ass checked you out every chance he got. He probably never seen a *real* woman since he married her ass."

Leilani laughed. "Girl, stop. She's pretty."

"Pretty fake," Camille muttered with a smirk.

Leilani sighed. "Moon, he's *such* a good guy. I don't want to mistake his politeness for anything more than what it is; being a polite gentleman. We have good chemistry together. But, we're just hanging out."

Camille watched her and Leilani returned the stare.

"He's *just* a friend," Leilani pressed with a raised eyebrow.

Camille raised her hands in surrender.

"*Okay*," she said popping a piece of brownie in her mouth, "That's how I used to talk about Russell," she pointed down, "And you see this belly as proof of what *just friends* can get you."

"No, that's what being a floozy can get you," Leilani corrected with a grin.

Camille tossed the rest of the brownie at Leilani's face.

"Okay, I'll just be waiting to say I told you so," Camille replied, pressing play on the remote.

Leilani ignored her comment and stared at the television; her mind far from the movie.

6
Battle of the Sexes

Leilani made her way to the front door, juggling with her keys to unlock it. She knew that Darnell was home, but she didn't want to announce her entrance. It had been nearly two weeks since she had spoken with her husband. She decided to come home because he surprised her by giving her a phone call earlier that evening asking how she was doing.

He was calm and friendly, so she took it upon herself to decide to make things peaceful with him again. She was committed to her marriage and despite the ups and downs, the flaws and frustrations, she was determined to give her best even if she wasn't always happy. She opened the door and stepped inside.

Their home was silent like a coffin. Leilani paced through the foyer, into their great room and found no one. She realized that Darnell may not be home, but out with Russell and driving one vehicle – leaving his parked. Either way, they needed to talk about the state of their union and the plans for their future, if there'd be one.

She heard male laughter and followed the sound to Darnell's office. His door was cracked, not enough to see in or out. So, Leilani decided to stop and listen once she realized he was on his telephone.

"Naw man, I didn't even think about that." Darnell laughed again. *"You the one that said she had the bubble guts."*

Silence.

Darnell laughed again. *"You still hit it though, right?"* Laughter, *"Yeah, I knew you couldn't resist! Gassy and all! What did she say was the reason?"*

Silence.

"Tacos my ass. You sure you didn't get her knocked up, man?" Darnell asked.

It dawned on Leilani that her husband was talking to his best friend, Russell. She closed her eyes and sat down on the single step, leaning in to hear. She wanted to see what kind of man her husband was when he wasn't in her line of sight or hearing. Even though she knew that Darnell was charitable, had a big heart, was a hard worker and believed in God. She also knew that with Darnell also came his arrogance, pride and ease of lying as to not taint his, what he thought to be, perfect image of a man.

Leilani continued to listen. She shook her head at the naivety that Darnell tried to show towards Russell about Camille's pregnancy while at the same time giving him clues to the result of his indiscretions. She hated how he acted innocent when he was really trying to use something to his advantage. Leilani knew that if Darnell planted the seed to Russell that Camille was pregnant, that would cause discord and thus, Leilani would be booted from her safe haven – Camille's place. There'd be no other person in Camille's eyes that could have told Russell, after all.

"Hey man, all I'm saying is, I've been checking out home girl and she looks like she's starting to get a big belly. That shit isn't bloat from that time of the month either," Darnell instigated and laughed. *"You might wanna hurry up and get that dog neutered before you end up in a kennel yourself."*

Leilani rolled her eyes in disgust; her husband was unpredictable. But, she did not believe that he could be this immoral. She heard Darnell laugh again.

"I ain't said nothin', man. Camille isn't bad looking and she

indeed has a phatty. But, you should've picked from another tree. Especially with her being friends with my old lady." Pause. *"No, she wasn't a bad choice. But, all I'm saying is this one was too close for comfort. You should've strayed much farther away from the home base,"* he laughed, *"A-ight, I married mine though,"* he paused, *"You damn right!"*

Leilani wished that she could be on the other end of the conversation, able to hear what Russell was saying into the receiver.

Darnell's cheerful tone changed.

"I think she's coming home," Pause, *"Yeah, I talked to her earlier to see what she was up to,"* he paused. *"I don't like conflict, Russ. So I just let her be. Give her time to cool off and we go from there. I don't have any interest in arguing and fighting over nonsense. I got bigger fish to fry."*

She stood, turning to exit the hallway and venture back into the great room when she heard the door open to Darnell's office.

"Lei?"

Leilani turned and they stared at each other for a moment. Her eyes scanned over his 6'0 slender frame, covered in a pair of jogging pants and a casual tee. His feet were covered in dark socks. It was the weekend and Darnell rarely dressed rugged. This was the most comfortable she had seen him in years, especially late in the afternoon. Darnell scanned her frame. She was wearing a pair of black Capri's and a baby blue tank; fancy cut out sandals on her pedicured feet.

"What are you doing home?" he asked.

Leilani raised an eyebrow, offended.

"I didn't think that I had to explain that to you."

"That's not what I meant," Darnell started, but she turned to exit the hall.

"I know what you meant. Sorry to disturb your peace and quiet," Leilani said.

Darnell followed her. "Unh-unh, don't even try to act like the victim."

She turned to look at him.

"The victim? I'm not acting like anything, Darnell. I'm just home. Is that a problem? Cause' if it is, then I'll gladly leave. Better yet, how about you get the hell out this time around and go stay with your boy, *Russ*!"

Darnell smirked. "You got jokes, I see," he mockingly said.

"No, I actually *don't*. I'm just tired of this joke of a marriage. That's what the big joke is."

"You know what, Leilani. The next time you decide to leave, don't come back," Darnell countered.

"*Excuse me*?" she shouted with a croon of her neck.

Darnell glared at her.

"I'm not fighting to keep you. So, if that's what you expect – for me to chase after you, hunt you down or *beg*, you got another thing coming! If you don't wanna be here, you're free to go!"

"I never asked you to beg, Darnell. All I've asked is for you to be a husband!" she yelled.

Darnell scoffed.

"Oh, here we go with this shit again! What do you want from me?" he snapped.

Leilani was silent, watching the dark skin of his cheekbones become taunt; the veins in his neck protruding. His fists were clenched and Leilani knew he would hit her if he were that type of man. He was fed up with her, but she could not determine how far his discontent measured. She didn't respond. There was nothing more to say. Darnell made it clear to her that she meant nothing to him.

"Huh?!" he screamed. "What do you fucking want from me, Leilani?"

"Not a damn thing," she snapped.

Darnell growled.

"I swear, sometimes I just…" he raised his fist and shook it in her direction. "Sometimes I just wanna knock the shit out of you! That's how *angry* you make me with this bullshit!"

Her husband didn't frighten her.

Leilani began to turn. "This conversation is over, Darnell," she said calmly.

Darnell grabbed her arm, snatching her back around to face him.

"No it's not. You wanna bitch and moan all the damn time - now you're gonna listen to what I've gotta say. I bite my tongue way too much around this damn house. Just to keep the peace! Just to keep you satisfied! But, no!" He shook his head. "That's not even enough for your ass! You're gonna hear me out. If I have to listen to you, *you* are gonna listen to me!"

Leilani snatched her arm away, her eyebrows raised high.

"First, don't you ever grab on me like that again, Darnell," she threatened. "Second of all, I don't bitch and moan to you—"

"Oh *please*! You're always complaining about how I don't do this or that. How I don't touch you enough, kiss you enough! I am always home! Every night! I don't pick fights with you—"

"No you don't. You're exactly right! You don't do *any*thing. You come home and you just walk around here like I'm your damn servant! You don't interact with me, Darnell!"

He laughed.

"See, there you go," he said, he raised his hands up in the air. "Cutting me off just so you can be right! You *always* do that!"

Leilani watched Darnell as he paced around, creating distance between them. The tension was thick in the room and her heart was heavy with emotion. She wanted to scream at the top of her lungs, release the anger and animosity that had built towards Darnell in all their years together.

At that moment, she realized she hated him. Hated him for all the hurt, frustration, denial, distance and neglect he had put her through in their most recent years together. She didn't know if she could go on anymore. Not with this much abhorrence. It cut deep into her soul. Leilani stood there. She was hesitant to move because she thought she might take one of their overpriced vases and hit him with it. Just to end things, just to close this depressing chapter that had invaded her life.

Darnell kept his back to her. He was now on the other side of the room. Intentional distance created, like always. Leilani gulped, seeking to calm the building anger. He turned and leaned against the wall, looking down at her.

"I don't know," he softly began.

He shrugged with a scoff.

"I don't even know what you want from me, Leilani. I give so much as it is."

She smirked and shook her head, but he continued.

"You just don't know how hard it is to be with you," he said. "How hard it is to love you when you seem to hate me so much and spit on everything that I do for you."

"I don't spit on everything you do," she muttered. "And you don't do much as it is."

"*Damn!* Why won't you shut the fuck up and let me talk for a change!" he shouted.

She glared at him. Her temper rose a few notches from his foul language towards her.

"Darnell," she warned.

"You always want somebody to listen to you, but you can't do the same!" He shook his head. "*Shit*, a person can only take so much before they just say fuck it—that this person isn't worth the bullshit!"

Leilani watched him. She took in a deep breath.

"Then I guess you've helped me make my choice then," she said calmly.

They stared into each other's eyes. Leilani tried to read her husband's expression, but it was stale.

"I'm not asking you to leave me," he finally said. His voice low.

"Yeah, but you're not asking me to stay either. Remember?" she reminded with a raised eyebrow.

He shifted, standing straight up and sliding his hands into his pockets.

"Lei, that's not what I meant—" he stopped when she held up her hand.

"Darnell," she began with her eyes squeezed shut.

She looked at him.

"Just stop. You've said enough as it is. We both have," she said and turned, walking out of the room and going upstairs.

He sighed and rubbed his forehead.

"You're always trippin' about nothing," he muttered.

❖

12:01 AM

Leilani couldn't cry. She just sat laid in their California King bed and stared at the wall. She felt helpless. She didn't want to lose Darnell, but she also didn't want to be with him. She knew there was happiness out there – someone that could give her those things that she longed for. But, the turmoil of a failed marriage that she once had unyielding faith in did not give her much hope in finding true happiness elsewhere. She no longer thought it existed. It was a farce – a fairytale ending that only happened in books and fantasies. True love did not exist.

She heard the soft footsteps of her husband entering their bedroom and the weight of his body rest upon the bed. Leilani closed her eyes, trying to force herself into a deep sleep. But, her mind was immeasurably energetic –thoughts swirling through it – fighting any chance of peace for the night. She twitched when she felt his hand slide underneath her pillow then the slow creep of his body easing closer to her. She didn't want to be bothered. She wanted him to leave her alone.

Darnell moved closer and his chilled hand began to glide down the dip in her waist and up the rise of her hip, down to her stomach. He tugged and shifted her body to lie on her back. Leilani took in a deep breath, squeezing her eyes shut and trying to take her mind to happier places. She knew where this was headed and there was no stopping him.

Darnell climbed on top of her and she felt the brush of his

erection against her thigh, feeling him ease his weight onto his forearms as he settled on her. The room was dark, so he couldn't see her stone expression. Her body was stiff, but he wedged his legs in between, shifting his weight to open her thighs farther. He tried to kiss her, but she turned her head away. He opted for her neck as he began to slobber against her skin, his breathing growing heavier as his excitement rose. He tugged at her nightgown, stretching the sleeve to expose her breasts, his mouth lingering over her nipples.

Leilani couldn't feel excited. She felt his weight shift and Leilani braced herself for his entrance. It had been nearly a month since she had sex and she knew he wouldn't do anything more to warm up her southern comfort to his erect visitor. She didn't want his intrusion.

"No," she said.

Her husband ignored her.

"Darnell, no," Leilani protested louder, attempting to push him off.

Darnell pinned her wrists down on the mattress and groaned when he thrust inside. Leilani took in a sharp breath. She couldn't bring herself to enjoy this moment. Her disdain for Darnell overshadowed her attraction to him and over the past few years of their marriage, she had to prep herself for sex with him. After the numerous droughts and lack of affection and attention, she had lost the feeling of a sexual connection with him.

Their sex had merely become just a space filler – a requirement being met at the bare minimum of their union. Rarely was it hot and steamy. It was more rushed and a waste of her time. She just had sex with him to say she simply was having sex and deep inside, she felt that Darnell regarded it the same.

There was no passion in their lovemaking and as Darnell's thrusts became harder and faster, she listened to the silence in the room. He never moaned, she was always the one making the noise.

For a moment, Leilani contemplated if Darnell ever truly enjoyed making love to her or was he that hell bent on proving he was such a man that he couldn't even allow himself to express the pleasures of sex. He tried to kiss her again, but she turned her head. Her arms still pinned by his vice grip.

"No," she muttered, moving away from his attempts.

His mouth followed and he forced her lips against his; sliding his tongue inside. His kiss was cold. No fireworks or electricity. Leilani refused to kiss him back. She snatched her mouth away.

"Darnell, stop." She wanted it all to be over.

Her mind drifted to Evan and she wondered what he was doing with his wife. She remembered the desperation that Sophie showed when she propositioned her – the fear of losing her husband was the only real emotion Leilani saw that evening. That was what drove Sophie's irrational behavior. Leilani's mind drifted to their patient profile notes and to how frequently they made love. It made her and Darnell's sex life look like a tortoise in a race.

Her husband ignored her; continued his enjoyment of her body. Leilani could feel her walls begin to throb. She was drier than the Sahara and the friction had begun to sting. Darnell wasn't the largest she had experienced, but over their years together, her body had adjusted to his dimensions. She freed her hands from his grasp and began to push at his shoulders.

"Stop. Get off of me," Leilani demanded.

Darnell didn't budge. Instead his thrusts became faster... harder. Tears sprung to Leilani's eyes at the realization that he didn't care what she wanted. Leilani shoved at his shoulders again.

"Darnell. Stop!" she growled.

"I know you like it," he hoarsely replied and pinned her wrists to the mattress again to halt her contest.

"I feel you coming," Darnell groaned.

He could not have been further out of tune with her body. Leilani's eyes filled with tears. He tried to kiss her and she sharply turned her head away.

"Please, just stop," she muttered.

Darnell's breathing quickened. She felt him thrust harder and Leilani squeezed her eyes shut, trying to block out the sensation of his release flowing inside of her. He groaned, huffing and puffing as he shifted his weight and walked into the restroom to relieve himself. He came back and slid beneath the covers, his body on the opposite side of the bed—the intentional space between them bringing with it a cold draft. He turned his back to Leilani after fluffing his pillow to his desired level.

She heard him mumble, "Love you, goodnight."

Leilani lay there, staring at the ceiling. She slowly exited their bed and walked into the bathroom; sitting on the toilet as she peed and began to clean herself. She stared ahead and the emptiness overwhelmed her, causing more tears to flood her eyes. He had gotten what he wanted and had no other concerns with her. She realized that was why he called her earlier that evening. He needed his fix – nothing more. She had fallen victim to the need of being wanted by her man. She closed her eyes in disappointment.

It was time for her to accept that her marriage was over.

***

She stared at him in disbelief.

"I've always thought highly of you, always trusted you. But, for the first time in my life I feel like I am looking at an impostor."

He looked away and shook his head.

"I haven't been happy for a long time, Sophie. You have known this for the past few years—"

"No! You haven't been happy since you met that minstrel show!" she yelled.

Evan looked at his wife.

"Would you stop with the racist rubbish?" he asked, growing more irritated.

Sophie stepped closer to him seated in their great room.

"*Such* valiance on her behalf!" She scanned his face. "How long have you been seeing her?"

Evan raised his eyebrows. "I haven't been *seeing* her. We're *just* friends—"

She scoffed.

"She's beautiful!" she interjected. "I don't believe you."

Evan looked away, sighing.

"Sophie," he said softly and pinched the ridge of his nose, squeezing his eyes shut.

"Please just sign the papers," he pleaded. "Don't make this any harder than it has to be."

Sophie snatched the packet off the coffee table and stood in front of him, opting to rip a few pages to shreds since it was too thick for her grasp. She tossed them at his feet.

"I am not signing *anything*," she hissed and leaned towards him, pointing her finger in his face. "You married me. Til' death do us part. Or did you forget that morsel of our vows?"

Evan watched her as Sophie backed up and stood defiantly in front of him, her hands on her narrow hips; her augmented perky breasts protruding from her much too low cut dress. Evan no longer found her attractive enough to be intimate. He hadn't touched her in nearly a month. He wanted to get as far away from Sophie as he could. Thankfully, years before, he had succeeded in having her sign a prenup, but now his battle was getting her to sign the divorce papers.

He stood, his over six foot frame towering over his below average height wife. Her blue eyes glared up at him; decorated with dark eyeliner and false lashes.

Evan took in a deep breath and exhaled.

"I cannot be with you anymore," he said calmly.

Sophie slapped him across his cheek, his skin flushing from the strike. Evan closed his eyes for a moment and looked at her.

"Sophie," he began.

"You think I'm just going to let you desert me?" she bit.

"*Desert you*? Sophie, you are getting far more than what you should. I don't see how I'm deserting you. You will have plenty of *my* money to keep you more than comfortable. I'm," he paused and raised his eyebrows. "I am not happy. It's over."

Sophie reached to slap him again and he grabbed her wrist.

"Strike me again and I will have you taken away this time," Evan threatened.

Evan had suffered his fair share of physical attacks from his petite wife. Even though she was much smaller than he, she packed a wrath that could topple a dozen buildings. He wasn't afraid of her. But, he knew that if cornered, his wife would strike. He had grown to deal with Sophie's abuse as she had never hurt him to the point that he had to seek medical attention. But, mixing that with all of her other unstable antics and he had developed immunity to her violent threats.

Sophie snatched her slender wrist away from his grasp.

"I never asked you to marry me," she began.

Evan turned to walk away. Sophie followed.

"I *never* asked you to marry me!" she yelled. "*You* proposed to me! *You* got down on your knee that night! I didn't make you do any of this, Evan Worthington!"

He turned and looked at her.

"You are precisely correct. But, you cannot make me stay with you," he animatedly replied.

Sophie's eyes filled with tears and they spilled down her cheeks; her face turning crimson.

"Evan, I love you," she said. "I love you so much."

"I know you do, Sophie," he said. "But, I can't do this anymore."

"Don't say that!" she demanded. "*Please* don't say that. I will be better. I will be better, I promise!"

He emptily stared into her eyes. Sophie recognized that expression. She knew he was done with her.

"We're supposed to be having a family. What about everything we have been through?" She fought.

Evan's eyes skimmed over her exposed belly ring and he smirked to himself at how serious she was not for having any children more then she would be to have a lobotomy. It was her ploy to keep him. He knew that the moment she began dragging him to fertility specialists. This was a desperate measure to salvage her marriage. Sophie stepped closer to him and she began to stroke his face, gazing into his eyes.

"Don't you still love me?" she asked her voice softer. "Don't you remember how happy we used to be?" She sniffed. "We can get that back." She nodded with a smile. "We can get back to that, Evan. Don't give up on us. Don't give up on me," she begged. "I can't lose you."

Evan looked around at their wedding, holiday and anniversary photos hanging from the walls. They looked happy – elated, on cloud 9. But, soon that faded and he was left with a wife that was only concerned with her reputation, looks, and his money and had no goals in life.

He wanted to be with someone who had purpose – not a leech. He looked down at her and cupped her face, leaning down and kissing her. Sophie's tense body relaxed and she attempted to undo his belt buckle. He reached down, held her hands still and looked into her eyes as he peeled his lips away from hers.

"Sophie, you're beautiful, one of a kind, bright and vibrant."

She began to smile.

"I will never regret getting down on one knee and proposing to you nor the day that you were my bride and we started our life together," he paused and she rested her hands on his waist, gazing into his eyes, mesmerized and hopeful.

Evan stared at her for a long moment and kissed her gently on the forehead, pulling back to look back at her, waiting for hers to open.

"The house is yours to keep," he said softly. "But, I need you to understand. I can't stay here anymore."

Sophie watched him as he turned to exit their front door. She snatched a vase from a nearby tabletop and flung it towards him exiting their home, it and its fresh flowers crashed against the wooden door loudly.

She released a guttural scream, beginning to smash things around the house.

"Bitch!" she yelled as the image of her seeing Evan and Leilani at the restaurant together flashed through her mind.

"You're going to pay for this!" she screamed.

"Man, I knew it was some shady shit going on."

"What you talking about?" Darnell asked, tossing a crisp fifty on the counter.

Russell signaled the bartender for another Corona.

"Cheryl's ass," he said.

"I thought you were talking about Camille," Darnell said, glancing down the row at a cute dark brown, short haired diva sitting with another friend that he had been eyeballing since they arrived.

His friend sucked his teeth. "Hell naw. I ain't studding her."

Darnell looked at him and raised a brow.

"What happened with that?" he asked, curious.

Russell laughed and sipped from his Corona.

"That trick's not giving it up anymore. But," he paused. "I'm working on her though."

Darnell shook his head, "You need to just leave her alone, man," he suggested.

"Not til' I get a replacement. I like *smooth* transitions," Russell said with a grin. "No down time."

Darnell laughed, shaking his head.

"So what's going on with you and the ole' lady?" He changed the subject.

"*Man,* check this, that two-timing bitch has been cheating on me," Russell confessed.

He laughed at Darnell's expression, nodding his head as he took another swig from his Corona.

"Yep," he said.

"Get outta here with that mess," Darnell said sucking his teeth. "You're lying."

"I swear on my mother's grave, man. We accidentally swapped phones – cause' you know how I just got that new Android like hers. She had voicemails and texts from some cat she met at some *yoga* class."

"Yoga class?" Darnell asked with furrowed eyebrows.

Russell nodded,.

"Bet you his ass is colorful like Fruity Pebbles, y'know what I'm sayin'," he said with another laugh. "Apparently, they been goin' out for a good three or four months now. I noticed she had some new jewelry and shit," he shrugged, "But I didn't think nothing of it. Figured she got em' off the QVC channel."

Darnell smirked, sipping from his jack and Coke; the ice clinking against the glass. They both had just finished long days at work in their legal firms. This was supposed to be time to unwind, but it had turned into a care circle for the two men to mend their wounds. He watched his best friend.

"It's alright though. I got somethin' for her ass," he talked. "D.i.v.o.r.c.e."

Darnell shook his head. "She's gonna drag you to counseling and ya'll are gonna work it out just like all the other miserable married people do. You don't mean that shit, Russ."

Russell sucked his teeth and looked at Darnell.

"*Shit.* Yes, I do. I'm already drafting up the papers. She ain't getting a dime. I'm taking the house, the car, the cat, those damn flowery panties she wears…I'm taking it *all*."

Darnell laughed louder as he looked up at the football game on the big screen affront of them; resting his forearms on the countertop of the bar. Russell stared at the screen, but his thoughts were far from the play action.

"You're seriously going to leave her?" his friend asked and Russell looked at him.

"Wouldn't you?" he asked with attitude, "Bet that you would drop Lei's ass with the quickness."

Darnell raised his eyebrows and shook his head.

"That's a tough decision to make, man. We already aren't seeing eye to eye. But, *divorce?"* Darnell paused. "I don't know. If it was for any other reason than cheating, I wouldn't. I do love her."

Russell sucked his teeth.

"Man, I ain't talking about other reasons. I'm asking if she was cheating," Russell said.

Darnell stared at him and then looked away, licking his lips before taking another sip.

"Probably," he answered.

"*Probably?"* Russell exclaimed, nearly jumping off his bar stool. "*Man*, Leilani has got your ass whipped."

Darnell laughed.

"Actually she doesn't. It's the other way around. She's not going anywhere. She talks all that yack, but it's just to get a rise out of me. Lei would never stray. I got her wrapped."

Russell smirked.

"Don't get ahead of yourself, bruh'. I thought the same thing about Cheryl. These women can be some scandalous bitches. No joke. But that's alright, Cheryl ain't gonna know what hit her when I get done with taking everything. Unlike you, *I* didn't hide money all over."

Darnell shrugged. He didn't agree, but he chose not to argue with his friend. This was something they'd never be on the same page about. Russell stroked his goatee, deep in thought.

"I thought I had her wrapped around my finger just like you think you got Lei. That's the tripped out part about it the most," Russell said. "Scandalous bitch," he muttered.

Darnell watched Russell in the mirror as he twirled the Corona in his hand, deep in thought.

"She's lucky I don't have a gun. I would blow her fucking brains out," Russell said.

Darnell shifted uncomfortably on the stool.

"Man, now you're *really* talking crazy," he said.

Russell smirked and shook his head.

"Bet you that'd really surprise her ass though," he replied.

"Does she even know you know?" Darnell asked, shifting the nature of their topic.

Russell shrugged.

"Nah. She's got her head too far up fruity pebble's ass to notice what I'm doin'." He laughed. "I swear that dude gotta be fruity. Any man that does Zumba gotta be sweet – up in there wearing tights and shit."

Darnell laughed.

"Man, you're thinking ballet. They don't wear tights in Zumba," Darnell corrected.

Russell glared at him.

"Whatever man. Since when did you become an expert in that *girly* shit?" Russell looked away. "Just be lucky you don't have any kids yet. That's one thing I'm most grateful for."

Darnell glanced down the row at the young brown again. She was in the zone laughing with her female friend – he was dead to her world. He was more curious to see her derriere when she stood than anything else. The torso and up was acceptable. He took another sip of his jack and Coke, looking back at the big screen.

"Why do you think I haven't got Lei knocked up yet?" Darnell asked. "That's no mistake."

His friend looked at him.

"That's cause' she's not giving you any," Russell replied with a smirk.

Darnell laughed and tilted his head to the side.

"No, I just know that babies really mean you're tied to that person and I'm not chancing that shit."

"You already stuck with her ass in marriage, man," Russell stated.

"No. I look at it this way, if I and Lei don't work out, it's a simple split. *But,* if I get her pregnant," he tossed his hand. "That's still child support up the ass I have to pay and I have to deal with her for the next eighteen damn years. This way, it's a clean break. We pay our agreed percentages and I'm out."

Russell raised a brow.

"Smart man. But, it doesn't bother you that you're gonna miss out on all her loot? Lei pulls major bank – more than you, dawg."

Darnell shrugged.

"I know, but we have T's and C's that I can't divulge at this present moment in time," he said with a grin. "Besides I have hidden bank accounts—to which, Leilani has no idea since our finances are separate. Divorce attorneys don't typically look for private accounts unless they're asked to do so and Leilani would really have to push for it. You're a divorce attorney, you know the deal."

Russell replied with a slight shrug.

"Besides, it doesn't bother me cause' her hand isn't in *my* pocket," Darnell added with a slight shrug of one shoulder.

"I thought you weren't even thinking about leaving her," Russell said.

Darnell scoffed softly and shook his head.

"I don't know. Lei has been *so* damn emotional lately. I can't get two words in without her going all PMS on me." He shrugged. "Besides, I honestly don't know if I wanna be bothered with any kids, man. I'm in my prime; making good money. Kids take up all your freedom. Your life completely changes. I can have kids til' I'm dead, why rush now?"

Darnell's friend nodded.

"But, I thought your ole' bitty wanted kids?" Russell asked. "And soon?"

Darnell sighed. "She's not getting knocked up until I'm good n' ready. That's plain and simple fact."

"So why you letting her think you want them now? All that baby making talk you entertain, those stupid ass calendars, all that bullshit?" Russell asked.

Darnell shrugged. "A happy wife," he began.

"Is a happy life," Russell finished. "And sure does beat a naggin' bitch *any* day."

They tapped their balled fists together and commenced to drinking their alcohol.

Darnell watched his friend's reflection in the mirror. He didn't like to be the bearer of bad news, but he considered the fact that since Russell was now planning to leave Cheryl, he should know what else is going on in the dark. Darnell shifted and took in a deep breath.

"Aye man, I do have something serious I wanna tell you," he started.

Russell looked at him. "You don't think me and Cheryl is serious?" he asked sarcastically.

Darnell shook his head. "It is, but, there is something else you need to handle."

Russell tossed a handful of nuts into his mouth.

"What? You planning on leaving your lady too?" he asked with a smirk.

Darnell laughed. "No, it's about your home girl, Camille and why she's been dodging you."

Russell looked at him and furrowed his eyebrows.

"She bitching to your old lady?" he asked Darnell.

"Naw. Nothing like that." Darnell paused. "Look man, you know I don't get all involved in other folk's business. But, you're my boy. And considering the foul shit that Cheryl is pulling on you, you deserve to know what else is going on."

Russell nodded, tossing more cashews into his mouth.

"Okay, I feel you. What's up?"

Darnell pivoted his torso in Russell's direction.

"Word on the street is that you got Camille knocked up," Darnell announced.

Russell stopped chewing, his mouth hanging open, his hand frozen in midair. Darnell watched him for a minute and then took a sip from his jack and Coke. Russell laughed, shaking his head and began chewing again.

"Good joke, man. You really got me on that one," he said, "Not the way I'd thought you try to cheer me up, but a-ight. I can dig it."

Russell laughed again. "Camille pregnant with my baby," he shook his head, "Now *that* is a good ass joke."

Darnell turned his body forward, taking another sip of his drink.

"It's not a joke, Russ. She's pregnant," Darnell flatly said.

Russell looked at him. "Get the fuck outta here with that bullshit," he said angrily.

Darnell looked at him and could see Russell's chest rising in growing anger. Darnell shook his head and looked away.

"Ask her if you don't believe me, then," Darnell said.

Russell tossed a fifty on the counter, pulling his keys from his suit jacket and stood.

"I for damn sure am about to," Russell said.

He patted Darnell on the shoulder.

"Thanks for havin' my back, man. I'll hit you up later. Make sure you get that phatty's number over there," he said, nudging his head in the direction of the woman Darnell had been admiring the entire evening with a wink.

Darnell laughed and topped off his jack and Coke, glancing down at the woman who was now looking in his direction. He licked his lips and glanced at his wedding band. His thoughts went to Leilani and their lack of communication over the past few weeks. He hadn't made love to her since the night of their argument because she intentionally found a way to fall asleep on the lounger in their family room or any place else other than their bed. She timed it perfectly. He sighed and signaled the bartender.

"I'll have another," the bartender turned, "And send the ladies down at the end a refill. On me."

Darnell looked at the woman and they made eye contact. She showed him her pearly whites, dimples accenting her diamond shaped face, high cheekbones and narrow eyes. She was picturesque. Darnell returned her warm smile with a slight grin;

barely noticeable and looked back at the game on tv. He was not going to approach her. He had bought her and her friend a drink. The ball was now in her court if she wanted to get to know him. After all, he was a married man.

"Somebody loves you baby. Whoa, whoa whoa! Somebody loves ya' baby," Camille sang loudly with a smile to her small bump as she lathered her stomach in the shower, the hot water soothing to her skin.

She always loved hot showers – didn't matter the outside temperature or the humidity that remained in her apartment despite the open windows and ceiling fans. Her bay window welcomed the sun and all its warmth, but being overly exposed with no tree coverage in the dead of the city didn't allow for many cool breezes to stop by and visit.

She continued to sing as she shut off the running water and began to dry herself with a plush towel. Tonight was going to be a quiet evening. Just for her. She wanted to unwind and enjoy the weekend without any interruptions – including those from Russell who was incessantly calling her phone for the past hour.

She chose to ignore him for the past three weeks, hoping that eventually she'd fade from his psyche and he'd move on to another piece of tail. Only Leilani knew that she had decided to keep her baby. The day they met at the practice for her appointment, she broke down into tears and begged her best friend to take her home. She couldn't bear the thought of killing her child – even if it meant being a single parent and hiding who the real father was.

She had already concocted a fairly believable explanation for inquiring minds. She went with Leilani on her medical conference in Vegas and slept with one of the Chippendale dancers after their show. She figured not only would that excuse be shocking to most, it wouldn't bear too many questions besides *"oh, which one?"* Of which, no one would have an ounce of a clue. It was better if she cut all ties with Russell. It wasn't as if the group of them had hung out since their college years.

Their unions were sporadic and at most, paired off with Darnell and Russell, Leilani and Camille or Darnell and Leilani with Russell. Camille rarely stayed knitted with them and didn't enjoy feeling like the third, fourth and fifth wheel seeing as though she typically was the single one out the bunch.

The ding of her doorbell brought her singing to a halt and she raised her head as she pulled on her underwear.

"I hope that's not Mrs. Jenkins' nosey fifty thousand cat having ass," she complained and tossed her robe over her bra and panties, tying it in a knot and briskly walking to her door.

"Okay, okay, *okay*!" she yelled due to the incessant ringing of her doorbell, "Don't wear the shit out. It ain't broke!" Whoever it was let off the handle once they heard her voice through the door.

She yanked open the door.

"Mrs. Jenkin—*Russell*? What are you doing here?" she was caught off guard by his appearance.

Russell scanned her from head to toe, his tongue against his jaw. He looked inquisitive, almost in disbelief as he stared at her. Camille returned the look and shifted her weight to one side, placing her hand on her hip.

"What do *you* want?" she asked, rolling her eyes.

He stared at her.

"Oh, you don't wanna let a brotha' in?"

She scoffed, irritated as she stomped in the other direction, turning her back to him. Russell entered and quietly shut her door, locking it behind him. He eyeballed her, watching her as her petite a buck ten body turned to face him, her nipples poking against the silk of her robe once she crossed her arms underneath them. She reminded him of Jada Pinkett; had her bone structure and build to match. That's what attracted him to her in the first place.

"What is it? I was about to have me a nice, *quiet* evening. But, here you go showing up here unannounced. Did you even consider that I might have company?"

"What's with the attitude?" he asked.

Camille sucked her teeth.

"I don't like uninvited guests. Especially not my booty calls popping up like they own me," she snapped.

"I'm not a booty call," he corrected, offended. "And you didn't have a problem with me showing up unannounced when I was making you speak in tongues."

She sucked her teeth again, releasing her arms and slapping her palms against her thighs.

"What do you want?" she nearly yelled. Since she started her second trimester of pregnancy, her temper was easily triggered. That was a large part of the reasoning of her wanting to be left alone.

Russell scratched his eyebrow.

"You got somethin' you wanna tell me?" he asked.

She furrowed her eyebrows and twisted her neck.

"Yeah, go on about your business so I can enjoy my evening."

He smirked and shook his head, rubbing his goatee.

"You knocked up, Moon?" he asked.

Camille popped her neck backwards. "*What*?"

"You heard me. Are you knocked up?" he asked.

She flipped her hand, turning to walk into her kitchen as he followed.

"Get outta here with that bullshit," she said.

Russell watched her.

"Answer the question with a *no, it's not true Russell,* and I'll gladly leave."

Camille looked at him.

"Why does it matter, Russ?" she asked. "We're obviously done with being cutty buddies."

Russell laughed.

"So it's true," he said shaking his head and leaning his hands on the countertop.

Camille watched him for a moment, her mind racing back to

Leilani. She was the only person that could have told her secret. Camille closed her eyes.

"Damn you and your big ass mouth, Lei," she muttered.

Russell looked at her. "When you getting rid of it?" he asked.

Camille quickly looked at him and furrowed her eyebrows and smirked.

"I'm not," she snapped.

He raised his eyebrows.

"Oh, you *better* be."

She scoffed and turned, opening her refrigerator to pour herself a glass of juice.

"You're not my daddy. You don't tell me what to do," she replied.

When she turned, Russell was standing inches behind her, catching her off guard. She nearly dropped the juice jug.

"*Damn,* back up!" she exclaimed, attempting to move forward, but he blocked her.

Russell stood nearly a foot taller than Camille and his weight was easily double her size. It never intimidated her nor did it come to her attention just how much larger he was until she couldn't get past him. He had never been a threat to her or anyone in all their years of knowing one another. He couldn't hurt a fly; or so they thought.

Camille looked into his eyes. "*Move,*" she said with attitude.

Russell stepped closer, forcing her to back against the refrigerator door.

"You're getting rid of it," he said.

Camille shoved past him, slamming the glass container on the counter.

"Go home – go somewhere, Russ," she said. "I don't have time for this."

Russell didn't budge and she turned to look at him.

"Get out! *Now!*" Camille yelled, stomping her foot on the floor and pointing to her door.

He walked towards her and she stepped back.

"Russell," she threatened with a raised brow. "If we were ever friends, you will leave, now," she recommended.

"You're not having that baby," he said.

She watched him for a moment.

"What the fuck you gonna do if I do keep it besides lying to your damn wife?" she challenged.

No immediate response and Camille laughed.

"Ya'll men really get me with that shit. Wanna be dogs, fucking any and everything that moves! But, then you wanna try to tell a woman what she *gotta* do. How about you do what you *shoulda'* been doing which is bein' a *married man* and get the hell outta my face!"

The mentioning of Cheryl resurfaced his rage from the knowledge of his wife cheating. Russell snatched her quickly by her forearms, pulling her towards him.

"Bitch, you're not having that fucking baby," he said angrily.

Camille tried to snatch away from him.

"*Bitch*? What is wrong with you?" she yelled.

"Moon, get rid of it," he said. "Or else I will."

"Russ, ain't nobody scared of you," she said.

Camille wiggled to get away and laughed when he held her tighter.

"Really? Are we really gonna do this?" she asked, looking into his eyes.

"What did I say? Get rid of it," he hissed at her.

Camille laughed again.

"That threatening tone might work with Cheryl's ass, but it ain't working on me. I don't *have* to do anything you tell me to do."

Russell gripped her wrists harder.

"Moon, don't fuck with me," he said angrily.

She pried herself away from his hurtful grasp.

"Get out," she said, her pulse quickening. "Get out or I'm calling the cops, Russell."

He laughed.

"You're not having it," he said. "So either you get rid of it or I'll get rid of it."

It dawned on Camille that he'd hurt her if he had to. She realized that was why he had come to see her this evening. She gulped and felt her breathing begin to become shallow. She felt cornered in her small apartment as she began to slowly back away from him, searching for her cell phone.

"Russell, for real," she said. "Just leave me alone."

He followed her, sliding off his suit jacket and placing it on her sofa.

"Not til' that baby is dead," he said calmly, his eyes glancing at the small bump of her belly.

The reality of her situation hit home. Camille bolted, sprinting to her front door. He chased her, grabbing her around her waist and yanking her backwards as she tried to hold onto the doorknob. She was screaming, kicking, squirming to get away from him. Successfully, she was able to break away and attempted to get to her door again. Russell grabbed her and she turned, swinging her fist at his face. He pinned her in his grasp and she caught a glimpse of the blood on his now busted lip.

They stared at each other for a split second and she saw the shadow of his fist. Russell punched her in the eye, watching her body fall to the ground. Camille cupped her eye; tears began to stream down her face, stinging the fresh bruise that she knew was beginning to form. He had hit her hard. She could barely see out of her right eye as she scrambled to her feet, rushing to the kitchen for something to defend herself. If this was going down, she wasn't going without a fight.

Camille reached for a knife and turned. Russell was too fast, covering ground and punching her in her face again. This time, her nose. She felt a crack and a pool of blood rushing out of her nostrils. It was undoubtedly broken. Camille was dazed from the strike as he had hit her harder than the first punch. She was stumbling around, trying to get away from him, frantically searching for her phone.

She could hardly breathe, she was frightened and knew that either she got away from him or this would be the end of her. She ran for her second floor balcony and he shoved her against the door before she could open it, snatching her back by her robe and tossing her to the ground. Camille began to crawl away from him, panting and crying.

"Russell," she begged. "Please. Don't do this."

He walked towards her and she saw him raise his foot. She shielded her face and grunted in pain when his size eleven shoe smashed down on her abdomen. Her hands flew to cover her stomach, but his continuous kicks and stomps were too powerful for her protection. She tried to yell out in pain, but her ribs were hurting beyond measure, restraining her lungs. She turned on her stomach; attempting to get away from him. He followed, kicking her in side and Camille balled herself in fetal position. Russell stopped after a few minutes of beating her body with his foot. He scanned her over, assessing his job and nodded, straightening his shirt before pulling on his suit jacket.

"I told you to either do it or I would," he said, buttoning his suit jacket.

Camille began to crawl, groaning in pain.

"You bitches really think ya'll run shit." Russell licked the blood from his cut lip. "Surprise. You ain't running a damn thing."

Russell snatched his keys and walked to her door to exit. He turned to see her reaching for her cell phone and he grabbed it before she could get to it, tossing it against the wall. It cracked in pieces upon impact. He looked down at her. Camille was defeated, helpless. This confrontation had completely caught her off guard and Russell grinned at his accomplishment.

"I told you not to fuck with me," he said. "And if one damn cop shows up at my door, the next time I see you, you won't be alive. You hear me?"

Camille began to sob loudly. The sharp pains with each inhale were beginning to surface and she could feel the severe cramps developing in her womb. She heard her front door click shut as

Russell exited and she looked at her phone, shattered in pieces on her hardwood floor. She slowly pulled herself to her feet, feeling a gush of fluid escape her body and slide down her inner thighs. She figured it was blood so she didn't look down. Instead, she grabbed her car keys and inched to the garage, the pain mounting from her injuries.

She couldn't see out of her right eye as it was now swollen; could scarcely breathe from her cracked ribs. But, she succeeded in getting to her Camry and making it out the garage. Her goal was to get to the hospital. She didn't want to wake her neighbors because she knew that would mean ambulances and police officers.

Camille pulled out onto the main road, crying and grunting from the excruciating pain she was now feeling. Her tears flooded her eyes and she could barely see the road in front of her. Camille was speeding, doing eighty plus in a fifty-five. She needed to get medical attention and fast as she could feel blood pooling on the seat beneath her and the lightheaded sensation easing in from lack of oxygen. She didn't see the red light until she was already in the intersection. She gasped when she saw all the headlights flying towards her.

DARKNESS.

* * *

8:45PM

Leilani laughed loudly, her eyes tearing up; her abs were aching from the hilarity.

"You remember her face when she saw Russell jump out the bushes on her with that Michael Myers mask on last Halloween? That was too funny!" Cheryl said with a huge grin on her face.

Their laughter subsided and they wiped tears from their eyes. She and Darnell decided to meet with Cheryl and Russell for their weekly couple's game night. The guys were in the kitchen, having their own separate chatter as Leilani and Cheryl talked and reminisced of their funny moments together as friends since she was married into the group. The discord in their relationships was obvious with the clear separation of the men and women in Leilani's and Darnell's home, but no one paid it any mind.

She never had an issue with Cheryl. Leilani had more so adopted her into their group by default. After all, one of their friends had found her special enough to marry. So, why shouldn't she accept her as a friend? She looked at Cheryl. She stood about 5'3 and was a little chunky. She had gained weight a year prior when she had found out that she was pregnant and unexpectedly lost the baby. The story that was told by Russell was that she was overexerting herself and had fallen down the stairs in their basement while doing laundry, causing her to go into early labor. She was only five months.

The weight had never come off of Cheryl's frame after that and Leilani equated that partly due to some level of depression from her lost child. Cheryl was cute. She had a round face and slanted eyes. Her bouncy hair in natural spirals, tinted with a light reddish orange color. She was a nice person and Leilani could always see how Russell was smitten with her unlike Camille who disliked her from the day they were introduced at their engagement party. Leilani now knew that it was because Camille secretly wanted Russell all to herself. But, beyond the hidden envy of his wife, Cheryl was a genuinely friendly woman. And like Russell, she too seemed completely harmless.

"Oh my God, Russell used to *love* to scare Camille. She was *so easy* to get," Cheryl said, still laughing as she drank from her glass of iced cognac.

Leilani cleared her throat; her thoughts going to the fact that Cheryl had no clue that her husband and Camille were doing more than just playing their usual pranks on each other. She glanced at the grandfather clock against one wall of her great room.

"I'm surprised I haven't heard from her yet. Usually she calls me. It's been like two days." Leilani said.

Cheryl laughed.

"She's probably trying to find her heart medication from Russell scaring her half the time!" Cheryl replied.

Leilani laughed and picked up her cell, speed dialing her bestie to hear it go directly to voicemail. She furrowed her eyebrows. "That's really odd. Straight to voicemail."

Leilani knew that her office was closed for the past few days for upgrades, but she still hadn't heard from Camille for them to do anything together on their time off. She chose not to bother her, thinking that she was probably laid up with a new piece since she had left Russell in the dust or basking in the joys of motherhood since she decided to keep her baby. Leilani dialed her number again. Voicemail. She began to grow concerned and she stood to head towards the kitchen where Russell and Darnell were talking, stopping in her tracks when she heard their conversation.

"What did you do?" Darnell asked.

"I just went to talk to her. She's getting rid of it." Russell said.

"That easy? How'd you convince her?" Darnell was taken aback.

"You underestimate my skills, man. No more baby momma drama, that's all I'm concerned about. That shit is handled." Russell bragged.

"Wow, I need to take pointers," Darnell said, surprised.

Russell laughed. "Well, hopefully your plan will work and you won't have to convince Lei to get an abortion anytime soon."

"Are you still going through with the divorce?" Darnell inquired.

"Hell yeah! Cheryl thinks everything's cool. But, when she least expects it, wham! Gonna serve her ass with those papers."

They both laughed.

"Man, I've been having her followed. I got pictures, emails, texts. She ain't gonna know what hit her." Russell vented.

"Make sure you videotape it for me. That's going to be priceless," Darnell requested.

"No doubt," Russell said with another laugh. "Scandalous bitches," he muttered.

Leilani stepped into view, both of them turning quickly to look at her, shocked by her entrance. Russell cleared his throat, taking a gulp of the vodka in his hand and glanced at Darnell. She could tell they both were uneasy out of the possibility of her hearing their discussion.

"Have you heard from Camille?" she asked Russell boldly.

Russell smirked. "Why are you asking me?"

Leilani glared at him. "Cute. Don't play games with me, Russ. Have you heard from her the past two days?"

His thoughts shot back to their altercation and he raised an eyebrow, giving off a slight shrug.

"Nope," Russell answered, taking another drink, the ice clinking against the glass.

Leilani rolled her eyes, turning to look at Darnell.

"I'm gonna head over there to check on her," she said quietly.

Darnell furrowed his eyebrows.

"No. You're not going anywhere. We have company and you're not her babysitter," Darnell ordered.

"Yeah, she's a grown ass woman," Russell agreed with a laugh.

Leilani looked at Russell.

"This is an A and B conversation. So, C your ass on out of it, okay?" she snapped.

"Hey, it's no need for all that," Darnell jumped to his defense.

She looked at her husband and raised an eyebrow.

"I'm going to check on *my* friend since ya'll don't seem to be concerned one bit," she said.

Darnell made a low noise in disagreement, shaking his head.

Leilani twisted her neck in irritation.

"What? I have to get permission now to leave the house?" she challenged her husband, attitude oozing from her body language.

Russell laughed.

"On *that* note, I'm going back into the living room," Russell said and exited.

Darnell watched him exit and looked down at Leilani.

"Don't ever do that shit again," Leilani said.

"What are you talking about?" Darnell questioned.

"Try to pull rank! You're not my father, Darnell. He's been dead and buried for over a decade now."

He rolled his eyes, turning his back to refill his glass with more vodka atop of the ice.

"I'm not trying to be your father. But, it'd be rude if you just left and we have company," Darnell replied.

"That's not all you said," Leilani snapped.

"Well, you're not her sitter. Shit, not gonna bite my tongue about it," he said.

"I'm not babysitting her," she stated.

"Yeah, but you go running to her like she's a wounded animal. You drop everything." He paused. "That doesn't seem weird to you?"

Leilani shook her head.

"No, no it doesn't. She's my best friend, Darnell."

He smirked.

"It almost seems like your lover the way she gets so much of your attention," he stated.

"What? Are you jealous?" she sarcastically asked, offended at his accusation.

Darnell looked at her and raised a brow.

"Should I be?" He shrugged. "I'm saying; if you like the bush more than the hot dog, more power to you. But, that's not what I prefer in my wife."

Leilani scoffed.

"You're such an asshole," she said. "No wonder you and *Mr. Suave* get along great. The two of you are just alike."

"You know what? What happened to this grand escape you decided to make since you were so tired of being with me?" Darnell asked, growing more irritated with her.

Leilani furrowed her eyebrows. "What?"

"The whole *psycho* breakdown you had a few weeks ago. You've been avoiding me, I've noticed that. I'm not stupid, Lei,"

Darnell confronted. "What? You can't find the front door without your *girlfriend* to help you?"

Leilani stared at him, not responding. Darnell returned the look and drank from his glass.

"Should I be babysitting you?" he asked with a straight expression.

She furrowed her eyebrows again.

"What are you talking about, Darnell?"

Darnell's mind rewound to the few months prior when she was working later hours, coming home at odd times of the night even when he knew that she had left her office already. He never thought anything of it. He figured it was her running around with Camille. However, when he learned of Russell and Camille, he knew exactly when Russell occupied Camille's time; times when Leilani was missing in action.

Not once did Darnell consider that Leilani was cheating, but after the recent news of Cheryl's infidelity, he became slightly suspicious of his wife's sporadic behavior and mood swings towards him. He knew it was easy to stray – no matter how in love a person was.

Darnell remembered the woman at the bar that he bought drinks for. They ended up flirting that evening and she freely invited him to her place afterwards. Sex was available a dime a dozen. Even more if you were attractive and had money; to which, both of them possessed.

Darnell knew that his wife turned heads. He had even caught Russell eyeballing her time after time, but it was never a concern for him because he always believed that Leilani was as faithful as they came.

"You're unbelievable," she said and rolled her eyes.

"Are you really going to check on Camille or are you running off somewhere else?" Darnell asked.

"You've had too much to drink. So it's best if we end this conversation now," she snapped, turning to exit.

Darnell's expression was mischievous.

"No. Let's not. Why you acting all *uptight*? You're the one always wanting me to talk. *I'm talking*."

Leilani turned to look at him.

"I've never cheated on you if that's what you're implying," she said angrily.

Darnell smirked, drinking more of his vodka. Leilani's eyes scanned his frame. She didn't appreciate his accusatory temperament.

"Maybe I should be asking you the same," Leilani said.

Darnell raised his eyebrows and smirked.

"Maybe you should," he said sarcastically.

Leilani scoffed.

"You're such an asshole," she stated, disgusted.

"You married this asshole," Darnell countered, standing from leaning against the counter. "So either love it or leave it, baby."

Leilani opened her mouth to speak, but Cheryl came running into the kitchen, interrupting them. Cheryl's face was pale, her eyes wide as if she'd seen a ghost. Leilani and Darnell looked at her.

"What's wrong?" Leilani asked.

"You guys remember that horrible accident the day before yesterday that was on the news?" Cheryl asked.

Leilani's heart sank and she immediately became panicky.

"No," Leilani said, shaking her head. "Please don't tell me— don't tell me that was Camille."

Leilani recalled seeing the news brief, but she had turned before listening to the rest of it. She didn't like hearing bad news and she felt that the news stations were full of it. So, like always, she chose to turn the channel and thought nothing else of it.

Cheryl nodded slightly.

"That was Camille. She's-she's in the hospital. In critical condition," she told Leilani and Darnell.

"What?" Darnell asked, shocked.

Leilani rushed out of the kitchen. Darnell and Cheryl followed.

"Lei," Darnell yelled. "Lei, wait!"

Leilani turned. "Why am I waiting? I knew I should've checked on her. Shit," she said, tears filling her eyes as she searched for her keys.

They all had been drinking Patron and Courvoisier on the rocks since Russell and Cheryl arrived. None of them were in the best position to drive. They typically played board games until late in the evening to sober up enough to drive home. But, it had only been an hour into their get together. They were all still buzzed from the liquor they had consumed. Russell didn't budge. He sat on the sofa, watching Leilani scamper around. Leilani was a wreck.

"Where are my keys?" Leilani yelled.

Darnell walked to her and grabbed her arm.

"Lei, you're in no condition to drive," Darnell said, "Let's just wait until we sober up a little bit and I'll drive you to the hospital."

Leilani looked at him, snatching her arm away.

"I'm going to see my friend *with* or *without* you!" she replied, finding her keys and stomping out the front door, leaving it open.

Cheryl followed behind Leilani.

"I'm coming with you, Lei," she said and exited behind Leilani.

Darnell sucked his teeth.

"What is with these crazy black women?" Darnell asked aloud. "Now if they get pulled over, both their asses are going straight to jail."

Russell shook his head.

"I told you before, they think they run shit," Russell said as he rubbed his hands together, thinking to the evening he attacked Camille. "You gotta put these bitches in their place."

7
Getting to Happy

Leilani rushed down the hallway, running past the receptionist's desk and leaving Cheryl behind.

"Camille? Camille?" Leilani yelled, looking in the rooms she passed.

A few nurses began to chase Leilani and grabbed her by the arm.

"Ma'am! Please, we can't have you running around in the ICU," one of them barked.

Leilani turned and looked at her.

"I'm looking for Camille Campbell," she said.

"Are you family?" the nurse questioned.

"I'm the only family she has left living that matters," Leilani replied.

The nurse opened her mouth and Leilani knew what came next – typical procedure.

"I'm listed as her next of kin," Leilani informed the nurse before the nurse objected to telling her information. "Dr. Leilani Mathews."

The nurse took in a deep breath.

"We couldn't find any identification on her, so for now, she's being listed as Jane Doe. Please wait here while I bring in her doctor."

Leilani followed her to the waiting area where Cheryl was already seated. Leilani stood immediately when the doctor entered and shook his hand.

"Hello doctor, am I able to see her?" she asked.

"Not at the moment. I'm afraid that Ms. Campbell is in a coma. She suffered severe trauma in the accident she sustained. She has eight broken ribs, a chest tube and isn't breathing on her own. We had to give her a blood transfusion upon admittance," he paused. "She also had slight brain swelling, so we're monitoring her brain activity very closely. She's in pretty bad shape, Dr. Mathews."

Tears filled Leilani's eyes and she wiped them.

"Um, Camille was—Camille," she glanced at Cheryl, and then looked back at the doctor. "Camille was pregnant – four months. Is…"

He exhaled.

"Unfortunately, we were not able to save her fetus. We believe her miscarrying to be the cause of the accident. We had to do an emergency hysterectomy to control the bleeding."

Cheryl sobbed and covered her mouth.

"Oh my God," Camille exclaimed in shock.

Leilani was calculating the physical trauma that Camille could have suffered and her rate of survival in cases that she had seen before.

"How bad was the car accident?" Leilani asked.

He glanced down at her chart, flipping through pages.

"It appears that Jane Do—I'm sorry, Ms. Campbell was doing about eighty five and ran a stop light, speeding head on into traffic on the interstate. She was struck by approximately ten oncoming vehicles. It was a horrible, *horrible* collision. The car was totaled. We are completely in shock that Ms. Campbell even survived the accident. She's a fighter."

Leilani gulped.

"When will she be able to have visitors?" Leilani asked.

The doctor raised his eyebrows.

"Not for a few days. Ms. Campbell is in very critical condition and we're trying to minimize any risks at the moment until we're able to get the swelling down in her brain."

Leilani stared at him and nodded.

"Please keep me posted. I want updates every hour about her condition – even if it's the same," she demanded.

The doctor nodded.

"Certainly. I'll have our nurses stay on top of that. Again, we are doing everything in our power to keep Ms. Campbell as comfortable as possible. This was a very unfortunate event and our medical team is working diligently to keep her stabilized."

Leilani faintly smiled.

"Thank you. I appreciate it," Leilani said.

The doctor exited and Leilani turned to take a seat next to Cheryl who was wiping tears from her eyes.

"She was pregnant?" Cheryl asked.

Leilani sighed.

"It's a long story, Cheryl. That's honestly not my main concern right now. Camille surviving this is what matters," Leilani replied.

Cheryl shook her head and wiped more tears.

"There's nothing worse than having your baby that you wanted to keep so badly snatched from you," she said.

Leilani looked at her, reached over and touched Cheryl's leg.

"Hey, it's okay Cheryl. She's going to pull through this," Leilani encouraged.

"You never forget." Cheryl shook her head. "You never can forget losing a child," she said.

"I'm sorry about your loss," Leilani comforted. "But that was an accident that was out of your control, Cheryl. The same that has happened to Camille. The two of you did nothing wrong."

Cheryl shook her head as tears poured out of her eyes.

"I should've left him," she said. "I should've left him before he hurt my baby."

Leilani moved her hand.

"What?" she asked Cheryl.

Cheryl's round face looked back at her.

"I didn't fall down the stairs," she confessed.

Leilani's eyes widened and she stared at Cheryl in disbelief.

"Cheryl, what…what are you saying?"

"Russell doesn't want any children. He never wanted me to have that baby. So, he came home one night after work and offered to help me do laundry," Cheryl sniffed, wiping her eyes. "We got into an argument because he tried to make me go and get an abortion and I refused," she paused. "All I remember… all I remember is him yelling at me and slapping me around. He knew better than to punch me, because he didn't want to leave any marks. But, when I got to the stairs, he," she paused and took in a deep breath. "He shoved me backwards and I…I fell. I fell down the stairs."

Leilani stared at her; she couldn't find words to reply to what she had just heard. Her thoughts were racing, wondering if something happened before Camille's accident for her to leave her apartment speeding like a mad woman. She recalled Darnell and Russell's conversation in the kitchen earlier that evening and she now wondered what Russell had done when he went to go "convince" her to get the abortion.

Leilani shook her head in repugnance.

"Cheryl…" Leilani began and looked at her distraught friend. "Why are you still with him?"

Cheryl looked at her and her lips twitched as she shrugged.

"I'm scared to leave," she answered. "Out of fear that he'll do worse. He's—he's threatened to kill me before."

"Is that the first time he ever put his hands on you?" Leilani asked.

Cheryl sniffed and nodded, wiping tears from her eyes.

"It came out of nowhere. Russell is usually the sweetest guy. I don't—I don't know what I did wrong that day. I didn't provoke him, I just…I just didn't want to get rid of my baby. I wanted to keep it so much. I thought he'd be happy. I didn't plan to get pregnant."

Leilani shook her head over and over.

"Don't blame yourself, Cheryl. Shit, that's the last thing you should do. Russell," she paused and took in a deep breath. "He needs help," she paused again and closed her eyes. "I can't believe this," Leilani muttered.

Leilani looked away. She was now immeasurably disgusted with Russell – far more than she had become in learning more about his despicable ways. They heard familiar voices and Leilani looked up to see Darnell and Russell entering the waiting room. Cheryl stood and quickly went to Russell, flinging herself into his arms and balling. Darnell and Leilani stared at each other, both unmoving. Leilani didn't want him to comfort her.

"How is she?" Darnell asked.

"We're not able to go see her." Leilani sighed. "I don't know if she may make it. She's in a coma."

Darnell's eyes widened. "A coma?"

Leilani nodded and looked at Russell who was now standing alone. Cheryl had excused herself to go to the restroom.

"Are you happy now?" Leilani angrily asked.

Russell laughed, glancing at Darnell.

"Why you all up in my face?" Russell asked.

Leilani stood and approached him, standing in front of him.

"I know you had something to do with this you piece of shit," Leilani growled.

Russell raised his eyebrows and looked at Darnell.

"You better get your girl, man," he threatened.

Darnell reached for Leilani and she snatched her arm away.

"This is between me and you," she said to Russell.

"Lei," her husband said and Leilani turned, looking at him.

"What? You don't think I have a right to be mad at your shitty ass friend?" she snapped.

Darnell shook his head.

"This isn't your busine—" Darnell began.

"Not my business?" Leilani yelled. "It doesn't seem odd to you that this jerk finds out that Camille is pregnant and she ends up in the hospital?"

Russell looked at Darnell.

"You told her about me going to talk to Camille?" he asked angrily.

"*Whoa*, we all just need to take a step back before this gets way out of hand," Darnell said.

Leilani looked at Russell.

"What did you do to her?" she demanded.

Russell laughed.

"You're crazy, woman," he replied.

"I know you had something to do with this. What did you do to her?" Leilani demanded, stepping closer.

Darnell moved forward and held his hand between their bodies.

Leilani looked at him.

"Darnell," she started.

"Lei, leave it alone," Darnell said.

She glared at Darnell.

"You're protecting this dirtbag?" she spewed.

"No I'm stopping you from accusing *our friend* of doing something when none of us have any idea what happened," Darnell argued.

Leilani's eyes opened wide for a moment and she scoffed.

"You've gotta be kidding me," she said in disbelief.

Darnell stared back at Leilani.

"Lei, there's no way Russ caused that accident."

Leilani scoffed.

"Yeah, just like he had nothing to do with Cheryl losing her baby?" she said.

Russell laughed and she glared at him.

"You're a little shit. Camille shouldn't have given you the time of day," Leilani insulted.

Russell looked at her.

"How about you ask your girl her opinion on that?" Russell covered his mouth. "*Oh wait*, you can't cause' she's in a coma."

Leilani lunged towards him and Darnell jumped in front of her as Russell laughed.

"I will fuck you up!" Leilani yelled. "You hear me? I will fuck you up if you had anything to do with this!"

Russell continued laughing and turned to exit.

"I'll catch you later, man," Russell said to Darnell.

He looked at Leilani and chuckled.

"Put your dog on a leash before she bites somebody," he said to Darnell.

Leilani looked at Darnell and shoved his hands away.

"Get off me," she said angrily.

Darnell watched her as she began to pace.

"Lei, you need to calm down. You're *way* out of line."

"I'm out of line?" she yelled. "Darnell, for once in your fucking life, take up for your damn wife!"

Darnell raised his eyebrows. "Not when you're wrong."

Leilani stopped pacing and faced him.

"When *I'm* wrong?" she yelled. "Tell me something, Darnell, when you heard about Russell cheating on his wife, did you tell him how wrong *he* was?"

Darnell licked his lips.

"Camille was just as wrong," he said.

"It doesn't matter who it was – he was still cheating on his wife!" Leilani fumed.

He pointed his finger at her.

"Don't try to put this on me," he snarled.

Leilani shook her head.

"You're no better than him."

Darnell scoffed.

"And you have completely lost your mind!" he yelled.

She nodded.

"You're right, I have. Except I lost it when I married you

thinking that you would be the person I'd spend the rest of my life with." She shook her head. "I now see just how wrong I was."

"Then do what the hell you need to do, Leilani!" Darnell yelled. "First and foremost, go get some psychological help because you've gone to Mars with these psychotic thoughts! Do you hear yourself?" He stared at her. "You're walking around here accusing our friends of assault and murder!"

Leilani scoffed.

"It's not an accusation," she snapped.

"Yeah, ok. You need someone to help you find your way back down to earth, Dorothy, cause' you're not in Kansas anymore!" Darnell barked.

"How about you grow some needed balls," she said angrily. "You get mad at me for expressing myself but you can't even be honest about your true feelings."

"This has got nothing to do with us!" he yelled.

"Yes it does! It has everything to do with us, Darnell! You can't even fight for this marriage! Yet, you'll go toe to toe with me to defend everyone else!"

"Whatever," he muttered, turning to walk away. "You just couldn't wait to try to make this about us." He paused. "I'm going home."

"When were you gonna tell me that you didn't want kids?" she asked.

Darnell turned and looked at her.

"What?" he asked.

"I heard you talking to Russell. About how he hopes *your plan* keeps working out for you. I'm not an idiot, Darnell. I know what's going on," Leilani quickly ranted.

"You don't know what you heard," he growled. "And you need to stop while you're ahead."

Leilani raised a brow and scoffed.

"What? Are you gonna kick my ass too if I get pregnant like your buddy did to Cheryl and possibly Camille?"

Darnell shook his head.

"Here you go again with the foolish accusations," he said.

Leilani stared at him and laughed, shaking her head.

"This is such a waste of my time," she muttered.

"You know what, Leilani? You're right. I'm done listening to your bullshit. I've been done a long time ago." Darnell admitted.

She nodded. Her heart was racing.

"I'm not surprised." She snatched her purse. "I'm *so* done with you too."

Darnell watched her storm out of the waiting room and he sighed, rubbing his head. He tossed his hands in the air.

One Month Later

Camille groaned, squinted her eyes as she shifted in the bed. She licked her lips, feeling the dryness of her lips. She opened her eyes farther to see through her blurry vision. She tried to raise her head and felt a cool palm touch her forehead, gently pushing her head back against the pillow. She looked up to see Leilani's eyes gazing back at her.

"Hey, hey, hey. Take it easy," Leilani's gentle voice coaxed as she stroked Camille's forehead.

Camille groaned again and looked around the room, remembering that she was still in the hospital. Camille had woken up from her coma two weeks prior, but was slipping in and out of consciousness since she had awoken. Leilani had been there with her to visit every day. Leilani didn't miss a beat.

"Here, have some water before you try to talk," Leilani said, offering her the straw.

Camille took a few sips, the sensation of the cool fluid moistening her mouth. She looked at Leilani as she sat down in the chair beside the bed.

"How long was I out this time?" she asked, her voice slightly hoarse.

"For about two days," Leilani answered.

Camille scanned her. Leilani was wearing boot cut, fitted jeans and a dressy cream blouse. Her curly hair pulled into a tight bun; her face lightly decorated with bronze makeup. Camille gathered that Leilani must've just come from the office on their usual casual Fridays. Camille pushed the button of her bed and slightly raised her torso in the air.

"How are you feeling?" Leilani asked.

Leilani wanted to control the pace of the conversation before rendering the dreadful news to her best friend.

Camille swallowed.

"Better. Much better than the last time I woke up."

"You weren't up for long. You came to and then went back under a few minutes later. You didn't even talk. You just looked around and then, bam. You were gone," Leilani explained and then smiled. "So this is great that you can remember being awake before and are talking."

There was silence. Camille looked around the room and touched her lower abdomen, feeling the tenderness of a scar. She raised the sheet and assessed her body. Leilani watched her. Leilani didn't want to have their first conversation be about her injuries, but she didn't expect Camille to check her scars. The swelling in face had gone down considerably, so that minimized the first shock that Cheryl had seen upon going to the restroom.

Camille gulped.

"I lost the baby?" she asked.

Leilani stared at her for a brief moment. She nodded.

"Yes. You lost the baby," she confirmed.

Camille's lips began to quiver as she started to cry.

"Why is there a scar?"

Leilani cleared her throat, feeling the sting of tears.

"Um, you…" she paused. "You had a bleed that they couldn't control. They had – the surgeons had to," she took in a quick breath. "They had to perform an emergency hysterectomy on you, Moon."

Camille gasped and sobbed loudly, her body shaking. Leilani stood and attempted to hug her, but Camille pushed her away.

"Don't," Camille said. "Leave me alone," she said.

Leilani backed away.

"Do you want me to call your doctor," she asked.

Camille shook her head.

"You've done enough." She looked at Leilani. "This is all your fault."

Leilani furrowed her eyebrows.

"What?" she asked. She was taken aback by the allegation.

"This is all your fault, Leilani. If you hadn't said anything to your husband, Russell would've never known about the baby," Camille seethed.

"What did he do to you?" Leilani asked.

Camille squeezed her eyes shut to squeeze out the memories.

"It doesn't matter," she said, fighting the tears. "What's done is fucking done and I can't do anything about it."

Leilani sighed.

"Moon, please don't let him get away with this," she begged.

Camille shook her head.

"Why did you have to say anything?" she growled.

Leilani stared at her. Camille opened her eyes, staring at the ceiling as tears streamed down her cheeks.

"Why did you say anything at all? No one had to know who the father was. I was doing fine hiding the pregnancy, but you," Camille paused and shook her head. "You just *had* to say something to Darnell, didn't you?"

Leilani licked her lips. She needed to steer this in a better direction. She did not like the view on the horizon.

"We were arguing and—I," Leilani began to explain.

"What did that have to do with me and my business, Lei?" Camille asked, her voice was louder.

They stared at each other and Camille's bloodshot eyes turned into slits as she glared at her.

"My baby had nothing to do with you and your fucked up marriage," she spit.

Leilani took in a deep breath.

"I understand you're upset, Moon, but I didn't—"

"You didn't what? Didn't mean for me to lose my baby? Is that what you didn't mean to do?" Camille snapped.

Leilani looked down at her hands.

"Moon, please know that I didn't mean for any of this to happen to you. I don't know what I can do to make you forgive me, but I can't rewind time."

Camille didn't respond, she continued to stare at the ceiling; her thoughts swirling back into her active mind. With these came a realm of emotions that she couldn't quantify. She was inundated with feelings of hurt, rage, resentment, denial, remorse, hostility and Leilani was to blame for all of it.

"I'm sorry for telling Darnell. I'm so sorry for all of this," Leilani said.

Camille shook her head.

"It's too late for apologies. You promised me that you wouldn't tell anyone. And you broke that promise."

"What can I do to make things right?" Leilani asked.

Camille looked back at the ceiling and swallowed.

"Nothing. You should've never said anything in the first place. I trusted you."

Leilani looked at her and Camille turned, making eye contact.

"I want you to leave," Camille said, "I don't want you here."

Leilani's heart sank. She stared at Camille.

"What?" she asked.

Camille looked away. "I want you to go," she said, "I want you out of my life."

Leilani furrowed her eyebrows. She was in utter shock of the turn of events.

"Moon, I'm your best friend. I'm—I'm the only one that has come to see you since you've been here."

"This is all your fault!" Camille shouted, catching Leilani off guard.

Even though Camille's ribs were still healing and her belting out her voice caused discomfort, she was outraged with Leilani.

"You were the only person that knew about the baby. *You* told Darnell. *You* started all of this. I asked you not to tell anyone – you promised me! What best friend does that?!" Camille yelled.

Leilani's eyes filled with tears but she forced them back. She licked her lips and nodded, picking up her purse and keys. She didn't want to argue. Camille still had a long road of healing in front of her both physically and emotionally. Leilani looked down at her friend and took in a deep breath, opening her mouth to speak.

"Just leave," Camille said. "Don't say anything else. Just leave."

Leilani stared at her for a moment and turned, walking to the door. She stopped. She couldn't leave without saying her piece. She turned and looked at Camille, her hand on the door handle.

"I know that I broke my promise and told Darnell and I'm sorry for that. But, I didn't make you sleep with Russell," she said. "This isn't *all* my fault. But, if you want to blame me for it, that's fine," Leilani finished and quietly exited the room.

Camille heard the door click and closed her eyes, tears flooding her eyes again. She began to sob; crying harder at the reality of her existence. She had lost her baby and there was nothing she could do about it and she'd never have another child of her own. She gathered from the accident that the doctors had more than likely concluded that all of her injuries resulted from it. There was no evidence of an assault. It was all erased the moment she was hit by the first car. She had lost all opportunities to send Russell to jail for his attack on her. There was nothing she could do but live with her regret.

Leilani guzzled down the cognac, closing her eyes and rocked her head to smooth melody. Leilani left the hospital and headed to her rented penthouse to park her Benz and take a quick shower. She took a private car with chauffeur to her favorite jazz club in town. She planned on drinking quite a bit and chose to take that route than to risk a DUI. Charlie O's was featuring a new and upcoming artist and she was feeling the vibe in every inch of this artist's music.

Leilani felt movement at her table, passersby bumping into the circular top as it was now becoming more crowded. She opened her eyes to see Evan Worthington strolling by, easing his way through the traffic jam of thin linens and sports coats. He was alone and did not notice her sitting there.

Leilani leaned back, hoping to ease more into the darkness. Leilani's waitress came by to check on the status of her drink. The waitress grinned flirtatiously at Evan once they came face to face, her average heighted frame gladly blocking his forward progress.

"Excuse me," the dark-haired waitress said to Evan with a slight wink, continuing to block the walkway.

The flirtatious waitress looked at Leilani.

"Are you ready for another?" the waitress asked.

Leilani didn't want to speak. She smiled and nodded at the waitress who grabbed her empty glass. Evan turned, glancing next to him at Leilani's table and did a double take. Leilani froze like a dear in headlights, feeling her heart skip a few beats. Evan furrowed his eyebrows.

"Leilani?" he asked, squinting due to the dimness in the club.

Leilani quickly looked away, acting as if she were searching for something in her booth. Evan moved in closer to the table.

"Leilani, is that you?" he asked again.

Leilani sighed and turned to look at him; making eye contact with those beautiful sapphire blue eyes of his. He smiled; his handsome face lighting up.

"*Wow*," he said. "It has been a while."

Leilani raised her palms and gave a slight shrug.

"It has," she replied with a forced smile. "How have you been?" She really didn't care to know.

Evan turned, easing into her booth and helping him to a seat at her private table.

"I've been pretty good," he glanced around, looking back at her. "You look amazing," he said, his eyes taking in her beauty.

He was promptly mesmerized by the emerald and pink silk sarong she had on her body.

"Are you here all by yourself?" he asked in disbelief.

Leilani looked around. Evan being this close to her was still quite unnerving.

"No. Actually, I was—I'm—I'm waiting for two of my friends. They're—they're on their way here," she fumbled with the lie.

Evan glanced at the crowd and looked back at her, his eyes scanning over Leilani's face.

"Cool. I'm actually meeting up with two colleagues and my older brother is in town until tomorrow. We all could just use this one VIP booth if you don't mind," he said.

Leilani stared at him for a moment, broke their gaze. She looked down into her cognac, her nails tapping against the glass as she cupped the cool goblet tighter. Evan noted her hesitancy and he grinned slightly.

"My brother is a riot. You will enjoy him the most. The two colleagues are really sociable and also happen to be fellow fraternity brothers," he said to lighten the mood.

Leilani nodded.

"Ah," she said disinterested. "Let me guess, Kappa Alpha Psi?" she asked with a faintly pleased grin.

Evan smiled one-sided at her cynicism, momentarily interrupted by the intentional brush of the waitress' body as the waitress passed Leilani her refill.

"Actually, I am a, Deke…" He watched Leilani's eyebrows furrow in confusion. "I'm a proud member of Delta Kappa Epsilon," he answered, ignoring the other woman's flirtatious grin altogether as she turned to exit their space; his eyes never parting from Leilani.

Leilani smirked softly, taking a slow sip of her cognac as his eyes relentlessly watched her every move.

"I'm not surprised," Leilani muttered.

Evan glanced at the entranceway of the cozy club.

"Anyway, I don't believe they are going to show. This isn't their ideal place to catch a few drinks," he said with a laugh as he slid his LG into his breast pocket. "Those guys are more into alternative and rock. And my brother," he shrugged with a laugh. "Well, he's just into women."

She glanced at her Breitling wristwatch.

"I guess you can wait here. But, like I said, my girls are on their way," she replied.

"Let me guess, Alpha Kappa Alpha?" he said with a raised brow.

Leilani glared at Evan from her sip.

"Yes," she snapped. "And they should be getting here any minute now."

Evan watched her, his gaze intense and unmoving. Leilani cleared her throat and shifted in her seat, turning her body slightly at an angle away from him. Her spiked 4" heel was tapping frenetically against the floor, twiddling her thumbs as she looked around the club. He still made her skin crawl. Unfortunately, it was in all the good ways that she sought to ignore.

"You're alone," he realized aloud. "You just don't want me here," he said.

Leilani shifted uncomfortably as Evan leaned closer and scanned her face.

"Or is it that you don't want to be seen with me in a place like this?" Evan pressed.

Leilani looked at him and raised her eyebrows.

"Excuse me?" she asked. "Stand corrected, I'm not ashamed of this establishment," she insulted.

Evan laughed and scratched his eyebrow.

"What did I do to you, Leilani? We were doing just fine and then unpredictably you put up this wall between us as if I somehow mistreated you."

She stared at him; a bewildered expression on her face. She couldn't believe that he was pulling her trump card.

"I don't know what you're talking about," Leilani calmly replied.

Evan laughed again and shook his head. He couldn't believe the breeziness of her dismissive behavior.

"We haven't spoken since the night I invited you to the martini bar," he reminded.

Leilani continued to stare at him, forcing her expression to remain emotionless.

"I've been busy," she retorted.

"No. You have been avoiding me," Evan corrected with a raised eyebrow and smirked. "It has been *months* since we've spoken. I find it hard to believe that you've been *that* busy. I am a president of a company and I find time to touch base with good friends."

Leilani looked away and sighed.

"Evan, I really don't think you understand what happened that night. Your wife—"

"My ex-wife," he interjected.

"*Your wife,*" she stressed, "thinks that we had an affair."

"Which we did not," Evan said simply.

Leilani closed her mouth and paused for a moment, exhaling roughly through her nose.

"No, we didn't. But, it didn't look right," she countered.

Evan raised his eyebrows.

"So you figured the best solution was to eradicate me as a friend altogether?" he asked. "Was that all you could assemble as an objective alternative?"

Leilani sucked her teeth. He wasn't letting her get off as easy as she assumed.

"Evan, I don't like drama," she said.

"And I don't either. But, I wasn't going to dispose of a good friendship ov—over some paranoid ex-wife's preconceived notions," he argued.

She smirked and rolled her eyes.

"You mean your wife," Leilani corrected with a twist of her neck.

"*No*, for the thousandth time, my *ex*-wife," he said, raising his bare left hand. "Sophie and I are divorced."

She felt her pulse skip a few beats. Leilani closed her eyes to calm her hopefulness.

"Evan, what do you even want from me?" she asked and looked at him.

They stared into each other's eyes for a moment and she leaned onto her forearms.

"You are a *grown ass* man," Leilani said with a twist of her neck. "Why do you need *me* as a friend? I'm sure you've got all the connections with the Bentley driving *multi-millionaire* execs and I'm pretty sure you have plenty of other acquaintances that are far more entertaining than I ever was."

"But, they are not you," Evan straightforwardly stated.

Leilani scanned his handsome face and laughed, sitting back. She didn't know if he was flirting or being facetious. She sipped from her refilled cognac.

"You're really a piece of work, Mr. Evan Worthington," she said, shaking her head.

Evan watched her, his eyes scanning over her body; down to the tips of her manicured fingers. They were a light shade of pink – the color blending perfectly against her creamy complexion and accentuating the pink tint in her dress. His eyes caught a glimpse of her bare left hand; the tan mark from her absent brilliant wedding set teasing his senses. He looked at her lightly decorated face as Leilani watched the budding crowd.

"How have you been?" he asked, hope coursing through his veins.

Leilani inhaled loudly and sighed.

"Let's see, I've been just peachy," she said sarcastically with a stiff smile.

Evan continued to watch her, now noticing the slight puffiness of her eyes and the nervous tapping of her fingernails against the tabletop.

"You need to release it," he said.

Leilani looked at him and furrowed her eyebrows.

"What?" she snapped.

"You need to vent whatever it is you are holding inside. It is going to slowly eat away at you until you let it go," Evan elaborated.

Leilani smirked.

"What? Are *you* the psychologist now?" she asked and took another sip from her drink. "I'm fine and you don't have the slightest insight into my life."

Evan reached over and touched Leilani's tapping hand. Leilani yanked her hand away and looked at him wide-eyed.

"Don't," she said angrily.

She didn't expect Evan to touch her and the electric jolt that shot clear to her crotch alarmed her. He raised his hands in surrender.

"I am just trying to help, Leilani."

"I don't want your help," she said quickly.

There was silence for a brief moment. Evan noticed the rapid rise and fall of her chest. Evan had created an upheaval of emotions inside of her that Leilani didn't wish to entertain. These emotions were fruitless and only exasperated her further. She couldn't have him. She never expected to and had grown to accept the loss of him as a friend. She was trying to move on with her life…without him.

"I'm here alone for a reason. I didn't ask you to come over here. I didn't ask you to stop and talk to me and I for damn sure didn't ask you to have a seat at my table," Leilani snapped and rolled her eyes. "Why don't you go and wait for your *frat* brothers somewhere else?"

Evan scanned her face in silence. Leilani raised a threatening brow.

"Are you deaf?" she barked.

He slightly shook his head.

"No. I am not," he answered.

"Then why are you still here?" she snapped.

Evan licked his lips and nodded.

"Fine. I will leave you alone if that is how you want it," he said.

"That's exactly how I want it," Leilani retorted.

Evan casually slid from the booth and stood, straightening his suit jacket.

"Have a nice life, Leilani," he said and turned, walking away.

Leilani watched him until he disappeared into the crowd and grabbed her phone and Burberry bag. Evan had killed her buzz and it was now time to head back to her temporary home. Evan glanced back, seeing her leave out of the club and climb into the backseat of a black Mercedes.

Evan shook his head and answered his ringing phone as he walked over to valet.

"Hey shit face, what happened to you guys tonight?" Evan snapped.

"Whoa bud! I'm stuck in traffic—there's a concert tonight in the city and, I'm still sitting on the freeway."

Evan rolled his eyes.

"Nice. You could've called me and told me that earlier, Nic. I would have stayed at home."

"What's your deal?" his brother snapped back.

Evan rubbed the back of his neck, glancing at the black Mercedes' brake lights. He hadn't noticed until now that traffic was a bit insane getting out of the parking lot and to the packed street.

"Nothing," he muttered.

"You saw her, didn't you?" Nicolas asked.

Evan raised a brow and sighed.

"Yeah," he paused. "I just ran into her at the same place we were meeting up."

"That blows. I could've played defense so you didn't see her with her new guy," Nicolas offered.

Evan shook his head.

"She was waiting on her friends," he corrected.

"She was alone?" Nicolas exclaimed. "So, why are you talking to me?"

Evan furrowed his eyebrows, ignoring the honking cars of irritated drivers in the background.

"She's leaving the club," he answered.

"Is she gone yet?" Nicolas asked.

"Her car is about to drive off," Evan answered.

"And where are you?" Nicolas asked.

"Valet just pulled my car around," he said.

"Follow her!" Nicolas yelled.

Evan grimaced at the absurd suggestion.

"I am not—" he began.

"You go to her place. You talk to her, dude. Then you fuck her brains out. Because you've been obsessed with this chick," Nicolas barked.

"I'm not doing that," Evan said, shaking his head.

Nicolas groaned in frustration.

"Then go home and be lonely. But I don't want to hear about her anymore," he retorted.

Evan sighed and looked at the Benz that was still sitting in traffic waiting for a friendly driver to brake.

"Baby bro, dude, come on. Don't let her get away," Nicolas encouraged.

Evan walked towards the valet attendant.

"I'll think about it," he replied, taking the key fob in exchange for his generous tip.

"Dude—" Nicolas began to object.

"I said I will think about it!" Evan interjected, hanging up.

1:34 AM

Leilani turned the volume up on the Bose surround sound system, humming along with a Jill Scott tune. She adored their music and tonight, she needed to unwind to their relaxing tunes. She was beyond aggravated after seeing Evan. She couldn't shake him from her mind and she was angry with herself that she couldn't accept the fact that they would never be an "us".

She had given up on love. Not only had she looked for it in the wrong places, but she had had her fair share of letdowns with men – men who only wanted her for what she could give to them and never valued her for the woman she was. She thought back to all of her short relationships and flings she had with a handful of men.

Leilani was never a wild woman. Surely, she did have her stent early in college where she accepted an offer from a few men to be an on call fling. But, it never went farther than that. Then, Leilani thought that was out of her character, but at the time she felt that she needed to listen to Camille and live a little. However, in all of her run-ins, she ended up having her esteem more beaten than the previous.

Darnell was the longest relationship she had ever had and he had done nothing more than become a longer spell of all of her previous dealings wrapped in one. Darnell had put her through emotional ups and downs, moments where she had grown to dislike her body and even attack her personality because it didn't appeal to him.

She allowed Darnell to make her feel less adequate, undeserving of real love and affection. Leilani had grown used to cold and distant men so much that she couldn't accept that men were capable of being loving. She had learned to stop believing that she was a beautiful woman and had attached to the notion that no man would ever be content with what she had to offer – looks and all.

Sure, Evan was now divorced from Sophie, or at least that's the story he told, but Leilani knew that Evan was nothing more than a short friendship at best and it'd be wise if she left it alone than to be disappointed anymore. Her favorite Marvin Gaye song came on, *I Want You.* Leilani snatched the remote and pressed repeat as she closed her eyes, leaning her head back against the plush chaise and sighing deeply. The warmth of the fireplace heated her body from the chilly evening. She began to hum along with the captivating tune, feeling her body ache from the tension pent up inside of her.

The cognac had long drained from Leilani's body during her extended shower and she now faced the harsh reality of her loneliness. She had left Darnell – sent movers to pack her belongings and move them into a vacation penthouse she was renting monthly from a fellow colleague until Darnell was gone. Leilani had given Darnell three months to move. After all, she had the most input on their designed home and Darnell was not in the least bit bound to it with any fond memories.

Despite all of her and Darnell's disagreements and shortcomings, Leilani missed the feeling of having someone – anyone to call her own. This song brought thoughts of Evan flooding her mind and she closed her eyes, trying to shake them and think of something else. She couldn't have Evan and she had to accept that.

Leilani inhaled deeply and opened her eyes, staring at the burning logs in the fireplace. It had been a long time since she felt alive and now her emotions were too dull to fathom the degree of her sadness. She no longer knew how to feel stress. She had been able to hide it in her marriage for years that her mind had become immune and she no longer knew how to release.

She thought of Evan again and his concern for her. She smirked and shook her head. Evan knew nothing about her but what she let him in on in their short friendship. Leilani couldn't understand how he could feel a connection with her knowing the little bit that he did.

Her doorbell rang and Leilani ignored it, thinking she was hearing things. It rang again and she sat forward, turning to look in the direction of the front door. Leilani snatched her Breitling off the coffee table, noting the time and furrowed her eyebrows. She had no idea who it could be.

She knew it wasn't her colleague that she was renting the penthouse from and no one else knew where she had been staying. Leilani stood, grabbing her mid-thigh length robe to pull over her Victoria Secret's pajama short set.

Leilani walked to the door, the song flowing into the foyer. *Nothing better than a Bose*, she thought. She peered through the peephole and froze momentarily at who was standing on the other side. She paused for a moment and took in a deep breath, trying to calm her anxiousness before opening the door to Evan.

Their eyes met and she felt chills run down her spine. Leilani deeply inhaled as she prepared for the shadiest performance of a lifetime.

"What are you doing here?" she snapped, disdain forcefully spewing from her pores.

Evan's magnificent eyes scanned her frame.

"I want to talk to you," his voice resonated to her core.

Leilani grimaced. She asked the obvious.

"How did you know I was here—how did you even get past security?"

Evan raised his eyebrows.

"I followed your driver and..." He gave a slight shrug. "I'm five hundred bucks lighter."

She rolled her eyes and released a disapproving stare.

"Evan..." she began.

"Hear me out," he interjected. "I just want a few minutes of your time. That's all I ask of you."

Leilani stared at him, her face stone. Her emotions were

doing somersaults but she refused to show it. Evan scanned her face, hoping to find a glimpse of delight. None.

He sighed.

"I don't like the way our friendship ended, Leilani. And to be honest, I miss having you around," he paused and cautiously added, "As—as a friend."

Leilani watched him, even though her heart was dancing with excitement to have him in her presence, she refused to expose her inner feelings. She nibbled her bottom lip for a moment, wanting to appear as if she were contemplating inviting him inside the penthouse. She had eagerly decided upon that moments ago. She shifted her feet, stepping to the side.

"Come in," she invited. "I can at least offer you a drink for all the trouble you went through to talk to *your friend*," she said.

An Hour Later

Leilani giggled, covering her lips to keep the sip of cognac from spilling out of her mouth. Evan laughed with her as he finished sipping the Pappy Van Winkle bourbon she had offered.

"How did ya'll *not* get expelled for that?" she asked, her smile wide.

"If I can have another glass of this awesome bourbon, I'll finish the story," Evan said.

Leilani playfully glared at him, taking his glass.

"I'm surprised you're not on your ass. I'm gonna send you a bill cause you've had damn near half the bottle," she lightheartedly teased.

Evan chuckled. He admired her switching derriere and the sensual sway of her hips as Leilani made her way into the gourmet kitchen. He sighed as his sexual tension rose.

"Doing what I do, you develop a high tolerance with all the Cuban cigar sessions that you attend," he said.

Leilani handed him his replenished glass, plopping down on the sofa.

"So, you've picked up a bad habit?" she asked, beginning to sip her refilled cognac.

"No. I still detest smoking. But, it doesn't dismiss me from those meetings. That's when the high and mighty *really* let it all hang out. They're not as put together as you would perceive them to be when they're in the public eye," he explained. "Some of them are pretty fucked up."

"And that's when you can reel them in," Leilani said with a soft smile.

Evan grinned.

"If I can accept their genuine persona, they trust me with their life," he elaborated.

"And *then* you make your move," she said with a wink, taking another sip.

He nodded.

"It's all about the right timing," he said and glanced at her glass. "I see you topped yourself off as well. That's what? Your second glass?" he asked.

Leilani licked her lips.

"As long as I pace myself, I can handle it," she replied.

Evan nodded, his eyes scanning her long, flawless, exposed legs. He cleared his throat before tossing back the remainder of the bourbon. He wanted to pounce on her and the smooth bourbon only increased his desire.

"I see. Slow and steady wins the race," he stated, watching her watch him.

Leilani skimmed his athletic frame. Evan looked sexy in his casual dark blue slacks and bright white button down, sleeves rolled up to his elbows. Evan didn't interrupt as she appreciated him. Leilani eyeballed the strong curve of his jawline, the fine strands of trimmed dark hair tapered flawlessly towards his neck.

He was indeed handsome—if not more from the last time she saw him months prior. The air between them was different this time around. They were no longer tied to their respective lovers and Leilani could feel herself growing warmer by the minute.

Evan raised a brow.

"You see something you like?" he boldly asked.

Leilani's heart skipped. She fumbled for her words.

"I—I'm sorry. I was—I wasn't looking at you," she lied. "My mind was…" She laughed. "It was—it was a—a thousand miles away."

Evan stared into her eyes and Leilani shifted awkwardly, hurriedly gulping the rest of her cognac and coughing at the potency.

"You wouldn't enjoy my career," he stated.

Leilani furrowed her eyebrows, Evan's topic change sudden and unpredicted.

"Why is that?" she asked.

"For starters, you have to be very perceptive of body language…" he began.

"Un-huh," she murmured.

Leilani hung onto his every word. Evan faintly smiled at her as he continued to gaze into her eyes.

"You're responsive…" He paused. "And can be quite evasive. You're definitely not one to make the first move," he assessed.

Leilani gulped. Speechless. She didn't want to jump to conclusions. Evan moved closer and Leilani swiftly sprung off the couch.

"I—I need another drink," she said. "Care for more?" she asked, snatching the empty glass from his grasp. "Yes? Great," she answered for him. "Let me get that for you."

Leilani high tailed it to the kitchen. Evan remained on the sofa and began to rub his palms together as he contemplated his next move. He didn't want to scare Leilani away. But, he couldn't back down. Not this time. It was the perfect opportunity. Evan patted his thighs, stood and followed her. Leilani reached the counter, quickly placing their empty glasses atop the granite and reaching for the bottle of Pappy Van Winkle. Evan moved closer and placed his hand on top of hers, easing the bottle back onto the countertop.

"That's not what I want more of," he said, his warm breath tickling the back of her neck.

Leilani's heart was racing a mile a minute. She stared at his hand on top of hers and breathed deeply.

"What do you want then?" she asked. "I can order a pizza if you're hungry."

Evan faintly smiled, finding her shyness amusing. Leilani turned to face him. The look in his eyes made her southern neighbor spasm. She slid her hand from beneath his and moved away from him. Evan watched her. He could see her nervousness. It wrapped her in a sheath. He stepped towards her and Leilani backed away until she hit the other counter, halting her escape.

She glanced at the neon clock on her Electrolux microwave.

"Wow, it's—it's really late. I think you should go hang out with your brother before he leaves," she suggested.

Evan gazed into her eyes and reached up, stroking her cheek.

"My brother is just fine," he replied.

She gulped.

"Evan, what are you doing?" she asked. "We've been drinking. I don't think this is a good idea—"

"We've done this dance long enough. I know you want me," he said and his thumb stroked her bottom lip. "I certainly want you and not just as a friend."

And there it was... The point of no return.

Leilani's heart began to beat faster. She stared into Evan's mesmerizing eyes. She didn't know what to do with his confession. He took advantage of her silence, leaning down and kissing her. Leilani couldn't fight the moan that escaped. *Oh, he kisses so good,* she thought as her knees grew weak. Evan's hands were on her robe, untying it and pushing it off her shoulders. Leilani broke their kiss.

"Evan, wait," she breathed.

He gazed into her eyes.

"Is that a no?" he asked.

Leilani was breathing heavily, her heart pounding against

her chest. Her body was hot with her desire for him and he noted her excitement.

"Evan, I—I don't...Shit, I've been drinking—*you've* been drinking. I don't know—God, I don't—I don't know about this," she stuttered.

"We are both adults here. There is no need for either of us to be juvenile about our attraction. I know exactly what I am doing," Evan replied.

The shocked expression that crossed her face was immediately erased with her flushed cheeks and dilated pupils. *Oh God, I really do want him,* she thought. Evan licked his lips and raised a brow.

"Shall we explore your bedroom?" he asked.

Leilani faintly nodded and turned, leading the way to the master. Once inside, she scanned his handsome face and rested her hands on his cheeks, leaning in and beginning to kiss him again. Evan pulled away from her and began to undress himself. She couldn't tear her eyes away. She wanted with every fiber of her being to see his naked body that she had been fantasizing about for months now. But, to her dismay, he pulled off just his shirt and tee. Her eyes soaked in his chiseled torso.

There was no doubt in her mind that he ever missed a day doing some form of physical activity. His body was athletic, lean and seamlessly toned. If he wasn't a white collar guy, he could easily be a model. His physique was breathtaking; almost unreal. Leilani raised her eyebrows in awed appreciation, nibbling her bottom lip in approval. She wanted to see the rest of his magnificence and silently prayed he wasn't lacking where she needed it most.

"Wo—wow. Shit," she replied. "I need to take my ass to the gym more often."

Evan laughed and stepped forward and they began to kiss again. Leilani eased backward onto the bed as he followed, his hands slowly undressing her until she lay bare beneath him on the plush mattress. He gazed at her in admiration. His sapphire blues took in the smooth, brown shade of her creamy skin; the darkness of the circles around her petite nipples leading down to the curve of her flat stomach which sunk into the dip of her narrow waist and soared out towards the sharp extension of her round hips.

His gaze slid down to her bare mound; the only remnant of hair being a short, perfectly trimmed patch directing his attention to her cocoa lips. He groaned softly in provocation—the look in his eyes causing Leilani's heart to skip a few beats.

"Are you gonna take your pants off?" she eagerly asked, looking into his eyes.

Evan glanced down and stood, swiftly pulling them off. He climbed back into the bed, giving her barely any time to make note of the bulge in his boxer briefs. Leilani raised a brow.

"You're not naked," she said with a soft smile.

He stared into her eyes and she rested her hands on his waist.

"Let me help you out," she said, eagerly pushing down the waistband of his boxer briefs as he climbed out of them, kicking them off his feet.

Leilani smiled.

"Much better," she said, reaching down to boldly palm his erection.

Her eyes widened and she looked at him.

"What?" Evan asked.

"Not what I'm used to," she said.

His heart sank.

"Smaller?"

She gulped in astonishment.

"Actually, no," she said.

The mystified expression on Evan's face made Leilani smile. This fine specimen was easily made unsure about his manhood and it amazed her that he had no idea what he had been blessed with.

"Let me give my doctor's opinion...you're above average. But, it's not frightening," she eyeballed his hesitant expression. "It's quite impressive," she reassured him with a smile. "Any larger and I'd be putting my va jay on lock down."

Evan laughed, relieved.

"Great medical evaluation. Let's make sure that makes it to the medical dictionary."

Leilani giggled at his humor.

"Were you not sure how I would respond?" she asked, curious.

Evan gave a slight shrug.

"Every woman is different. You never know," he replied.

"You're good…" she raised her head and pecked his mouth, sucking on his bottom lip as she retreated.

She gazed into his marvelous eyes and sighed in awe.

"*Mmm.* You're actually *more* than good," she said softly.

Evan's eyes gazed at her face and scanned down her body.

"You're undeniably splendid," he muttered.

Evan began to passionately kiss her, hearing her moan in response. He moved away from Leilani's mouth and began to kiss her neck, feeling her shiver. He made a mental note of each spot that brought a pleasurable response. Leilani could feel him making his journey to her southern comfort. She figured he would stop, but to her surprise, he pushed her legs wider and began to tease her—his tongue gliding around her inner thighs.

"Oh my…You…you don't have to do that," she breathed, his soft kisses making her shiver.

Leilani was anxious for Evan to make his grand entrance and she was uncomfortable with his unforeseen detour. Darnell's visitations to this region were few and far between. When he did make the venture, it was hasty and uneventful. Darnell had made it perfectly clear that it was not his favorite pastime and Leilani had developed a self-conscious outlook towards up close and personal visits to her nation's capital. Evan's tongue moved closer to her apex and she tensed.

"Evan, you don't….*Oh….Oh shit,*" she breathed.

Leilani gasped as his mouth made contact with its final destination. She soon realized that Evan was quite talented as he worked his magic, moving his tongue and lips in assorted ways to ascertain what she enjoyed. He then manipulated the hell out of those annotations.

Leilani's body arched, her breathing grew heavy and deep. *Damn, he's so good at this,* she thought, gripping the sheets and biting her bottom lip to maintain her composure. It was short lived. She let out a loud moan when she felt him slide a finger inside, his tongue continuing its sensuous laps around her engorged knob.

"Oh....oh...*oh God*," she cried, reaching to clutch a pillow as her body arched higher.

"You have a tiny cunt," he moaned, in awe of his finding. "I'm going to enjoy filling it with my cock."

Evan's lustful dialect jolted her over the edge. No matter how Leilani tried to fight the rapture, it was an imminent fate. She kissed heaven when Evan easily made her vigorously come the first time. She was puzzled when she brazenly skidded into a second. Evan didn't stop there. The third time had Leilani's head reeling and her body quivering from head to toe. She hadn't realized that Evan was on top of her and between her legs until the fullness of him entering her yanked her back to reality.

"Ah," Leilani cried, pushing against Evan's hips to stop him from going further.

Evan moaned at the immense sensation of her compact sex stretching to accommodate him. He thrust again, her shaky palms halting his full entry as she cried out. Leilani was taut. Her narrow void hadn't been stretched beyond what Darnell had to offer in years and Evan's prize surpassed him in both length and girth. Evan began to kiss her neck, feeling her hands relax. He thrust again, this time, deeper and Leilani loudly gasped.

"Oh shit," she cried. *Oh my God, his dick is huge,* she thought.

"Shit," Evan groaned, as a chill ran down his spine. "You're so wet and," he groaned again with another thrust. "Oh *fuck*, so tight."

Leilani gasped, pushing at Evan's hips when he tried to thrust again. It was too much, too soon. The ampleness felt marvelous. Her previous partners didn't take their time with her. They all rushed into her southern neighbor like it was the first day of hunting season and all seemed determined to permanently stamp their seal of approval in it.

She wasn't confident if she could handle all of Evan's manhood without losing complete and absolute control. His proficiency and awareness of her cues caught her completely by surprise.

"Please let me," Evan moaned. "You feel amazing."

Leilani continued to restrict his penetration, but Evan knew how to stop her combat. Evan swiftly shifted, raised her legs and hooked her thighs with his forearms. He eased inside, slowly and felt her hips jerk as she gasped, her hand going to his waist to halt him. She didn't have as much leverage in this position.

He gazed down at her staggered expression as he began to thrust until her void was at full capacity with his rod. Leilani's body quivered and her cries began to escalate. The sound of his heavy breathing and sensual moans amplified the experience. The throbbing and full sensation was heightened with this position. It was overwhelming.

"Oh m—my God, w—wait," she panted, gripping his biceps.

Leilani needed a moment to collect herself. She was losing her restraint as his thrusts increased in intensity. Her body was shivering in delight and her voice defied her aim to remain poised.

"Oh God, Evan, wait," she pleaded. "Oh shit! Wait."

He groaned, hearing her curse again.

"*Oh Leilani*, don't stop me," Evan moaned. "I don't want to stop."

She felt powerless, all control of herself adrift in this moment. His movements were concentrated, slick and precise. She was stupefied at the blissful awareness of what was happening between them, but she didn't for a second want it to stop.

Leilani knew she probably sounded as if she were coming entirely unglued. But, this was unadulterated pleasure. Her eyes rolled into the back of her head at the incalculable sensations of the friction of Evan's manhood massaging her walls. Her body had welcomed every inch and he knew precisely how to work his masterpiece.

The pressure began to build with each steering thrust of his hips, urging her closer to another climax. She could no longer contest it. Her body had abandoned her and had succumbed to this incredible man.

This was just the beginning...

* * *

9:47 AM

The Morning After

His smartphone buzzed repeatedly, waking him from his slumber. Evan shifted and squinted as he opened his eyes to the bright daylight. He glanced beside him at her lying there—his eyes scanning down to her exposed backside.

He felt a twitch of his manhood at the exquisite view of her slender back leading to her narrow waist and ample bottom. She was truly a sight. His phone distracted his thoughts and he reached down to grab it from his pants, slowly pushing aside the covers and climbing out of the bed as he answered it.

"Hey Nic," Evan said quietly, easing out of the bedroom in hopes of not waking his sleeping beauty.

"Baby bro! I hope that you not coming home last night meant you nailed her," Nicolas yelled excitedly.

Evan groaned in disgust.

"Good morning to you too, brother," he replied.

"Aw, enough of that. Are you at her place?" Nicolas asked.

"I am," Evan answered.

"Did you nail her?" Nicolas inquired.

Evan ran his fingers through his hair, peeking into her bedroom. Leilani was still sound asleep. He closed the door behind him and stepped further into the hallway.

"What time is your flight again?" Evan blatantly ignored the question.

"I'm boarding the plane now. Your driver took me since *someone* was too busy *getting busy*," Nicolas said with a laugh.

Evan rolled his eyes at his brother's immaturity.

"But, I won't keep you, dude," Nicolas said. "I wanted to make sure you were alright since I didn't hear from you after we talked last night."

Evan raised his brows.

"Thanks. I'm great," he said with a faint smile as he recalled the evening prior.

Nicolas laughed.

"I'm quite sure you are!" Nicolas exclaimed. "I will let you know when I make it home. Make sure you nail her again before you leave her place!"

"Jeez, is that all you think about?" Evan asked.

His brother laughed.

"I doubt you were thinking about anything else when you woke up next to her. Anyway, I hope to meet her someday. She sounds special."

Evan nodded.

"I hope you will," he said. "She's very special."

"Alright. Love you, baby bro. *Enjoy!*" Nicolas said.

Evan smiled as he hung up his smartphone. He glanced at it again, noting the hour and decided against returning to bed. He would let her get her beauty rest.

Ten Minutes Later

Leilani opened her eyes, squinting at the light flooding in from the rays outside. Her drapes were wide open. She groaned and stretched, the soft cotton sheets sliding away from her covered legs. She pushed her hair out of her face and opened her eyes wider as they adjusted to the brightness of the room.

She groaned again as her grogginess began to drain from her

and awareness set in. She furrowed her eyebrows when she sat up and looked around the bedroom, trying to piece what happened the night before.

Leilani looked next to her at the empty space in the bed and sighed, somewhat relieved. Evan was gone. She didn't know how she could face him after the way he handled her the night before. She was totally embarrassed as she recalled her reaction to his lovemaking.

Evan probably felt pity after such a deprived performance. Even though his talent was indeed one for honorable recognition, she doubted Sophie or his other partners responded in the way that she had.

She slid from under the sheets, stepping into the restroom and pulling on her robe. She walked into the living room, making her way into the kitchen, the smell of eggs and toast hitting her nostrils. She sniffed and furrowed her eyebrows, *I thought he was gone,* she thought as she stepped into the kitchen.

"Holy hell!" she yelled, jumping backward and covering her eyes.

Evan turned to face her, a flawless smile on his handsome face to greet her entrance. Leilani turned away, her breathing elevated, her pulse was racing. The night's events came rushing back into her memory. Her face flushed immensely and she was even more embarrassed.

Evan was naked, not a stitch of clothing on his body and she couldn't look at him. With all her years of being with Darnell, they never freely walked around nude with each other. They were always covered with something – never fully exposed unless they were getting dressed or undressed.

"Evan, why aren't you dressed?" Leilani asked.

He laughed.

"Good morning to you too," he said with a confident grin, strolling towards her.

Evan stroked her face, leaning in for a kiss, but Leilani kept her head turned. She wouldn't look at him.

"I-I need you to put some clothes on," she stuttered.

"Why?" he asked, raising his hand again to touch her and watching her move away.

Evan furrowed his eyebrows.

"I still make you nervous?" he asked.

She opened her eyes, staring at the wall.

"Evan, I...I really need you to put something on."

He sighed and walked into the bedroom. Leilani took in a deep breath to calm herself. Her emotions were torn now that she was face to face with Evan the morning after. She couldn't acknowledge that she had slept with Evan the night before, but the memories of their lovemaking crowded her thoughts. She covered her mouth, her eyes slightly wide with astonishment.

"Shit," she muttered. "Why did you do this?" she asked herself.

She could hear Evan's footsteps on the hardwood floors as he made his way back into the kitchen, walking over to the stove to check on the food he was cooking. Evan glanced at Leilani, trying to read her awkward behavior. He wasn't sure if she regretted last night or if she simply was in shock from the realization of what happened between them.

"I made you breakfast," he said, turning and placing scrambled eggs on a plate. "It's just eggs and French toast. You didn't have much food in the fridge, so this was all I could pull together before you woke up."

Leilani turned to look at him. He had only pulled on his boxer briefs. She admired his superb body and closed her eyes for a moment, shaking her head. *What have I done,* she thought, *he's a good friend. There's no turning back from this.*

"Damnit," she mumbled.

Evan looked at her.

"What? You hate French toast?" he asked lightheartedly.

Leilani awkwardly laughed. She was growing increasingly uncomfortable. He watched her in silence.

"Are you okay?" he asked.

Leilani was fumbling with her words, trying to find the right thing to say that matched her mixed feelings. She looked at Evan, her eyes scanning over his body again. She looked away and inhaled deeply.

"I can't believe this," she said softly. "I can't believe that we slept together."

Evan laughed nervously and scratched his eyebrow.

"You say that like it's a bad thing," he said, "As if the sex wasn't enjoyable."

Leilani looked at him. She needed to set the record straight.

"I shouldn't have done this. This was wrong...*so wrong* on so many levels. We crossed the line," she said.

He stared at her for a moment, offended.

"Let's address the latter first. Precisely what line did we cross, Leilani?" he questioned.

Leilani sighed.

"Evan, this shouldn't have happened."

He scoffed.

"You didn't say that last night," he said.

"I said a lot of things last night that I shouldn't have said," she commented.

Leilani gulped at his dubious expression.

"I had too much to drink," she justified.

Evan scoffed.

"For fuck's sake..." he muttered and shook his head. "Is this a twisted joke?" he exclaimed.

Leilani stared at him, wide eyed as he returned the gaze; assessing her.

"You were not drunk, Leilani!" Evan shouted in response to her bewildered expression.

She closed her eyes and sighed.

"Evan, don't argue with me about this. It shouldn't have happened. Plain and simple." she gently said.

He scoffed.

"You and I wanted what happened last ni—" he began.

"I'm—I'm trying to let you down easy. Don't make this more difficult than it needs to be," she interjected.

Evan stared at her for a short moment and licked his lips.

"Let me guess, it's the white thing, right?" he asked the inevitable.

Leilani looked away and crossed her arms underneath her breasts. Evan's eyes scanned her and he nodded.

"Yet you were the one calling *me* a racist," he commented, slamming down the spatula.

She jumped slightly and closed her eyes.

"Evan," she said softly. "We're supposed to be friends."

He scoffed and nodded.

"Yeah? You *sure did* make that very clear last night," he said sarcastically. "Was that before or after your fifth orgasm?"

Leilani looked at him and tilted her head to the side.

"That isn't fair," she said.

He raised his brows.

"Fair? That is the last word you should try to throw out as a measuring stick," he snapped.

"What do you want me to say?" she asked.

Evan scoffed and shook his head.

"Nothing at all, Leilani. But, let me make this real easy for you. I don't fuck my friends. And since you can't swallow the fact that you even slept with a white guy—I have no reason to be here because you obviously have a problem being *just friends* with a white guy too!"

"Evan, it's not like that…"

"I don't—I don't get what your qualm is about it," he snapped. "You're biracial. You aren't one hundred percent anything."

"Don't you dare try to label me—I'm black," Leilani snapped.

Evan stared at her for a moment and looked away.

"I wasn't labeling you, Leilani. I was trying to make a point because all I see is a beautiful woman when I look at you. I don't—I don't see black or white or—or any race. I see *you*."

Leilani watched him as he threw away the food he had

prepared, tossing the dishes into the sink. He flipped on the water and he began to wash them. She stepped forward.

"You don't have to do that," she said. "The maid is coming today."

Evan smirked.

"Consider it payment," he snapped. "Don't worry. I am leaving once I'm done with these."

She could see the tautness in his shoulders – the serious expression on his face. He was clearly upset and undoubtedly frustrated with the way she was treating him. Leilani realized she had offended him because of her own foolishness and insecurities. She watched him and was overwhelmed with a funnel of emotions; none of them being regret. She stepped closer to him and touched his forearm. His hands stopped moving and he stood still.

"Evan, I don't want you to leave," she said quietly. "You don't have to go."

He didn't look at her, he took in a deep breath.

"Leilani," he began.

"I don't want you to leave," she interjected.

Evan looked down at her and scanned her face. He sighed and wiped his hands.

"How am I supposed to be sure you're not going to change your mind again? You're so," he paused. "You're so unpredictable. I don't know if I can deal with this."

She wanted to kick herself if she could. Leilani looked away. She didn't know what to say. She knew that she was all over the place with him emotionally – considering the way she dismissed him at the club and how she was now stomping on the passionate moment they shared the evening prior. She didn't regret it. But, inside she had no hope that anything could come of them besides the moment they had shared. They were from two different places – places that she didn't believe could merge.

"You need to figure out what you want," Evan continued. "I am not going to be your scapegoat. Nor am I going to be involved with someone that cannot decide if she wants to be with me," he paused and sighed. "I want you, Leilani. But, I can't do this again. I was already with someone who didn't know if she was going or coming. I have been there and I am not willingly stepping into the same situation again with someone else."

Leilani looked into his eyes and they stared at each other. She reached up and placed her hand on his bare chest, feeling his pulse quickening. She kissed him gently, leaning back and gazing into his eyes. She repeated the soft kiss. Evan stared into her eyes, his pulse was racing the minute he felt her hand touch him. He licked his lips and stepped closer to her, pivoting their bodies and placing her back against the counter.

"I do want you," she said softly, reaching up and placing her palms on his pectorals.

The heat between her thighs was growing and she could feel herself becoming moist. She hadn't felt this way with a man in a long time – never did she feel a strong connection with Darnell. But, Evan made her feel butterflies in her stomach at a quick thought of him – made her pulse skip beats just from a glance. He stared into her eyes, trying to gauge the seriousness of her tone. He didn't want to be dumped again with her regrets of the possibility of them. But, he didn't want to leave either. He began to kiss her. He yanked open her robe and lifted her to his waist, wrapping her legs around him.

"You don't know how much I want you," she moaned when his kisses made their way to her neck.

Evan's hands caressed her breasts, her hips, her thighs – he grew more excited at the feel of her curvy body against his. Evan didn't care for being with skinny women and the moment he laid eyes on Leilani, he was in awe of her curvaceous physique. He admired the way that it moved and fantasized about how she looked in the nude and how her skin felt against his touch. He yanked down his boxers and thrust himself deep inside of her, both of them crying out at the pleasurable sensation of their bodies merging together.

Their lovemaking was wildly passionate, their breathing loud and their moans hungry with excitement. The more Leilani dug her nails into his skin, the harder he thrust. Her cries escalated and she buried her face in his neck, attempting to muffle the sounds. Evan was an amazing lover and she couldn't contain the pleasure he brought her. It was as if he was in tune with exactly what her body needed, knowing the way to thrust to make her squeal, the way to grind to make her quiver and how deep to go to make her lose all control...

Leilani stared at the ceiling in a daze. She felt like she was floating on a cloud. She hadn't felt this way in a long time and she didn't know a true peacefulness and calmness within her could ever exist again. She had finally released all of the anger and loneliness that she had harbored for the disappointing years with Darnell – all the negativity and hurt flowed away from her. She felt alive, she felt free. The tears continued to fall from her eyes and Evan looked down at her.

"What's wrong? Did I hurt you?" he asked; his voice full of concern.

She closed her eyes and shook her head as she began to sob. She couldn't explain or find words about how she felt at this moment. She covered her face with her palm and Evan didn't know what to do.

"Leilani?" he asked.

She was embarrassed atop of her relief, but she realized that she couldn't let him feel that this was his fault. She sniffed and tried to stop her tears, looking into his eyes and shaking her head.

"You didn't hurt me," she answered.

He watched her and began to wipe her face.

"What did I do?" he asked.

She laughed at herself.

"You're wonderful..." she paused and looked at the ceiling again. "You're so wonderful, Evan."

He leaned down and kissed her gently.

"I thought I was too rough," he said stroking her hair.

Leilani laughed again.

"No, this is..." she looked into his eyes. "Honestly, this is the best I've ever had," she answered. "You're just—you're—" she closed her eyes for a moment and looked into his eyes again. "It's *so good.*"

Evan grinned.

"I've been told that a lot," he teased.

She looked at him, speechless and he laughed at the alarmed expression on her face.

"I'm just joking... kind of," he said with a boyish grin.

Leilani hit him gently on the shoulder and laughed. Evan kissed her again and shifted, helping her off the counter and walking her to the bathroom. Leilani followed and watched him flip on the overhead shower. He turned and looked at her, his eyes scanning her nude body; her robe was hanging from her arms, pushed completely off of her front. She had no makeup on. She was completely naked to him and he appreciated her natural attractiveness. Leilani became uncomfortable with him looking at her and she pulled her robe back up, covering her body. She felt self-conscious; felt that he'd see every blemish of her body now that they were no longer making love.

She laughed, embarrassed.

"Sorry," she apologized.

Evan stepped forward and stopped her hands.

"Don't," he said. "I want to see you."

Leilani laughed nervously as he pulled her robe off of her, his eyes taking in all of her nudity. He admired the perkiness of her breasts, the smooth complexion of her almond toned skin, the contrast of the dark brown of her nipples against the rest of her even skin tone. He reached up and began to stroke her full lips, his eyes scanning, marveling at the shape of her face, her high cheekbones that flowed into her slightly pointed nose was sheer precision in his eyes. She had a crevice underneath her nose that led to her lips that he had never noticed before and it accentuated the heart shape of her supple mouth.

She laughed again.

"Evan, what are you doing?" she asked, immensely uncomfortable.

"Has anyone ever told you how beautiful you are?" Evan asked.

She laughed nervously again and he looked into her eyes.

"You're gorgeous, Leilani," he said.

She raised her eyebrows and shrugged slightly. She didn't agree.

"I'm okay," she replied softly.

Evan furrowed his eyebrows as he caught a glimpse of how deep her insecurity ran.

"You don't know how to take a compliment?" he asked.

Leilani broke eye contact, attempting to pull the robe over her body to cover herself. She was uneasy; felt exposed to him – like she was in the spotlight and he was silently pointing out every flaw of her.

"I feel like you're inspecting me," she answered.

"No, I'm admiring you," he corrected. "Leilani, you're perfect."

She laughed louder.

"Cute. Now you're just being funny," she said, attempting to reach for her robe again.

His hand held it still, not allowing her to move it. Evan stared into her eyes and Leilani looked away, her hands covering her breasts.

"Don't cover yourself," he said softly.

"This feels weird," she complained.

"Why? I love what I see."

Leilani laughed again.

"Alright, you can stop with the jokes. I already know I'm not perfect," she said.

Evan stared at her and she attempted to back away. He was making her more self-conscious with his intense gazing.

"Come here," he said and pulled the robe from her arms, letting it drop to the floor.

"Evan," she began to object, moving away and reaching for the fabric.

"Trust me," he said and pulled her into the shower with him.

Evan placed her in front of him, his back to the wall. He saw the hair clip in the shower and grabbed it, lifting her hair and securing it out of the way. Leilani watched his hands reach for the body wash and begin to lather up her sponge, beginning to run it over her body. His hands caressed her and she could feel his strong frame standing against her, his hardness now pressing against her back. He finished washing her from head to toe. He finally soaped up the washcloth and handed it to her.

She turned to face him and began to wash his body; her eyes taking in his physique. She noticed the definition of his lean muscles than she had seen briefly when they were making love. Her hands reached between his legs and she looked down, her eyes admiring his manhood. She had never done this before with Darnell – with any other man for that matter. And never had she had a man bathe her.

Whenever she showered with Darnell, which was less than she could count on one hand, she found herself getting rudely splashed with the water; him having no regard for her presence with him. Darnell would only join her when he wanted to have sex. Not once did he partake in anything intimate unless that was his final reward.

He knew nothing of romance that extended beyond the tip of his penis and Leilani had grown accustomed to only receiving affection when it was time to satisfy him. He didn't make her feel appreciated – only to the degree of what she could offer him. And most times, he treated her as if that was not enough for him.

Leilani gazed in Evan's eyes and he reached for the shampoo bottle, beginning to wash her hair. She cringed for a moment at the thought of how much effort she'd have to put in flat ironing her kinky hair after they were done. But, she didn't want to be the typical black woman that yelled bloody murder whenever she got her hair wet. Besides, this was well worth the cause.

She leaned her head back, closing her eyes to the relaxing strokes and he leaned down, kissing gently down her neck. His hands and mouth continued to caress her body. She breathed deeply, feeling herself falling victim to his seduction. She didn't think this was going any farther. After all, they had just had sex not even an hour ago and the night before and she was used to at least one to two days in between acts with Darnell. She didn't expect Evan to be any different despite his prowess.

To her surprise, he began to kiss her, swiftly lifting her and edged her back against the granite, interlacing their fingers and holding them above their heads against the wall. She rested her foot on a shelf on the side of her, offering herself to him and he pulled away, gazing into her eyes. Leilani watched him as he descended; his face disappearing between her thighs. She moaned, her eyes fluttering shut at the sensation of his tongue dancing against her sensitivity. She held onto the wall for dear life as he immaculately sampled her sweetness. Leilani didn't resist. She was going to let him take her to heights that she had never seen.

8
The 4-1-1

1 Month Later

*L*eilani stared ahead, nibbling on the pen in her hand. She was in a daze, her thoughts on Evan and their past month together. It was nothing less than incredible. He had wooed her beyond belief and for once in her life, Leilani's future looked bright and promising. She had broken free from the mundane routine of her existence and Evan was to thank for it. He made every day feel like a dream; one more step closer to truly being in love.

She admitted; their time together was sheer perfection. He'd meet her at the penthouse and cook dinner together nearly every night of the week. She enjoyed how he called her during the day to check up on her or sent a quick text message to simply say he was thinking about her.

Leilani felt chills run down her spine when she reminisced on their lovemaking. She hadn't had a sex life like this and never did she have a man cater to her without hesitation and without payment. Evan made love to her nearly every night of the week – sometimes twice in one day. She couldn't understand where he got his stamina from, but she didn't complain. Typically, Darnell grew bored with partaking in sex more than three to four times a week if she was lucky. But, Evan had awakened her latent drive and they found the craziest, sometimes riskiest places to fit in a quickie if it was a mid-day pick me up. She giggled at the memory of him urgently calling her to meet him for a bite. Little did she know, she was his delicacy of choice and he sent her on her merry way once he had satiated himself with her nectar.

She smiled and a soft knock on her office door snapped her back into reality. Leilani looked up and cleared her throat.

"Come in," she said and the door opened with her new assistant.

Leilani had received a resignation letter from Camille once she was released from the hospital. It was expected, but Leilani at least thought that her friend would render it to her in person. They hadn't talked since their disagreement at the hospital and Leilani did miss their friendship. But, Leilani didn't want to bother someone that didn't want to see her. She had learned that lesson all too well after being with Darnell for so many years.

"A Ms. Charmaine is here to see you," Leilani's assistant announced.

Leilani wasn't familiar with the name, but she wasn't going to turn down a new patient either. She began to open the patient folder for review when a familiar southern drawl caught her immediate attention.

"Well, well, well, if it isn't the home wrecker," the voice said angrily.

She looked up to see Sophie standing in front of her. Leilani glanced at her assistant who was now standing wide eyed in the doorway. She had concluded that today would be her assistant's last day as Leilani now stared at Sophie Charmaine in her office. The assistant quickly exited and shut the door behind her. She and Leilani made eye contact.

"Sophie," Leilani began, keeping her voice calm. "What are you doing here?"

"How are you enjoying my husband?" Camille snapped.

Leilani stood.

"Sophie, you and Evan are no longer married," she cautiously reminded.

"Thanks to your two-timing, *oh I look forward to helping you be a mother,* conniving attitude," Sophie said angrily. "How long did it take before you got my husband to succumb to your whorish ways?"

Leilani stepped from behind her desk.

"Sophie, I didn't steal Evan from you and I think it's best if you leave now."

Sophie laughed loudly. The look in her eyes made Leilani uneasy. Sophie looked demented as she reached inside of her bag and Leilani balled her fists, preparing to defend herself if she had to against the smaller woman. Sophie pulled out a packet; one that after being married to an attorney, Leilani had recognized all too well.

"Consider this payback," Sophie spouted, throwing the packet at Leilani's feet and storming to the door. "You'll be hearing from my lawyer, you nigger whore."

Leilani bent down and picked up the paper, unfolding it and skimming it over.

"You've gotta be kidding me," Leilani said. "A discrimination suit." She laughed. "*Really?*"

Leilani read down further and squeezed the paper in her hand.

"Son of a bitch," she said angrily and snatched her keys, storming out of the office.

"I have it under control, you don't have to worry. Just stand firm in your decision and let me handle the rest," he said into his Bluetooth.

Darnell's office door flew open and Leilani burst inside with his assistant chasing her. Leilani stomped over to his desk, slamming the packet on top.

He fumbled for his words, distracted at the sudden interruption.

"Let me—let me follow-up with you later." He nodded. "Yes, I'll take care of it. You have nothing to worry about," he said and quickly hung up his call, signaling his assistant to exit.

Leilani glared at him.

"What the fuck is this, Darnell?" she demanded. "You're suing me?"

He leaned back in his leather office chair.

"It's a fair suit, Leilani," he simply replied.

"There is nothing fair about this lawsuit! And you just *had* to put your two cents representation on it, didn't you!" she fumed. "Do you know what this can do to my reputation? I could lose patients—investors, who knows what else!"

Darnell shrugged and smirked.

"The last time I checked, we were separated so I honestly don't care. I hope you go bankrupt."

She glared at him.

"You son of a bitch," Leilani hissed. "How dare you?" she yelled.

Darnell snickered and held his palms in front of him.

"Wait a second before you go blowing your lid," he paused. "Correct me if I'm wrong, but didn't *you* leave me? Weren't *you* the one that sent movers to pack your things and gave me the three months to be out of our house?" he asked.

Leilani stared at him and Darnell stood, coming to walk to her side of the room.

"Leilani, I am representing someone that was mistreated by her doctor simply on the basis of her race and financial status. *You* chose to abandon Ms. Charmaine's treatment without notice. That was your choice and now you have to pay the price."

She shook her head.

"You don't have a clue about this situation. You couldn't wait to find a way to sink your teeth in me," she seethed.

Darnell laughed.

"And apparently you couldn't wait to sink your teeth into her husband after you met him," he retorted.

Leilani's eyes widened.

"Excuse me?" she asked.

Darnell's eyes scanned over her frame.

"My client let me in on the entire deal," he paused. "No wonder you were so quick to leave me."

"No, Darnell, I was ready to leave you a long time ago. I just hoped that we had a fighting chance of surviving."

"Surviving what? You were the one that had all the issues and complaints," he argued. "And now, I see that once the ole' cowboy started sniffing up your skirt, you didn't know how to control yourself."

"That's what this is about? You have a problem with him being white," Leilani stated.

Darnell smirked.

"Trust me, I'm quite sure he ain't packing like me," he said. "And that he's not breaking you off like I did."

"If that helps you sleep at night, I won't bust your *little* conceited head," she insulted.

He glared at her.

"I can't wait until this blows up in your face, Leilani. Because it is," Darnell threatened.

Leilani stared into his eyes. Darnell was resentful for her leaving him and she knew it. The day that she sent the movers, she had to call the police to make Darnell open the front door. He was nearly violent with them when they tried to touch Leilani's personal belongings.

"You really thought that I was going to stay with you? After all the neglect and lack of interest in me?" she asked, her neck crooning.

Darnell sucked his teeth, looking away.

"Nobody was neglecting your ass. You just didn't know what a good thing you had. I am a good man, Leilani. *You* left that and decided to go running off with the pale face cowboy."

Leilani loudly sucked her teeth.

"I didn't run off with anyone. I fought for us. But, you chose to let me go. You chose to not raise a hand to save our marriage, Darnell! Why would anyone stay where they're not appreciated?"

Darnell shook his head.

"You've changed," he said, his eyes scanning her physique. "This cat really has your nose wide open."

"No, I'm happy, Darnell," she snapped back. "Which is more than I can say I ever was in our relationship."

He scoffed.

"We'll see how long that lasts. I'm quite sure he's not gonna marry you," he glared at her. "In case you didn't realize it, you're black and I'm sure he's not gonna taint his comfy, preppy lifestyle with a nigger on his arm."

His callous words cut to the bone. Leilani knew Darnell was intentionally being malicious in his commentary. He wanted to hurt her – make her feel less deserving of what she had with Evan.

"Fuck you, Darnell," she said angrily.

"Oh remember, you did and you did it *very* well," he retorted.

She scoffed in disgust, looking away and crossing her arms underneath her breasts.

"You'll *never* get a piece of this again," she replied.

Darnell glared at her.

"When are you gonna tell him you're still married?" he asked.

Leilani's mouth slightly opened and Darnell raised his eyebrows in realization, a sinister grin forming on his face. He stepped closer to her.

"*Oh,* wait a minute. So, Mr. Rogers doesn't know we're only separated?" he chuckled. "What? Are you still hanging on to a chance for us to get back together?"

She glared at him, her pulse racing. Darnell could see her anxiety; immediately noticed the tension in her stance.

"Why haven't you filed for divorce, Leilani?" he pressed, peering at her face to read her emotions.

Darnell stepped closer.

"Admit it, you still don't want to let me go," he said and smirked. "I wouldn't want to either."

Darnell leaned in close to her lips as if about to kiss her. Leilani didn't back away; she continued to glare at him; breathing heavy and deep.

"I know you miss me," he said. "And I know you're coming back after Mr. Wall Street is done exploring the other side of the plantation."

Leilani rolled her eyes. Darnell raised a brow.

"You're way out of your league on this one. And you don't even know how the game is played. He's not gonna stay with you. You're just his little black toy that he's gonna throw away when he's ready for a white woman on his level," he continued.

Leilani stared at him. His words were swirling around in her mind, causing tears to well inside of her. She forced them down with a gulp. She wouldn't allow Darnell the satisfaction.

"Why are you even kidding yourself thinking you have a chance with someone like him?"

He laughed at her assumed naivety.

"Successful, *white* men don't marry black women. They fuck them. I see it every day at this firm."

Darnell moved closer and caressed her jaw. He felt Leilani flinch beneath his touch when he cupped the back of her neck.

"Now, if you stay put where you belong, I will excuse this little *excursion*. You didn't know any better, I know. You were acting out to get my attention," he said with a faint grin.

Leilani didn't move as his lips pressed against hers. Darnell deepened their kiss and slid his tongue into her mouth. She struggled with her whirlwind of emotions. Darnell was right; she was still hanging onto the possibility of them mending things. But, she was happy with what she had with Evan. Yet, the realization that she and Evan were not officially a couple slammed into her core. Even though it was by her doing, the reality of it still stung. She had no claim to Evan, but she did still have Darnell as her husband. She shoved him away, slapping him across the face. Darnell laughed at her.

"I don't miss you," she said forcefully.

He laughed again.

"Sure you don't," he said sarcastically and scanned her body again. "I could make this all go away," he offered. "All you have to do is come back."

Leilani stared at him and Darnell came towards her again. This time, she backed away and grabbed her keys, shoving past him and storming out of his office. Darnell watched her exit and chuckled.

He knew he had her under his thumb.

***

Two Days Later

Leilani watched him as she chopped celery on the block of wood. Evan was deep in thought, he hadn't said more than a few words to her the entire evening. They were doing their usual routine. He called her before he left his office to see what she wanted for dinner. He went to the store and met her with groceries in hand. He greeted her with a warm kiss hello as soon as she opened the door to her penthouse and let her unwind as he began to set up for their meal.

They were in the kitchen as she helped chop the vegetables and he manned the stove, preparing their decided main dish of lamb, homemade mashed potatoes, black eyed peas and collard greens. She couldn't shake the comments from Darnell out of her mind, yet she didn't know how to quite feel about what was said. Part of her knew that Darnell was intentionally driving at her to make her regret leaving him and leave Evan alone, but the other part of her believed that there was truth in his statements. Leilani had witnessed herself the practices of the wealthy men she had been around – typically, even the black men who were successful were rarely seen with their own kind. She always saw them reach outside of their race as if a black woman was not good enough for their caliber.

Leilani's eyes scanned over Evan. He was polished and groomed; someone that would turn heads and take charge of any room he entered. He was powerful and influencing – so was his monetary worth. She knew that he could have any woman he wanted from his looks alone, but add that with his seven figures salary and he was a keeper by any sane woman's standards – no matter her race.

Now that she had experienced him firsthand, she clearly understood why Sophie would fight tooth and nail for him. Not only was he educated and lucrative, but he was highly skilled in the bedroom—demolishing every possible assumption and rumor of his race. He was a generous man; affectionate and kind. Evan knew what it took to keep a woman content and he had no qualms with giving to a woman exactly what she needed. It was almost as if he was a tailor-made gentleman; effortlessly adjusting himself to match the needs of his counterpart.

Leilani never thought men like him existed. Surely, she had talked to her friends who told her stories of romantic acts by their men. Leilani used to laugh thinking that it was all for show or simply driven by what the man was receiving in return for his acts of valor and sensitivity. She didn't believe that men could show appreciation of a woman beyond providing sexual gratification. Intimacy, in her mind, simply did not co-exist with m.e.n. It was all a fallacy that the female species had created in order to feel some worth in their existence. It was a standard held above men to weed out those that were unwilling to attempt at intimacy's feat.

Her eyes scanned over Evan; observing his relaxed demeanor. His dark brown hair was neat, his face slightly scruffy from him rushing out in the morning after making love to her and not being able to shave off the stubble. It made him look sexier in her opinion; but no more would be necessary. Her eyes glided down his muscular torso covered in Burberry and his powerful legs draped in matching slacks. His shirt sleeves were rolled upward as to not get them in the way of his cooking. She was sure that he was still wearing his size twelve Fendi loafers that coordinated with his attire.

Evan was incredible and Leilani couldn't imagine why he'd have anything to do with her beyond the magic that happened in her bedroom. She realized in their time together as lovers that they hadn't gone out on the town. All of their interactions were limited to the privacy of her penthouse and their smartphones. She had never been to his place; all of their encounters were at her abode. Leilani hadn't noticed it until this moment, but the reality settled into her mind. The more she analyzed it, the more she equated to the truth that she was Evan's house pet.

Evan looked up and their eyes met. His smooth lips turned upward, spreading into a sexy grin. He leaned over the counter towards her, holding a piece of the sauteed meat for her to taste. Leilani leaned in and allowed him to feed her. He topped it off with a kiss and she stared into his stunning eyes as he smiled at her and then moved back to focus on his cooking. Leilani watched him, wondering how long this would last between them. She'd miss this immensely, but she knew that it wouldn't make it to forever. Darnell was right; Evan was out of her league.

"What are you thinking about?" she heard his voice ask.

Leilani looked up from her slicing, dumbfounded. She didn't know that he was paying attention to her as deep in thought he had been the entire time that he had been cooking. She shrugged slightly, searching for a reasonable answer.

"You," she said simply.

They looked at each other and he grinned, slightly blushing.

"And what exactly about me are you thinking?" Evan inquired.

Leilani sighed and licked her lips.

"Nothing in particular. Just," she shrugged again, looking down. "Just about us," she answered.

She couldn't bring herself to lie to him. Evan washed his

hands and came around the counter, walking behind and wrapping his arms around her waist. He nuzzled his cheek against her neck and gently squeezing her body in a bear hug. She giggled at his playfulness when he nibbled at her ear, making a low growling sound.

"Am I going to have to force it out of you?" he asked with a smile.

Leilani couldn't wipe the smile off of her face. It was glued to her expression. Evan's warm embrace felt comforting. He made her feel safe with him; she had no other cares in the world when he was near.

"I'm just having a really good time with you," she answered; avoiding all of her other thoughts.

"Hmmm, is that a request for sex?" he said jokingly, nuzzling her neck.

She giggled.

"No, it's not," she turned and faced him, gazing into his sapphire blues. "You're just a really great guy."

Evan cupped the back of her neck, pulling her to him as he kissed her deeply. They both moaned, but he could still feel the tension in her body.

He pulled away and looked into her eyes.

"Hmm. What's wrong?" he asked.

Leilani tried to hide the outward expression of her inner battle. But, Evan saw right through it. She was taken aback and how he could read her like a book. She gulped and broke their gaze; his eyes were too intense.

"Um, nothing," she tried to lie.

"Then why won't you look at me?" he asked.

She looked into his eyes and pulled away from his embrace.

"I'm fine, Evan. It's—" she laughed nervously, placing hands on the counter behind her. "It's nothing."

He raised his eyebrows.

"For some reason, I find that hard to believe," he said peering at her.

Leilani looked away and shook her head.

"I don't…" she paused. "I don't wanna talk about it."

Evan furrowed his eyebrows.

"Why not?" he pressed.

Leilani groaned slightly and closed her eyes. She was used to the way that Darnell had no concern for her feelings and thoughts. He easily backed away if she told him she was fine, even if it was an obvious lie. But, Evan didn't back away so easily. Granted, it was an endearing quality for a man to possess, but Leilani didn't know how to handle it from her familiarity with Darnell.

"Evan, really. It's nothing," she said softly.

He furrowed his eyebrows.

"Did I do something to offend you?" he asked.

She chuckled.

"No. You're amazing," she replied.

"Then what is it?"

"Don't you—don't you need to check on the food?" she asked in hopes of detouring his mind.

"The food is done. Why are you trying to change the subject?" Evan said.

She laughed again, uncomfortable—she felt cornered as she glanced at the ceiling.

"Evan," she said and shook her head, staring at the wall.

Her heart was heavy. Darnell's words had started to eat away at her esteem and she was trying to fight the tears that were building inside of her. The more Evan showed his concern, the more it caused her to feel more depressed. She looked at Evan and bit her bottom lip, nervous and fighting the tears. He stepped forward and stroked her cheek, staring down at her as she avoided eye contact.

"Don't," she said quietly, placing her hands on his chest to not allow him any closer.

"Lei, whatever it is, you can talk to me. You can always talk to me. About *any*thing."

She couldn't hold them back any longer and the dam broke;

tears pouring from her eyes. She tried to hide her face, but he bent down, trying to look at her. She tried to move away from him, but he followed.

"Lei, what's—are you crying?" he nearly exclaimed.

"Evan, don't," she said, feeling his hand grab hers.

He pulled her to him and placed his hands on her lower back, holding her body against his. Leilani stared at his chin, she refused to look into his eyes and he gently kissed her on the forehead; causing more tears to spew. His coziness was staggering but she knew it wasn't hers to keep.

"Why do you have to be so perfect," she asked, trying to push him away, but he wouldn't budge.

Evan lifted her face to his and began to kiss her, slowly taking off her clothes even though she continued to back away from him. Leilani pulled her mouth away.

"Evan, you don't," she said when she felt his hands begin to unbutton her blouse. "I don't want…don't…"

Leilani wanted him immeasurably, but she knew that it would only be for a short period of time that she could have him to herself. Her heart grew heavier at the realization that she had fallen in love with Evan and she hated herself for being so weak. He lifted her in his arms and carried her to the bedroom, laying her down; his mouth finding hers as he began to kiss her passionately.

Leilani moaned, but continued to squirm beneath him. She had to break free from this or else she knew she'd suffer an even larger heartbreak than she did when she realized her marriage was over. At least then, Darnell had never shown her real love and her emotional void gave her the ability to manage the loss of their union. But Evan had caused her to feel renewed. He opened up a world to her that she thought she had lost forever – a world that made happiness and love seem impossible to not have.

"Don't," she muttered.

She felt the warmth of Evan's hand on her thighs as he reached beneath her skirt, hiking her skirt up to her waist and pushing aside her thong. His hand moved as he unzipped his pants, repositioning himself between her thighs and easing into her wetness. Leilani's body tensed and she bit her bottom lip, trying to constrain the pleasure. She couldn't give in. This had to be over.

Evan looked down at her and pulled his hips back, thrusting deep inside of her to watch her expression transform, her cheeks flushing. He saw that she was intentionally resisting and he repeated the motion until she began to gasp with each thrust, her cries beginning to follow.

He kissed her moist cheeks.

"I hate seeing you hurting," he said softly. "I can't bear it."

"Please...don't do this to me..." Leilani begged, his gentle words causing more tears to spew from her eyes.

Evan didn't want to see her in pain. Her tears made him want to make her smile all the more – make her feel pleasure versus whatever Leilani was harboring that caused her disheartened tears. He desired for her to know satisfaction beyond her wildest dreams – not only in the way he pleasured her, but also deep in her soul. She deserved that much and Evan wanted to be the one to provide it to her.

***

Leilani watched their fingers dance together, the striking contrast of her brown skin against his lighter complexion mesmerizing her. Evan's skin wasn't pale, but there was still a stark difference in their skin tones. Leilani lay in Evan's arms after his sudden and unexpected love making and she felt at peace once again. She was sure that their food had grown cold, but her mind was far from satiating her stomach.

"Tell me about your parents," she heard him quietly request.

She sighed, her gaze not moving from their intertwined fingers.

"Well, I am actually an only child. Both of my parents died before I turned eighteen. My dad from a heart attack and my mother," she paused. "Well, I uh, I would've had another sister, but my mother lost her when she was about six months pregnant. She had preeclampsia and well," she paused. "One day she was cleaning and her placenta pulled away and she bled to death while my dad was at work – the night shift."

"Where were you?" Evan asked.

Leilani was quiet for a moment as she reminisced.

"I was home with her." She gulped. "I watched her die right in front of me."

"I'm sorry," he said.

"Don't be. In my line of work, I see it happen all the time. It's actually a common occurrence."

Evan watched her for a moment.

"How can you be so robotic about it?" he asked.

She looked into his eyes.

"What do you mean?" Leilani asked.

"The way you just spoke about that – about your mom's death. That's more than just a patient," he said.

Leilani looked away. She didn't want to appear callous. Her mother's death had hurt profoundly.

"It is, but, what can you do about it? I can't become all depressed and sad thinking about my parents dying," she shrugged slightly, "They weren't..." She paused. "They weren't really my parents anyway. I found out I was adopted. So..." She shrugged. "Anyway, I'd rather think about the good times that I had with them; the times when they were alive and I was with them. It's pointless to focus on the loss of a person than the life that they actually lived."

Evan raised his eyebrows.

"You have a point there," he said.

"My parents worked hard to get me where I am. I didn't come from a long line of money. We struggled," she paused, raising her eyebrows in memory. "We struggled a lot and as a child, I never understood why because both my parents had decent paying jobs. But, turns out my dad and mom were busting their asses to help save up money for me to go to an Ivy League school so that I can be where I am now. And, the ironic thing is that, despite them nearly killing themselves working, when they died, they both had insurance policies that paid for both my undergrad and med school. That's how I was able to make so much money so quickly once I finished." She sighed. "I am *forever* grateful to them for what they've sacrificed for me. They always put me first which is more than I can say for anyone else in my life."

"Where is the rest of your family?" Evan asked.

Leilani smirked.

"Family? What family? When they died, my *family* came after me for money. They didn't feel I deserved any of it since I wasn't blood."

Evan raised his eyebrows, taken aback.

"Seriously?" he asked.

She sighed.

"*Yep.* They tried to sue me, I had to go to court...It got ugly. That's why I broke ties with all of them." She raised a brow. "As far as I'm concerned, I don't have any family. I never really did in the first place. They were borrowed."

"Have you ever tried to find your birth parents?" Evan asked.

She smirked.

"My adopted parents didn't cover up the truth when I found out I wasn't theirs. My birth father was my mother's *boss*, if you catch my drift. I was taken away from her and was a ward of the state the day I was born. She was a crack head prostitute who overdosed years later. My father..." She sighed. "I don't want to get into what happened to him. Shit, I was lucky that my parents even took a newborn who was an addict. I was hell on wheels as a kid. Tantrums, mood swings..."

Leilani became quiet. She wasn't sure why she was letting this man into her deepest and darkest secrets. He was only a side piece. She needed to close her mouth before she sent Evan running for the hills.

"I have moved on. I'm in a better place," she muttered.

"That's why you're such a strong woman," he said.

She looked into Evan's eyes and smirked.

"Sometimes I don't feel like that. Most times, I don't, in fact," she said quietly – almost talking to herself.

Leilani's thoughts began to wander back to Darnell's words to her in his office the other day and she tried to shake them away.

"Why? What about you?" she asked to distract her mind.

Evan licked his lips.

"Unlike you, I do come from a long line of money. My family has had wealth down through the decades. But, we're a hardworking family. My dad died while I was in the Air Force—" her soft gasp caused him to pause. "What?"

Leilani was surprised.

"No way! A Zoomie?" she asked.

He grinned and nodded.

"I enlisted after I finished undergrad believe it or not," he elaborated.

Her eyebrows rose.

"Impressive," she said. *That just makes you even more sexy. Damn,* she thought.

Evan shrugged.

"My family hated me for going. I didn't re-enlist. Instead, I went on to earn my MBA at Yale," he added.

"Don't downplay it. That's amazing," she said.

He smiled in response.

"Please continue your story," she said.

"Well, my mom..." He paused. "She's still alive, but she has Alzheimer's and it's really starting to take its toll. My oldest sister takes care of her back home. It's four of us and I'm the youngest. But, we are a close family. A *very* close knit family – always were."

"I honestly don't know how to respond to that... It sounds nice to have family that loves you and is there for you," she said softly.

Evan watched her for a moment, his smile faint.

"It is very fulfilling to have that," he replied.

Leilani began to stroke his arm, observing the veins in his forearm and the tints of green in them from the flowing blood. She thought of Darnell and his dark skin. She barely could see the blood in Darnell's; only saw the outline of the veins.

"What about your friends? Are they white collar, preppy guys like you?" she teased.

Evan laughed.

"I don't consider myself preppy. I'm just..." He shrugged slightly. "I am just me. My friends are more selective with who they hang around with. They're more into rubbing shoulders with the big wigs. Whereas for me..." He paused. "I guess you could say I just like to be a normal guy who enjoys philanthropy and I do my own shopping at the local Farmer's market. I even seem to recall a moment of utter devastation at a Dunkin' Donuts involving an armed civilian with hot chocolate."

They both laughed in remembrance.

"Being normal is kinda hard to do when you're making the money that you make," she said.

"It is, but it's not like I'm on a Hollywood celebrity..." Evan sighed. "Moreover, I don't care for some of the things that my friends do. They're very arrogant and they just..." He shook his head. "They're still in their partying frat mindset and we're in our thirties."

Leilani raised a brow.

"So you don't have a wild side?" she asked with a grin. "You didn't sew your *wild oats*?"

Evan glanced at her and smiled.

"Of course I did. But, that's no longer a part of my life," he replied.

"Hmm," she muttered, somewhat in disbelief. "What do you think this is then?" she asked.

He looked at her.

"This is not sewing my oats, Leilani."

Leilani didn't respond nor did she look at him. She didn't

believe what he was saying. They weren't dating. They were simply two people fooling around.

"Have you always gone for older women?" she inquired. "I'm older...Sophie is older than the both of us..." her voice trailed off.

Evan raised a brow.

"That has tended to be the case. It is no way a conscious choice," he replied.

Leilani chuckled.

"What?" Evan asked.

"Most men in your position would be after all the *young* pop tarts. I guess you want women who are established or out of the ditzy phase so you can keep your money," she assessed.

Evan stared at her for a moment and Leilani noted the slight flare of his nostrils. He was offended.

"I am not like that," he replied. "I like who I like."

Yeah, O.K. she sarcastically thought in disbelief.

"What about your friends? What are they like?" he asked, shifting gears.

Leilani laughed.

"You don't even wanna know," she said.

Evan smiled.

"Why not?" he asked.

She glanced at him.

"Let's just say it's probably too much drama for you to handle," Leilani said.

"What? You don't think *my kind* of people have drama?" he asked. "You think all we do is line dance and go hunting?" he teased with a smile.

She laughed again.

"No. But, I don't think you all have the kinda drama that black folks have."

Evan raised his eyebrows.

"You'd be surprised. Half the time, ours is worse. Soap operas have *nowhere near* the degree of foolishness that we can get stirred up," he commented.

She laughed and he scanned her face, unable to resist the smile that formed on his own.

"So, what kind of drama comes with your friends? Give me the juicy details," he said with one-sided grin, curious.

Leilani took in a deep breath and exhaled as her mind drifted to thoughts of Cheryl's attack and Camille's tragic incident. She felt tears tickle her eyes.

"Some things are just better left unsaid," she said. "No point in talking about my crazy friends."

"Well, are you ready to talk?" she heard him ask.

She took in a deep breath and moved out of his embrace, lying on her back and staring at the ceiling. Evan watched her.

"Talk about what?" she asked.

They both clearly knew the obvious issue at hand. Evan turned on his side and gazed at her face. Leilani glanced at him.

"What?" she asked.

Evan placed his hand on her hip and turned her body to face him, both of them gazing into each other's eyes. Leilani was lucky if she ever had Darnell this close to her after sex – typically he'd blow his load and immediately move away from her. And if Darnell did hold her, it was until she fell asleep and she'd awaken with him in his normal, distant position on the bed – his back to her. She never had Darnell stare at her, watch her, look at her the way that Evan did – especially not this close in proximity.

Most times, she felt self-conscious sitting directly in front of Darnell because she could see him not wanting to look at her. It made her feel ugly, unwanted and displeasing to the eye. So much, that she began to place herself in a seat beside him – even at restaurants to avoid the awkwardness between them.

"What was bothering you earlier?" Evan asked.

Leilani looked away and Evan pushed her chin up gently with his finger.

"Don't look away," he said. "Look at me, Leilani."

She returned the stare, fighting the tears that were beginning to make their way back into her eyes. She licked her lips and blinked, forcing them away. She needed to ask him, but she was afraid of his rejection.

"Evan, um…" She cleared her throat softly. "Where…where are we going with this?" she asked.

Evan's eyebrows rose.

"Where are we going with what exactly?" he asked.

"Where is *this*, what we're doing, where is it headed?" she elaborated.

Evan stared at her for a moment.

"Well, where do you want it to go?" he returned.

Leilani scanned his face. His expression was relaxed – emotionless. She took in a deep breath.

"Hmph, wow. I guess that's my answer," she said, turning on her back and propping her forearm on her forehead.

Evan watched her.

"What are you talking about?" he asked.

She closed her eyes and shook her head.

"I'm so stupid," Leilani said softly to herself.

Evan furrowed his eyebrows and raised himself on his arm.

"What are you talking about, Leilani?" he asked.

She smirked.

"Nothing… You just answered my question with a question," she stated.

"What's wrong with that?" he asked.

Leilani shook her head again.

"My husband used to do that all the time when he wanted to avoid telling the truth," she explained.

Evan raised a brow.

"I'm not your ex-husband," he said, offended.

"You're exactly right," Leilani snapped. "But, I at least thought coming from you, that you could give me a straight answer."

He chuckled.

"Lei, I said where do you want this to go," he said with a faint smile.

"No, you asked me," she quickly corrected.

Evan stared at her for a moment, making note of the seriousness of the conversation. His smile faded.

"Okay, so I *asked* you that… Again, how is that problematic?" Evan said, bewildered.

She closed her eyes.

"Evan, I don't expect anything from you," she replied.

He furrowed his eyebrows, increasingly offended.

"Pardon me?" he asked.

Leilani sat up, covering her breasts with the cotton sheets. She sighed.

"I already know this isn't going anywhere," she said. "I just assumed you'd have the balls to be honest about the fact that all this will ever be *is* sex."

Evan stared at her, astonished. He scanned her face and sat up swiftly.

"What the hell are you talking about?" he asked; his voice louder.

Leilani pushed her tousled hair backwards. It had been a few days since she had put a hot comb to her unruly locs. Evan liked it that way; told her many times he preferred her tresses untamed. But, Leilani felt that it made her unprofessional to let her hair be wild and free. She made a mental note to make a wash and flat iron her number one priority once he was gone.

"We don't belong together. You need to just go find you a nice, little white woman and—and have tons of light haired, funny colored eyed babies. Don't waste your time on the *black* side piece," she said.

He was speechless. Leilani looked at him. Evan's expression was priceless. She could clearly see he was caught off guard with her at this moment.

"We both already know this isn't gonna work. Besides, you already don't wanna be seen in public with me since we started messing around," Leilani added.

Evan scoffed. He was in a state of shock.

"For fuck's sake, where is this coming from?" he exclaimed.

"We don't go anywhere. I've never been to your place. All we do is screw here or in all these hidden places like I'm your little whore. But, I get it." She laughed. "I get it. I'm just your curious fling on the side. So, job well done, you fucked yourself a nigger."

Evan yanked off the Egyptian cotton sheet, stepping quickly out the bed and pulled on his boxer briefs. He was livid. He turned and looked at her.

"Leilani, you really have issues that you need to sort out," he snapped.

She laughed loudly.

"Congratulations! Now you and my husband at least agree on one thing about me," she said sarcastically.

Evan stared at her for a moment in disbelief.

"Are you listening to yourself?" he asked.

Leilani looked at him, his sapphire blues were nearly burning a hole into her eyes.

"Evan, you don't get it. I already know that I'm just helping you fulfill a *fantasy* here. I know how this *whole game* works. I know how it plays out in the end. You get your fill and then you go and snag a pretty, ex-cheerleader, homecoming queen *white*, prissy lady to put on your arm and parade around. And—and all this—this mega fuck fest, or—or *whatever* we had gets swept under the rug like it never happened," she elaborated, her hand flailing dramatically in the air.

Evan scoffed.

"Seriously?" he yelled.

"Yes, *seriously*!" Leilani mocked.

"Do you really think that all I want to do is fuck you because you're black?" he asked.

Leilani closed her eyes.

"I'm not stupid, Evan."

"Most definitely not! Nonetheless, you *do* need help!" he yelled.

He was angry with her beyond measure. Leilani felt tears

sting her eyes. Those words were all too familiar from Darnell. Leilani sat there, unmoving and he watched her. Evan shook his head.

"I cannot believe you. I am not one of your exes. Especially not your ex-husband," he spouted.

She rolled her eyes with a smirk.

"You're all the same," she said.

Evan nodded.

"Yeah?" he asked.

"Yes! Absolutely!" Leilani challenged.

"So if that's what you have thought all this time, why did you continue to see me? Why did you continue this?" he argued.

She didn't answer.

"I gave you the out. I told you what I did not want to walk into again. I made that *perfectly* clear to you, Leilani!" Evan yelled.

Leilani looked at him with pity.

"Evan, what more could you possibly want from me besides sex?" she asked. "Cause' I've been through so much bullshit that I don't know if I'm any good for you or for anyone for that matter. Besides, we both know that all it takes is for the right *white* woman to catch your eye or give you some *magnificent* head and *all* this great fucking you're having with a simple *minority* will be an afterthought."

He laughed in disbelief, shaking his head as he began to pull on the rest of his clothes.

"I never in a million years thought that I'd be hearing a woman so beautiful speak so lowly of herself," he said.

She stared straight ahead, her pulse was racing. Leilani knew she was making a mistake, but it needed to be done. Evan turned and looked at her.

"Why do you hate yourself so much?" he asked. "Why do you think you can't be happy? Are you really that damaged?"

Leilani scoffed, his words stung.

"Wow! Damaged?" More tears filled her eyes. "Thank you, Evan. I *really* needed to hear that."

He stared at her for a moment and sighed.

"I am not trying to hurt you..." Evan paused. "I have never wanted to hurt you. I have only wanted to be with you. Since the moment I first saw you, I wanted you."

She shrugged and looked at him with a trembling grin.

"Well, congratulations Evan, you got me. *Damaged* and all," Leilani replied.

Evan exhaled deeply.

"There is no winning with you, is there?" he asked.

Leilani stared into his eyes.

"Maybe you should just leave," she said. "Just go."

Evan stood there and shook his head. Defeated.

"Unbelievable," he muttered, rubbing his jaw as he scanned the room.

He looked at her.

"You're really going to do this?" he asked.

Leilani nodded.

"It's just best if you leave, Evan."

He scoffed again and shook his head as he ran his fingers through his unkempt hair.

"I cannot believe this," he said. "Are you--are you..." he stuttered.

Evan stared at her, his heart galloping a thousand races.

"Are you serious, Leilani?" he asked.

She looked away. Evan nodded and scoffed, blinking quickly to fight the tears.

"This is absolutely stupefying," he said and turned, beginning to exit.

Leilani looked at him.

"Before you go, there is something I need to tell you," she said.

Evan kept his back to her as he stared down at his keys.

"Unlike you, I'm not divorced," she announced. "So all this time, you've been fucking a married woman."

Evan laughed and shook his head even though the news hurt him to the core. He turned and looked at Leilani.

"Bravo," he said.

Leilani thought for a second that she saw his eyes saturated with tears as well. She concluded that she was hallucinating. After all, in her world, men didn't cry – especially not over a booty call. At least Darnell never shed a tear for his own wife. Evan turned and walked out; slamming the bedroom door behind him. Leilani closed her eyes with a heavy sigh.

Mission accomplished.

3 Weeks Later - 10:01 PM

Leilani stirred her hot cocoa as she watched her friend. She accepted the invitation from Cheryl to meet her at her and Russell's house. It had been a long time since any of them had spoken; mainly due to Leilani spending her time with Evan. Now that their fling was over, Leilani had found time to check her voicemails and return phone calls to those trying to reach her; one of them being her friend, Cheryl.

"How have you been?" Leilani asked.

Cheryl smiled stiffly and shrugged.

"I've been doing. How about you? Whatever happened with the lawsuit?" Cheryl inquired.

Leilani sighed.

"Luckily, Darnell was able to get her to drop the suit. It's amazing what a little coercing can do."

Leilani knew that word had gotten back to Sophie that she and Evan were over. Darnell phoned Leilani a week after she dumped Evan and she agreed to meet him for dinner. She and Darnell were now on speaking terms and Leilani had moved back into their home. Darnell was now staying with Cheryl and Russell for the interim. Leilani hadn't spoken to Evan since their argument; one that she had caused and Leilani figured that he had moved on to bigger and better things.

Cheryl smiled.

"That's awesome, Lei. At least now you don't have to worry about your practice and all of that. I wonder what made that lady drop it."

Leilani raised her eyebrows and shifted in her seat.

"Who knows?" she lied. "I'm just glad it's over and done with."

Cheryl watched Leilani for a moment.

"Is it true that you were dating a white guy?" Cheryl blurted out.

Leilani looked at her and laughed. She felt blood rush to her cheeks.

"Excuse me?" Leilani asked.

"I'm not—I'm not trying to be nosey. But, I overheard Russell talking to Darnell a while ago..." Cheryl paused. "And well, I heard some things and was just wondering if it was true."

Leilani licked her lips.

"Wow...Um..." Leilani deeply inhaled. "No. It's not true. I wasn't *dating* a white guy."

A little white lie. She was getting away on a technical. Under Leilani's definition, she and Evan were just sex buddies. Dating was never officially on the definition table.

"No?" Cheryl pressed. "Because Russell made it pretty clear like they knew who the guy was and how you were running around with him for like a few months—like ya'll were dating..." she stopped when Leilani held up her hand.

"Cheryl, don't go there," Leilani said and paused. "It was nothing."

Leilani sighed, beginning to feel melancholy.

"It was nothing," she added.

Cheryl laughed.

"Okay, whew! Because I was thinking, *no way* is Leilani putting cream in her coffee! You can have any brotha' you want. I wouldn't know why you'd want a white guy *anyway*. They usually working with a two incher at most which is a waste of my time," she said with another laugh. "And they all seem like dorks or they're wannabes which..." Cheryl smirked. "Is hilarious to watch. I'm sure they all are lousy in bed."

Leilani raised her eyebrow in disagreement. Cheryl could not have been more incorrect in her judgment of white men. Evan was far more endowed and experienced than all of her previous encounters, but Leilani didn't want to put her business out there. She sipped from her cocoa as Cheryl laughed; continuing her jokes.

"I don't think I could ever be with a white guy." Cheryl faked shivers. "I have to have me some dark meat. There's nothing better," she said. "These white boys ain't got nothin' for me but a signature on my paycheck."

Leilani licked her lips and shifted again.

"So, how are you and Russell?" she asked, changing the subject.

Cheryl's smile faded and she shrugged.

"We're okay. You know, he's always busy with work," Cheryl said with a nervous laugh to follow.

Leilani watched her.

"Has he put his hands on you anymore?" she bluntly asked.

Cheryl sighed and pulled her sleeve over her hand.

"No. Well," Cheryl paused, gulping. "Um, we've had our spats. But," she shrugged and stopped talking.

Leilani raised a brow.

"But?" she asked.

Cheryl looked at Leilani and laughed nervously.

"I don't wanna talk about it," she answered.

"Cheryl," Leilani began, shaking her head in disgust.

"We just...we're just having a few disagreements. I've done some things that I shouldn't have and," she paused and took in a deep breath. "Lei, I was messin' around on Russell," Cheryl blurted out.

Leilani stared blankly at Cheryl, not expecting her admittance of guilt. Leilani slowly sat down her mug and repositioned her butt on the sofa.

"You...you what?" Leilani stuttered.

I can't believe this shit, Leilani thought.

Cheryl laughed.

"I know. It seems crazy, right? Considering that he's been abusive before. But, um..." Cheryl nodded. "Yeah, I was cheating on him."

"How..." Leilani paused and raised her eyebrows in disbelief. "Does he know?" she asked.

Cheryl's eyes filled with tears.

"He *sure does*." She paused again and gulped, her eyes squinted. "Russell's divorcing me, Lei."

Leilani's mouth dropped open.

"*What*?" she nearly yelled.

"He's taking everything. He's already drawn up papers and, obviously, he's handling our divorce." Cheryl laughed, more tears falling. "I'm not gonna have a pot to piss in when he's done with me."

Leilani closed her eyes; she was utterly appalled with Russell's antics. Granted, Cheryl was equally in the wrong for cheating on her husband, but Cheryl had just as much leverage as Russell appeared to make it seem he had. She looked at Cheryl and took in a deep breath.

"Cheryl, you need to fight this tooth and nail," Leilani said, disgusted.

Her friend looked at her and Leilani noticed the dismay.

"I don't have the money for my own representation. And no lawyer is gonna do pro bono work on me. Not against Russell, at least. He's ferocious. I for damn sure am not asking your husband to help me," Cheryl said with a laugh. "I cheated on him. So..." She shrugged. "I'm screwed."

Leilani watched her as Cheryl continued to cry. Leilani shifted.

"Did he hit you again when he found out?" she asked.

Cheryl looked at her.

"Lei," she closed her eyes, "Don't go there."

"Cheryl…" Leilani said softly in disbelief.

"Has Darnell always been perfect?" Cheryl snapped at her.

Leilani raised her brows. Her friend could not have been far from the truth with her observation of her marriage. Leilani sighed.

"*No one* is perfect, Cheryl. But, there should be limits to what they're going to do to you that will cause harm. Whether it be physical or emotional."

Cheryl scoffed.

"Of course *you* can say that. Russ would force me to have sex with him, Lei. He'd laugh and say I couldn't do anything about it because we're married…" Cheryl paused, staring at her friend's stunned reaction. "Has Darnell ever violated you?"

Leilani did not want to drag out the skeletons in her marital closet. After no response, Cheryl rolled her eyes.

"I thought so," she muttered.

Leilani stood and sat next to her, placing her hand on Cheryl's thigh.

"I'm your friend. I'm here for you, Cheryl." Leilani thought of Camille and closed her eyes. "You *don't* deserve this."

Cheryl laughed.

"Convince Russ of that because apparently, he thinks I deserve every moment that he does it."

Leilani scanned her friend over. Cheryl was wearing long sleeves and long pants. The only area exposed being her feet and face.

"How long has this been going on?" Leilani asked.

Cheryl shook her head.

"I can't remember…about a month ago?" Cheryl nodded. "Yeah, he confronted me about it about a month ago. Right after Darnell moved in with us."

Leilani furrowed her eyebrows.

"Has Darnell been here when Russell put his hands on you?"

Cheryl closed her eyes.

"It doesn't matter, Lei."

"*Has he?*" she pressed.

Cheryl sighed.

"Yes. He's been here. But, he doesn't intervene. He stays out of our business, Lei; like he *should* be doing."

Leilani rolled her eyes and sucked her teeth.

"Cheryl..." she began.

"Don't be mad at Darnell. He just doesn't want to be involved," Cheryl said quickly. "I don't—I don't want this to affect your marriage. What I've done...I deserve what I'm getting. I deserve it. I shouldn't have cheated on Russell. He's just angry with me."

Leilani stared into her eyes.

"Enough is enough...Cheryl," Leilani took in a deep breath. "Russell was cheating on you."

Cheryl stared at her and then laughed.

"You're lying," she replied.

Leilani shook her head.

"I'm not. He was cheating on you. I know because I know the woman he was cheating with."

Cheryl furrowed her eyebrows.

"Who--who was it?" Cheryl asked, her voice breaking with a soft sob.

"You better not say another motherfucking word!" they both heard an angry voice yell.

Leilani and Cheryl turned to see Russell standing in the doorway of the den. He stepped forward and Cheryl walked towards him.

"You were cheating on me?" Cheryl asked angrily.

Leilani stood. Russell reeked of alcohol. She gathered that he had just come back from the bar. They both glared at each other. He barely noticed Cheryl in front of him.

"I want you out of my house," he said to Leilani.

"I'm not here to see you," she snapped back. "I'm here for Cheryl."

"I don't give a fuck who you're here to see. You're still in my damn house and I want you out of here."

Leilani stepped forward. She could feel the adrenaline rushing through her veins. She was up for a battle if need be and she was not afraid. She had had her fair share of spats...with women, of course, in her younger years.

"And if I don't? What are you gonna do about it? Huh?" she challenged.

Russell laughed.

"Bitch, don't try me," he threatened. "Darnell ain't here to help you."

"Bitch? Who are you calling a bitch?" Leilani yelled, offended. "*You're* the bitch!"

He stalked towards Leilani, but Cheryl blocked him.

"Russell, Russell, no. Don't—don't do this Russell," Cheryl said, trying to calm him down.

He noticed Cheryl and shoved her to the floor.

"Bitch, ain't nobody thinking about your slutty ass. Now get the fuck out my way," he spouted.

"You keep your hands off of her," Leilani said angrily.

Russell looked at Leilani.

"You're in *my* house! I can do whatever the hell I want! You ain't gonna stop me!"

Leilani glared at him.

"Put your hands on her again and you'll see what I'll do," Leilani threatened.

He laughed.

"Yeah, and you'll get fucked up just like Camille did," he warned.

Leilani lunged towards him and Cheryl jumped in the way, blocking Leilani.

"Leilani, don't! Just leave. Please just leave," she begged.

Leilani stared down at her, seeing the fear in her eyes. She grabbed Cheryl's hand.

"You're coming with me. I am not leaving you here with him," Leilani demanded.

Russell snatched Cheryl by her shoulder and punched her in the face. Leilani gasped in shock as Cheryl fell to the ground and he and Leilani looked at each other.

"I told you to leave," he said to Leilani. "Now look what you made me do."

Leilani backed away from him.

"Put your hands on me and I'll fucking kill you," she threatened.

He laughed as he continued to walk towards her.

"You always starting shit, Leilani. Always running around here thinking your shit don't stink. I've told Darnell, I've told him he needed to put you in your place. But, now I see that I'm gonna have to be the one to have to tame your ass," he said angrily, his eyes scanning her over.

She glanced at Cheryl who was whimpering as she crawled to pull herself up. Cheryl's nose was bleeding profusely. Leilani was sure that he had broken it with his blow to her face. Leilani looked at Russell and he snatched her by the forearms. She fought back and they struggled.

"Get off me," Leilani yelled.

Russell began to snatch at her clothes.

"You wanna act like a fucking bitch then I'm gonna give it to you like you're a bitch!" he said angrily, forcefully bending Leilani over the sofa.

It dawned on Leilani that Russell planned much more than to hit her. She increased her fight. She refused to let this happen. Leilani tried to pry herself from his grip and he grabbed her hair, yanking on it until she screamed in pain.

"Don't move," he said angrily, holding her head backward.

Leilani squirmed and Russell yanked her head back harder by her hair, hearing her yell in pain.

"Bitch, move again and I'll snap your fucking neck," he threatened.

Leilani saw movement out the corner of her eye, but she continued to tussle with Russell. She didn't care if he threatened her. She was not going to allow him to have his way with her. He'd have to kill her first. She held down the pain of him yanking on her hair and elbowed him in the ribs, causing him to let go and stumble backwards. Leilani broke free, moving away from him and reaching for her phone. She looked up to see Cheryl standing behind Russell. What Leilani saw made her eyes open wide in shock as she dropped her cell phone.

"Cheryl, no!" she yelled.

The loud blast caused her ears to ring as Russell fell to the floor. Leilani began to shudder uncontrollably as she went into shock. She touched her face, feeling moisture. She looked at her blood-spattered fingertips and made eye contact with Cheryl. Cheryl was standing there, holding the .45 in her left hand, staring down at Russell's lifeless body. Leilani stared at her. Cheryl was quivering as tears flooded her eyes.

"Cheryl," she said quietly. "Cheryl, what have you done?" Leilani asked.

Cheryl looked at Leilani and laughed hysterically as tears poured from her eyes.

"I couldn't let him hurt you too. Not my friend," she said to Leilani. "He's a rapist...he beat me... I—I couldn't let him do that to you."

Cheryl looked down at Russell's motionless body and they made eye contact again.

"We—we need to call the cops, Cheryl. We—we need to—to dial 9-1-1," Leilani stuttered. Her mind was scrambled.

Cheryl shrugged and frowned.

"My life's over. I'm sorry Leilani," she said and no sooner than Leilani could take her next breath, Cheryl put the gun to her temple and pulled the trigger.

3:13 AM

Leilani looked at her hands, they were still shaking uncontrollably. She sat in the police station, waiting for the detectives to come back after her interrogation. She was crying, her eyes bloodshot and swollen. She couldn't shake the images of Russell and Cheryl dying in front of her. Above all, she couldn't rid her thoughts of the image of Cheryl taking her own life.

She remembered the helpless look in Cheryl's eyes before she pulled the trigger and it caused Leilani to cry harder. Leilani wished that she could have done more for her and blamed herself for not returning her calls or going to see her when she was spending her time with Evan. She felt that she still should've been a better friend – regardless of the fun she was having with her temporary lover.

Leilani heard swift footsteps coming towards her and she raised a trembling hand to her face, attempting to wipe the tears and her runny nose to make herself somewhat presentable.

"Lei," she heard and looked up to see Darnell standing there.

Leilani stared at him and felt dullness within her. The last words from her conversation with Cheryl jolted her memory. She caught a whiff of the alcohol on Darnell's breath despite her stuffy nose.

"Lei, Bae, are you okay?" he asked, sitting down next to her and touching her hand.

She snatched it away and shook her head.

"Darnell, don't touch me," she said angrily.

Darnell stared at her for a moment and reached to touch her hand again. Leilani slapped his hand away.

"Don't touch me!" Leilani yelled, looking at him.

He noticed the disgust in her eyes and Leilani scoffed.

"You knew about him abusing her. You were there and you did *nothing*!" she barked.

"Lei, that's not true," Darnell quickly replied.

"You're a liar," she said and stood to leave.

"Lei, it's not true," he repeated.

"You're a damn liar!" she yelled turning back to him and pointing her trembling finger in his face. "Cheryl told me! She told me how you didn't do anything when they were fighting!"

Darnell sighed and rubbed his head.

"Lei, I didn't know he was hitting her," he said.

She scoffed, walking away and he followed.

"I thought they were just arguing!" he defended.

Leilani laughed and shook her head.

"I'm sure that's the perfect excuse! First, you knew about Russell cheating and you said nothing and now you wanna play naïve about him hitting on Cheryl." She shook her head, glaring at him. "You're despicable and I don't want to talk to you ever again!"

Darnell followed her again, snatching her back to face him.

"You've got some nerve!" he shouted.

Leilani glared at him.

"I have nerve? *I* have nerve?" she yelled.

Darnell nodded.

"Yeah, you! You were the one running around with Mr. Johnny Rocket and you wanna get on *me* about Russell cheating? You're just as bad as he was."

Leilani laughed.

"Darnell, we were separated."

"Separated! Not divorced! Was Russell wrong for screwing around? *Absolutely*! But, you were just as wrong as him! You had no business seeing someone else! But, no, you and your, *I need affection, I need this, I need that* just had to go out and screw the first thing that showed you some serious interest!" he yelled.

She shook her head.

"You know? You've always talked about how tired you are of my insecurities and *my* issues. But, Darnell, not once have you looked in the mirror at your own shit."

"What are you talking about?" he asked.

"I know about the woman you were seeing when you were out

of town doing that pro bono work. I saw the texts and the random late night phone calls. You may think you have your shit on lock. But, I got into your phone!" Leilani yelled.

Darnell laughed.

"You have no idea what you're talking about, Leilani—"

"No! You wanna throw in my face what I did when we were *separated*! How about what you did when things were fine between us?" she shouted.

"Things have never been fine between us! There's always some bullshit you're stirring up!" he yelled.

"How are her kids?" Leilani snapped. "Are you still checking in with them every birthday? Still playing doting father? When was the last time you paid some of her bills?"

Darnell stared at her in silence. He knew he was caught red handed and the only way she'd seen it was if she was able to get into his phone. No one knew about that situation but Russell. He licked his lips and stepped forward. Even with this realization, he would not be proven guilty unless she had hardcore evidence against him.

"You don't know everything! Matter of fact, you don't know shit," he seethed.

She raised a brow.

"Oh really?" Leilani challenged.

"Yes," Darnell snapped. "Show me the texts, show me my call log! Until you can do that, you don't have a damn thing to accuse me of that can stick! I'm not admitting to anything that you don't have proof of me doing!"

Leilani glared at him. She shook her head, disgusted.

"You're a piece of shit," she said. "I never should have married your selfish ass."

"In case you haven't noticed, we're *still* married," Darnell hissed, hatred in his eyes.

Leilani snatched off her wedding set, grabbing Darnell's hand and slamming them into his palm.

"Oh yeah? Not anymore," she said angrily and stormed out.

9
Never Make a Promise

Weeks Later – 1:01 AM

*L*eilani stared at the number. She didn't want to press dial, but she knew that she needed to make a move. Since the death of Cheryl and Russell, she had officially filed for divorce from Darnell. She needed to break away from the negativity and get a fresh start in her life. Camille didn't show for the funeral, which was expected and Leilani had accepted that they would probably never speak again.

Their friendship was permanently damaged for whatever reason that Camille felt necessary to do so. She sat on her chaise outside on her deck, the sounds of the crashing waves filling her ears as she continued to sip the wine from her glass. She missed Evan and regretted the moment that she rejected him. Her life would never be the same without him in it and she knew she needed to make amends.

She took in a quick breath and pressed dial on her screen, listening to the ringing of Evan's phone and hopeful that he would answer. She knew it was late in the hour to be calling, but from their interactions, Evan was never in bed before one a.m. He was a night owl. She heard the click of the pickup.

"Hello?" Leilani said when there was no welcome.

There was silence and Leilani furrowed her eyebrows.

"Evan?" she asked.

"No. He's unavailable at the moment. May I ask who this is calling?"

Leilani gulped. She didn't respond.

"Who is this?" the female continued to question.

Leilani's heart sank when she recognized the southern drawl in the voice on the receiving end of her call. It was Sophie. Leilani quickly hung up and stared at the screen of her phone as tears filled her eyes. Her heart felt as though it was breaking and she inhaled deeply, fighting the tears. They were stronger, forcing their way out of her and pouring down her cheeks. She sniffled and looked back at her phone, deleting Evan's number. It was time to move on completely; just as Evan had.

Evan groaned softly as he turned over in the bed. He opened his eyes and peered out through his grogginess at Sophie's nudity as she stood with her back to him next to the bed. She stared at his phone for a moment as she pressed delete and placed his LG on the nightstand.

"Who was that?" he asked as she crawled back into the bed beside him.

"It was a wrong number," Sophie said softly. "Just go back to sleep."

He shifted; raising his neck and looking around at the dimness of what used to be their bedroom.

"What time is it?" Evan asked and sat up higher. He didn't realize that he had dozed off.

"It's after one," Sophie answered.

He began to recall the events prior.

"I need to leave," Evan said.

His mind was groggy from the mix of the buzz of his hangover and his unplanned nap. Sophie gently pushed him back down on the mattress.

"Stay the night, honey," she said with a smile.

Evan looked at her and sighed.

"Sophie," he began.

"I want you to stay. *Please* stay," she begged, gazing down at him, a stiff smile on her face showing off her bright veneers.

"I don't know," he said and then shook his head. "No, it's best if I go. I shouldn't stay here."

Sophie stared at him for a moment and then gulped.

"But, we just made love," she said with a shaky smile.

Evan inhaled deeply.

"I'm sorry, Sophie." He gulped. "I'm so sorry." He paused. "I need to leave."

Sophie was silent as he stepped out of the bed and walked into the restroom. Evan closed the door and stood to look at his reflection in the mirror, shaking his head.

"Shit," he cursed and groaned in frustration.

Evan opened his eyes and walked over to the toilet, preparing to relieve himself when the light flickering off the condom wrapper on the floor caught his attention. He bent down and picked it up, noticing the small holes poked in the packaging.

Evan closed his eyes and balled it in his hand, his mind recalling Sophie pulling the condom out of the nightstand drawer. He stepped over, opening her cosmetic case to view the all too familiar fertility calendar and noticing the circled days. He dropped his head in dismay.

"*Fuck me*," he muttered in disbelief.

He slowly stepped out of the restroom and came to stand by the bed, still holding the shiny gold wrapper. Sophie's back was to him.

"What is this?" he asked.

Sophie looked at him.

"Why, it's one of your condoms, sweetie," she said with a grin.

Evan flung the wrapper at her and it landed on her lap. Sophie sat up and grabbed it. He watched her.

"Care to elaborate?" he asked.

Sophie looked at him and raised a brow.

"Whatsoever do you mean?" she innocently asked.

Evan furrowed his eyebrows, growing angrier by the minute.

"Don't play coy with me, Sophie. Explain the holes," he snapped.

Sophie came from under the covers and stood.

"What did you think I'd do, Evan? Just sit back as you left me for another woman?" she questioned.

Evan quickly scanned her nudity. Sophie wasn't ashamed of her body. She boldly paraded her six pack abs and toned physique like it was a piece of art.

"Sophie, I was never leaving you for another woman. I was simply leaving," he corrected.

She stepped closer to him, her chin elevated to look in his eyes.

"Did you expect me to just let you walk away from me so easily?" she asked.

He stared at her for a moment.

"Why would you do something like this, Sophie?"

Sophie laughed and threw the wrapper in the wastebasket near the nightstand.

"Call it insurance," she stated and looked at him with a wink.

Evan inhaled deeply and closed his eyes. He was trying to calm his nerves.

"Sophie, I gave you plenty of money," he said.

"It's never just been only about your *money*, Evan." She looked into his eyes. "In case you haven't realized it, even if you may have fallen out of love with me, I still love you. And I will do anything—*any*thing to get you back," she proudly stated.

Evan turned and began to pull on his clothes, shaking his head.

"Meeting you at the bar tonight was a *huge* mistake," he said.

Sophie watched him and laughed.

"I didn't make you sleep with me," she said. "I didn't make you call your driver to take me home and you come in my bedroom and take my clothes off! I didn't make you do any of that, Evan!" She began to yell. "You did what you wanted! And trust me; I wanted it *just* as much."

Evan turned and looked at her.

"You made sure the drinks kept coming! And you know I wasn't going to just leave you there alone. C'mon, you know me better than that, Sophie. Whether we're divorced or together, I'd never let anything happen to you," he said.

She grinned.

"You're right. I do know you. I know you very well. And I also know that you'd never leave your child, even if it means staying with me," she said.

Evan closed his eyes and groaned as the magnitude of her actions weighed in on his mind. He looked at her.

"You have utterly lost all logic. I can't believe you did this," he said.

Sophie continued to grin.

"Oh honey, believe it," she said angrily. "You're not going *any*where. You're stuck with me now. I can't wait to see our *beautiful* baby."

Evan stared at her for a moment.

"You don't know if this even worked," he stated and stepped closer to Sophie. "And if it did, you will be hearing from my lawyer because I will be damned if my child is raised by you," he snapped and stormed out, slamming the door behind him.

Months Later - Blind Date #3

7:41 PM

"I can't believe a woman like you is single? You're absolutely *stunning*!"

Leilani stared at the piece of spinach stuck between his slightly crooked and overlapping bottom teeth. She closed her eyes for a moment and looked away, glancing at the clock above the entrance to guage just how long her torture session had been going on. She had signed up for online dating to increase her odds of meeting a nice man. She refused to do her own screening and since all the Eharmony's, Match.com's, and Zoosk's were paid to do it for her, she decided to give a few of them a shot to prove themselves worthy of their advertised skills. However, the longer she sat with Gregory Mc'Stuck on Himself," she concluded that this, along with the dating sites, were becoming nothing more than a waste of her precious time.

She sighed as Gregory kept yapping his gums, the spinach in his teeth taunting Leilani and reminding her of how much she would've enjoyed a glass of Chardonnay and an episode of the Real Housewives of Atlanta than to be sitting here with disaster date number three. The first was a complete flop. Leilani walked into the restaurant and spotted number one sitting at the bar guzzling down tequila and bourbon shots like he was suffering from severe dehydration. Granted, his profile did say he was a liquor connoisseur, but he failed to mention that it meant he was two steps away from being an alcoholic. She didn't step anywhere near where he sat, she didn't want to entertain another chameleon. She had jet set out of the restaurant before the concierge could greet her with a smile.

She stared at Mr. Gregory Who Gives a… her eyes scanning down his lint painted suit jacket, noting the ash on his knuckles and the dirt beneath his unkempt fingernails. He was similar to number two who showed up with wrinkled velour pants and a slightly stained shirt. Leilani didn't understand what part of neat and clean did these men not comprehend in the questionnaire.

"Why are you single, Ms. Mathews?" the question snapped her out of her trance the moment she felt his hand touch hers.

Leilani sat back, sliding her hands closer to her and forcing out a stiff grin.

"I'm recently divorced," she replied.

He grinned.

"Lucky me," he said with a wink.

She laughed and looked away, shaking her head in disbelief of her disappointment. Gregory smiled and leaned closer.

"So tell me, Ms. Mathews, what will it take for us to have another date?" he asked, gazing into her eyes.

She stared at him and raised an eyebrow.

"Gregory," she began. "There won't be a next time."

His smile faded and he laughed, embarrassed.

"Did I say something to offend you?" he asked.

Leilani stood and gathered her Louise bag and jacket. She turned to face him.

"You said nothing offensive. Trust me," she watched him for a moment and felt emptiness within her. There was no level of attraction towards this man and it was time to go.

"It was very nice meeting you. And I truly appreciate all of your kind words and compliments. But," she paused. "I don't feel a connection with you. I truly am sorry. But, I think it's best if I don't waste your or my time. Good luck to you in finding love."

As quickly as she dismissed him, she departed from the restaurant; her thoughts wandering to Evan. She missed him, but their time had already passed. She hadn't given up on finding her happiness, but she knew with Evan, it'd never be. She walked quickly to the parking garage, her stilettos dancing against the concrete pavement. Leilani could not get home fast enough so she could get out of the pencil skirt and high heels and into her Jacuzzi tub. She needed to desperately erase this evening from her mind. Gregory would not be missed.

Leilani heard a familiar voice call her name and she ignored it, chalking it up to being her imagination. The parking garage was filled with others evacuating from the neighboring restaurants and stores; their voices intermingling.

"Lei," the voice called again, causing her to stop in her tracks.

She turned to see Camille standing there. She too was dressed in a one piece, A-line black mini dress that accentuated the curves she barely possessed on her petite frame; the tall heels sending her soaring easily past average height – nearly eye level with Leilani. They stared at each other in silence and Leilani didn't budge from her stance. Camille stepped towards her, covering the space between them.

"Hey," Camille said softly, hesitantly.

The air was awkward between them; tense and thick with uncertainty. Leilani's eyes scanned over her. Camille looked renewed, refreshed, revived; a complete 180 from the last time Leilani had laid eyes on her – after her car accident. Her hair was freshly oiled, the natural curl silky and shiny with the pomade she used to tame its wildness. Her fair skin flawless from all the scars she had endured months prior. Her lips lightly drizzled with slick lip gloss and a touch of bronze eyeliner accentuating her round eyes. Leilani cleared her throat and stepped backwards, putting distance between them. Camille's eyebrows furrowed slightly in Leilani increasing the space.

"Um," Camille paused and took in a deep breath. "How have you been?" she asked, her eyes scanning Leilani's taller frame.

Leilani raised a brow.

"I've been well," she answered flatly.

Camille stared at her for a moment, trying to read her straight expression. She saw no reaction in Leilani's face. It was stone – reminding her of Darnell's uncaring demeanor. She cleared her throat and smiled nervously.

"Can we—can we go somewhere and talk?" Camille asked; hopeful.

Leilani didn't respond. She inhaled deeply and looked away,

glancing at her Mercedes which was only a few feet from them. She then noticed a Camry identical to Camille's parked a few cars down. She must have arrived shortly after she had parked in the garage. Where she was coming from; Leilani had no clue nor did she have a care. She exhaled and looked at Camille. Leilani rolled her eyes.

"We haven't talked in *months*, Camille," she stated.

Leilani's voice was not angry. It was flat; emotionless; cold. Camille could feel the chill from her ex-friend and she knew that in the months of their separation that their relationship was nowhere near the same. Camille shifted her keys to her next hand.

"I know," she began. "But..." Camille closed her eyes for a moment and looked back at Leilani. "We just need to talk."

Leilani stared at her, her gaze unyielding. Camille returned the look.

"Look, I know you probably don't want to have anything to do with me. But, we have so many years behind us. I was—I was out of line for what I said to you that day in the hospital—"

"You mean when you kicked me out the hospital?" Leilani corrected with a raised brow.

Camille stopped talking and inhaled sharply with a slight nod.

"Yes. And...I was wrong for that. You were just trying to be there for me, Lei. I should've recognized that."

Footsteps and boisterous laughing of an entering younger crowd distracted them. Camille glanced in their direction and looked back at Leilani who was now observing the crowd.

"Can we please go somewhere quieter to talk?" Camille requested.

Leilani looked at her and shrugged slightly.

"Fine," Leilani snapped.

Coffee Shop

Leilani's heel tapped repeatedly against the floor as she sat with her arms crossed on the opposite side of the table from Camille. Leilani was being impatient as her ex-best friend was talking to the waitress ordering herself a half-caf.

"And for you, Miss?" the polite younger woman asked.

Leilani raised her hand slightly and shook her head.

"No thank you. I'm fine," she replied with a quick smile.

The barista exited from their table and Leilani turned her vision back onto Camille who was fidgeting with the napkin on her side. Leilani took in a deep breath and looked around the café.

"What do you want, Moon?" she finally asked, irritated at the drawn out silence between them.

"I miss us being cool, Lei," Camille answered.

Leilani rolled her eyes and looked away. Camille watched her tense demeanor, but chose to continue.

"Lei, I miss our friendship—"

"And what do you expect me to say to that?" Leilani snapped. "You're the one that dismissed me, Moon."

Camille leaned back in the chair and nodded.

"You're right. And you have every right to be angry with me," Camille replied.

"Angry with you?" Leilani chuckled. "You think I'm *angry* with you? No, no. I'm fed up. I'm fed up with people doing whatever the hell they want to do and then turning around and coming to me with the *I'm sorry* and the *please forgive me.* I'm done with dealing with people's bullshit."

Camille's eyebrows rose.

"Well, damn. Excuse me for trying to make things right," Camille muttered.

"Make things right?" Leilani asked and shook her head. "Moon," she began and closed her eyes for a short moment. "We have been friends for years...*years*. Through thick and thin and all the in between, we were there for each other. I would've never turned my back on you. No matter what you did or said. You'd have to have done a whole lot to make me hate you."

"I don't hate you, Lei," Camille stated.

Leilani smirked.

"Yeah and the fact that we haven't spoken in months proves just how much you don't hate me, right?" Leilani asked with a raised brow.

Camille looked away and cleared her throat, her eyes focusing on her lap. Leilani exhaled and shifted in her seat.

"Moon, you were like a sister to me. I could talk to you about *any*thing – especially when I couldn't even talk to my own husband," Leilani stated.

Camille looked at her.

"I never thought that we'd ever stop being friends – especially over nonsense. *Especially* over shit that we both made a grown ass decision to do on our own. I never blamed you for the shit going on with me and Darnell. I never pointed a finger at you or—or threw back in your face the entire lousy ass, shitty ass comments you've made in the past about my marriage. Not once did I ever judge you based off of your opinions of the type of person I was or how—how weak or scared you described me to be," Leilani said.

Camille shook her head.

"Lei, I didn't mean—"

Leilani held up her hand.

"Don't, you meant *every* single word," Leilani interjected.

"I'm sorry, Lei," Camille said quietly.

Leilani shook her head.

"Don't apologize for something you meant to say. You know that's one thing that I hate the most for someone to do," Leilani replied.

"Okay. I did mean it. But, it was out of line for me to say," Camille rephrased.

"You were being a concerned friend, Moon. That's why I never held it against you. You were trying to be there for me the same way that I was trying to be a good friend to you."

"I realize that now, Lei. My mind was all fucked up over what happened and I was angry. I wasn't..." Camille paused. "I wasn't angry with you. But, I shouldn't have taken it out on you. Then, after I showed my ass, I didn't—I didn't know how to face you after the way I treated you. I felt stupid. So..." Camille shrugged slightly. "I just stayed away from you. I understand if you don't want to have anything to do with me anymore. But, I just wanted to get this off my chest before it was decades later."

There was an awkward moment of silence between them and Leilani stared at her. Leilani licked her lips and glanced at her watch.

"Well, are we done? I have to get going," Leilani said quickly.

Camille stared at her in surprise.

"Wha—what?" Camille stuttered.

"It's a simple question." Leilani slapped her palms against her thighs. "Cause' I'm done listening to you."

Camille scoffed and nodded. "I see how it is."

Leilani furrowed her eyebrows.

"That's exactly how it has been since that day in the hospital. Unless you haven't realized it, we *were* friends. We're not friends anymore. We haven't been for a long time, Camille," she said angrily.

Camille stared at the table and her eyes slowly rose to make contact with Leilani's. She began to glare at Leilani and tapped her nails against the table.

"You've got some nerve," Camille said and scoffed again, shaking her head.

Leilani folded her arms underneath her breasts.

"Oh, now this, I wanna hear," Leilani said, attitude spewing from her pores as she shifted her torso against the chair back.

Camille looked at her.

"You *really* got some nerve sittin' here like you're miss high and mighty ain't never done shit wrong – folks always doing *you* wrong," Camille snapped.

Leilani rolled her eyes, looking away.

"Really?" she asked, looking back at Camille.

The smaller frame sat forward, her dark green eyes in slits.

"Yes. *Really*. The last time I checked, what happened to me was your fault – your doing – *your* damn big ass mouth," Camille seethed.

Leilani stared at her, her face expressionless.

"Nobody asked you to go blabbing to Darnell. You butted into my business, Lei. You took it upon yourself to try to fix *my* situation. Nobody asked you! But, no, that wasn't good enough for *Ms. Know It All;* you just *had* to go putting your two cents in cause you thought it was ammo to use against your two-faced, asshole of a husband. You thought you could use my life to fix yours. I didn't ask you to do shit for me or my baby," Camille snapped. "So, thank you for how you royally fucked things up for me, *friend*."

Leilani didn't respond. She inhaled deeply, calming her rising temper. They were in public and she refused to make a fool of herself. Leilani softly cleared her throat and uncrossed her arms and exhaled.

"It's nice to know just how forgiving you actually are. So, tell me, which part of your apology and the whole, *I want to make things right* was even truthful?" Leilani asked quietly.

Camille stared at her. It was her time to be silent. Leilani raised her eyebrow and scratched it; she smirked and sucked her tongue against her teeth.

"You know, out of all the years that we were friends, Camille. Not once did I think that you'd stoop so low to avoid taking responsibility for your own actions. Like I said to you that day in the hospital, I didn't make you fuck Russell."

"That was out of line then and it is now—"

"Yeah? But, you know what? I'll never apologize for saying it – cause it's one hundred percent *truth*." Leilani paused and shrugged. "I have taken blame for busting you out to Darnell. I'll even take blame for intruding on your *situation*. But, I will not take responsibility for what happened – for you getting pregnant because *you* chose to fuck a married man – and you chose to fuck him *repeatedly*."

They stared at each other, both glaring. Leilani licked her lips.

"Camille, I'm sorry for what happened to you. But, the bottom line is, you made the bed that you had to lay in that night. I didn't make you do any of that. Yes, I may have blabbed. But, I didn't make you get pregnant. And how exactly were you gonna hide your pregnancy, genius? Huh? How were you going to do that when we *all* were close friends?" she pressed.

Camille sat silent and Leilani could see her gulp. Leilani nodded.

"Exactly what I thought," Leilani stated.

Leilani turned, reaching for her purse.

"Now, if you will excuse me, I'm going home. I thank you for your time and I *truly* and *sincerely* hope that someday – one day, we can be friends again and you can stop blaming me for the consequences of your indiscretions. God knows we both have our own bad choices to live with…" Leilani paused with a sigh as her mind briefly drifted to Evan. "But, I obviously see, that now is not the time for that and I honestly don't have room for anymore drama in my life right now."

Camille smirked.

"Oh so now Ms. Thing doesn't have time for any *drama*," Camille said sarcastically.

Leilani exhaled deeply.

"Camille, when you get to a point that you're able to forgive me for what I said to you and to Darnell where we can move forward, then…" Leilani shrugged slightly. "You know how to find me. But, I am not going to sit here and go back and forth with you about how much me, you and everybody else was right or wrong. Feel free to live in the past on your own."

Leilani stood and watched Camille's flushed face for a moment as she continued to glare at the table.

"You take care," Leilani said and turned.

Camille didn't watch her leave. She stared at the tablecloth, feeling the tears flooding her eyes. She wiped them away angrily – refusing to cry.

A Month Later

4:32pm

Leilani continued to scribble her transcriptions in the patient folder. She paused for a moment when she felt a wave of nausea hit her unexpectedly and reached into her drawer for a Tums – about the fifth one she had tossed back before ten am. She closed her eyes for a moment to let the white pill begin to work its magic and inhaled deeply to focus back on her notations. Today was a slower day than the rest of her week had been, so she was grateful to be able to have privacy and silence in her office than the usual hustle and bustle of the week. The stress of this week was having its fair share of havoc on her.

A soft knock on her door distracted her for a short moment, but she continued to write.

"Come in," Leilani said.

"Dr. Mathews," her assistant's voice caught her attention.

Leilani looked up to her assistant with a smile.

"I have Ms. Camille here to see you," her assistant said cheerfully.

Leilani sat back in her chair and inhaled. She glanced at her desk clock and exhaled.

"Send her in," Leilani said softly. "And you can go ahead and head out for the day. The head nurse is going to stay with me until closing."

Leilani's assistant smiled.

"Why thank you, Dr. Mathews," her assistant said happily and bounced out of the doorway, leaving it open.

Leilani waited for Camille to enter, unsure of what she would be visiting her for. But, she knew one thing; she refused to argue - especially in her place of work. Plus, she was not feeling up to a dispute with anyone. Leilani wanted nothing more dearly at this moment than the softness of her plush California King in the master bedroom of her house.

Leilani heard footsteps and then the shadow of Camille enter the office. Camille was dressed in khakis and a three quarter inch length v-neck ribbed shirt, fire orange red in color which contrasted dramatically against the milky complexion of her skin. Her hair was laid in its usual natural curl and her face covered in mineral powder. Camille looked radiant as always – the slightly tinted gloss on her lips accentuating their puffiness.

They made eye contact and Camille slowly took a seat at one of the chairs in front of Leilani's desk, crossing her thin legs as she eased into the soft leather fabric covered cushion. Leilani watched her, unmoving, not speaking a word. Leilani was trying to gauge the other woman's mood as well as tone down her nausea that had come back with a vengeance – slaying the Tums that she had popped a few minutes prior to this meeting.

Leilani cleared her throat.

"To what do I owe this unexpected visit?" she asked Camille.

Camille took in a deep breath and Leilani's eyes noticed her fingers fumbling against one another nervously.

"I, uh," Camille paused for a moment. "I just wanted to come by and speak with you."

Leilani raised her eyebrows.

"Okay," Leilani said slowly. "Speak to me about what?"

"I've really put some thought into what you said at the coffee shop and…" Camille paused and raised a brow. "And you were right, Lei." She looked at Leilani. "You were right."

There was silence. Leilani released an uneasy laugh and shifted in her seat.

"Camille that was over a month ago," Leilani stated.

"I know, but," Camille paused. "It doesn't take away the fact that what you said was the truth. I just, I felt the need to come here to tell you this," she replied.

"Camille, I didn't say those things just to be right. I said those things because that's how I feel about all that went down," Leilani explained.

"But, you made a good point. And it was something that I hadn't been doing – it was something that I haven't even thought about doing. I needed to stop living in the past. I needed to move on and even though I survived what happened to me, I went to counseling and am now able to at least hold a phone conversation with a guy of interest, I..." Camille paused with a shrug. "I was still holding onto the past and the feelings that came along with it."

Leilani watched her. Camille uncrossed her legs.

"Lei, I really do miss you as my bestie, as my confidant, as my—as my roll dawg. I just, I miss having my sister," she said.

Leilani didn't respond, she sat watching her and Camille furrowed her eyebrows.

"I mean, are you—are you even listening to what I'm saying?" Camille asked.

Leilani gulped, battling the nausea and nodded.

"Yeah. I hear you. But, our conversation started just like this the last time and it went to shit not even ten minutes into it if you don't recall," she replied.

"I do, but, things are different now. I'm—I'm in a different place," Camille said.

Leilani stared at her and then raised a brow.

"Um, I need some time to think about this," Leilani said quietly. "We both said some pretty rough things that day at the coffee shop and..." She licked her lips. "I just—I need a day or so to think about this whole second apology."

The beeping of the alarm on Leilani's cell phone distracted her and Leilani picked up the device and placed it on silent. Camille watched her as Leilani stood and hung her lab coat in her closet, glancing at her reflection in the mirror and readjusting her blouse and walking back to her desk. Leilani didn't sit down; she began to gather her things as her friend watched her.

"I uh…" Leilani began and paused to clear her throat.

What the hell is with this nausea, Leilani thought before continuing her dismissal of Camille.

"I do thank you for coming by, Camille. But…" Leilani looked at her. "I just need some time. You were very angry with me and I…" She shrugged. "I don't think that just goes away overnight."

"It wasn't overnight. It's been a month!" Camille exclaimed.

"I know, but I still think we both need more time to get back to the old us, you know?" Leilani said.

Camille stood, taking Leilani's signal of grabbing her keys as it was time for her to leave. Camille skimmed her friend over from head to toe. Leilani wore pointy stiletto heels and a form fitted pair of black capris with a sexy rose-colored blouse – teasingly low cut in the front.

"You're going on *another* blind date?" Camille asked.

Leilani raised an eyebrow.

"Excuse me?" she asked, offended.

"I just…I heard through the grapevine that you had been going on blind dates. That's all," Camille explained, treading lightly as to not trigger Leilani's temper.

Leilani scoffed and shook her head.

"Let me guess, my blabber mouth assistant told you." Leilani shook her head, "I've gone through about five of them and I hired *her* ass back. She's gone permanently now that I know she's spreading my personal business to total strangers."

"Well, I'm not a *total* stranger," Camille replied. "I told her we were best friends and asked where you were…and she gave me a little bit too much information."

Leilani shook her head.

"I'm calling Manpower tomorrow," she muttered.

"I tell you one thing; I didn't think men who wore velour pants would be your cup of tea," Camille stated unexpectedly.

They stared at each other for a moment and burst out laughing;

the tension between them breaking. Despite the disappointment and hard feelings, Leilani and Camille could never be mad at each other for long. They had a sisterly connection that surpassed any drama they faced – even if it was between the two of them.

"I told her not to tell anyone about that," Leilani said, laughing as she shook her head.

Camille continued to laugh.

"Yeah, well, your assistant can't hold water. You just might wanna get rid of her or else you'll end up with a problem on your hands if she blabs to the wrong person," Camille replied.

Their laughing subsided and Camille could see the cold exterior of her best friend waning.

Camille shifted her feet.

"Are you still hiring?" she asked.

Leilani looked at her and nodded.

"Why? Do you want your job back? I'm not as nice and lenient as I was before to forewarn you."

Camille shrugged slightly. "*Well*, let me think about it and get back to you…I had an offer to be a prostitute in Vallejo, but now that I think about it; going back to my old gig might be a little bit of a better fit." They both laughed. "Besides, I don't think my bony legs would look quite right in fishnets."

Leilani laughed.

"You are right about that one," Leilani said with a raised brow and chuckle.

There was an awkward silence between them and Camille looked around and Leilani shuffled her keys in her hand. Neither of them wanted to leave, but also neither knew how to continue the conversation from this point.

"So, what's with the blind dates, girl?" Camille blurted out.

Leilani looked at Camille and shook her head.

"It's nothing. I mean, you know that Darnell and I are divorced now?"

Camille nodded.

"I do. Sorry to hear," she stated.

Leilani raised a doubtful eyebrow.

"*Yeah right.* I know you're grinning from ear to ear on the inside," she replied.

Camille laughed and shrugged.

"I didn't say anything of the sort. I just wanna know why you're going on blind dates," she replied.

"Why can't I?" Leilani asked. "People do it all the time. It's the *in* thing now."

"I understand that. But, you're gorgeous and you're a great catch...Plus, from what your assistant told me, it doesn't sound like you've been snagging too many trophy fish. At least not ones that don't think suede pants are out of style."

"You are *so* wrong for that," Leilani said with a smile. "That was *one* date!"

Camille chuckled.

"You need to just leave blind dates to everybody else cause' you are having *no* luck with these! Besides, I'm sure you can have much better than what you've been getting hooked up with."

Leilani shrugged.

"I was just bored, I guess. Figured that'd be a good, innocent way to entertain myself and have some company." She paused. "Besides, we both know that most of the *good* men are already taken," Leilani said quietly.

They both laughed again and Leilani shook her head, sitting down on the sofa typically used for her more in detail patient consults. Camille stared at her for a moment and proceeded with caution.

"Whatever happened with Evan?" she asked.

Leilani sighed and shook her head.

"I *really* don't wanna get into that," Leilani said softly.

Camille could see the sadness begin to loom over her best friend. Camille sat forward.

"You need to get back with him," Camille encouraged.

Leilani stared at her and inhaled deeply, composing her

thoughts as she looked out the window at the view of the city lights. Camille watched her intensely, taking in her every move.

Leilani exhaled and scratched her eyebrow.

"We just…" She paused. "Evan and I had a little fling and…" She shrugged. "And it just—it didn't work out," she explained.

"A *little* fling? Really, Leilani?" Camille replied sarcastically.

Leilani looked at her.

"Camille," she started and stood, walking over to the window and looking outside.

"That's bullshit, Lei and you and I both know it. Don't try to sit here and convince me that you didn't catch feelings for that white dude," Camille retorted.

Leilani laughed. "That white dude?" she asked, turning to look at Camille.

"Yes," Camille said with a grin. "Your knight in *white* shining armor. Your vanilla latte," she teased.

Leilani laughed, but her smile faded immediately.

"He went back to Sophie," she replied. "They're expecting a baby."

Camille sucked her teeth again.

"I'm sure you had something to do with that," she stated.

Leilani shifted, slapping her thigh.

"Moon, I would've been a fool to think that he and I actually had a shot at something serious."

"Why?" Camille asked simply.

Leilani scoffed.

"A lot of why's," she said.

"Oh I forgot…He's a cat and you're a dog. Oh wait, no, he's a horse and you're a—you're a…" Camille snapped her fingers. "You're a goat! That's right! You two are totally different species! Not just different races like normal human beings who don't go around focusing on somebody's *ethnicity*."

Leilani sucked her teeth this time and rolled her eyes.

"It's not that simple," she said.

"How ain't it?" Camille asked.

Leilani looked away and shook her head.

"It's just not," she said quietly. "I would've ruined things at some point. So, it was just best if I ended it before it even got started."

Her best friend laughed and shook her head.

"Well, according to your *assistant*, rumor has it you were happy as hell with him," Camille stated.

Leilani opened her mouth to interject.

"*Even* if it was a little fling or whatever the hell you wanna downplay it as," Camille finished.

Leilani sighed.

"It doesn't matter. He's back with his wife; where he belonged in the first place and they will be a happy family in a few months," she said.

Camille shook her head.

"I can't believe you sat back and let that fine man go back to that ditsy ass, psychopath woman," she said. "I tell you what? I'd been on the first thing smokin' to get his ass back. Bump that. You know good and well he doesn't belong with her cray cray ass," Camille said.

Leilani was silent; her emotions running deep at the loss of Evan in her life. Camille watched her for a moment and licked her lips.

"You really miss him," Camille stated.

Leilani looked at her and inhaled deeply, forcing the tears that were trying to form in her eyes back to their origin.

"Oh well. That doesn't matter anymore," she said softly and sighed again. "And that's exactly why I'm taking a year off."

Camille's mouth opened suddenly.

"A year off from what!" she exclaimed.

Leilani raised a brow.

"I'm going to spend a year traveling. I'm taking a sabbatical from everything. I just…" Leilani shrugged and closed her eyes. "I need to purge and refresh myself."

"What? You think you're Julia Roberts now?" Camille asked and laughed.

"You don't understand," she said and closed her eyes. "This year has to been *too* crazy. I need a break from *every*thing," Leilani explained. "I can't go a day without thinking about Evan... about my marriage failing, about what happened to you, about Cheryl and-and Russell. I just..." She paused. "I really need to just dump all this out of my soul and be renewed."

"Any guests welcome?" Camille hopefully inquired with a friendly grin.

"*Absolutely* and *positively* not," Leilani replied. "This is for me and me only."

"When do you leave?" Camille asked.

"In a few weeks. So, that is more than enough time for you can get settled back into your job at the office to keep things afloat. I have a stand-in colleague that will be taking over my patients. You've worked with him before, so you guys should get along just fine. Just *don't* screw him with your fast tail," Leilani said, shaking her finger at Camille.

They both laughed. Camille raised her eyebrows.

"Wait a second," Camille began. "You—you want me to just sit back in the office while you're out seeing the world? *Without* your bestie?" she complained.

Leilani nodded.

"Yes, *without* you and don't go calling yourself a bestie yet. Just cause we're laughing and talking now doesn't mean we're back to being bosom buddies."

"What kinda shit is this?" Camille exclaimed.

Leilani shrugged.

"The kind of shit it just is, Camille. It doesn't work that easily."

"Well, I think if I came with, it'd be easier for us to be cool again like before," Camille said.

"You're not invited. No one is invited. This is *Leilani's* time," she said touching her chest. "Besides, be glad that I even hired your bipolar ass back."

Camille's mouth dropped open in shock and they both laughed. Camille sat back and crossed her arms beneath her breasts, forcefully pouting as Leilani continued to laugh at her.

"*Awwww, poor baby.*" Leilani laughed again. "Wait, let me think...do I have an extra ticket?" she asked reaching for her Louise Vuitton.

Camille's eyes lit up and Leilani laughed.

"Oops! I don't. Sorry, but you're counted out on this one. But, at least you got a job out the deal!"

Camille laughed.

"Fine. You just better send post cards," she replied.

Leilani nodded.

"I *most definitely* will. But, this is something that I have to do by myself," she said turning to stare at the moon. "Something I have to do alone," she said softly to herself.

Weeks Later

10:57 PM

Leilani began to meticulously lay her folded clothes into the Louise Vuitton duffle bags. She stopped for a moment and looked around, sighing in exhaustion and frustration at the stacks of luggage scattered around her living room. Taking this year long trip had turned out to be more than she could handle as far as packing was concerned.

She contemplated for a moment purchasing her belongings upon arrival to her destinations instead of lugging all of these items along with her. She glanced at her grandfather clock and sighed again. If she didn't finish tonight, whatever didn't make it into the luggage was going to be left behind.

Her doorbell chimed throughout her vaulted ceilings and she furrowed her eyebrows, glancing at her wristwatch. Leilani had no idea who would be visiting her this time of the night. Even though she and Camille had forgiven one another and were on cordial terms, she had not gotten to a point in their friendship that Leilani was comfortable enough to go back to exactly where they were.

Leilani loved her friend dearly, Camille was like a sister. But, even in relationships like these, it was always best to take a break from one another and re-establish your individual identity as the lines tend to become too crossed and blurred as to whose life is whose. They both needed this break.

Leilani was on a mission, so she ignored the chiming of her doorbell. If it didn't ring again, it was not important. To her surprise, it began to ring frantically and Leilani stomped to her front door – glancing through the peephole. Her pulse skipped a thousand beats and she immediately felt her breath escape her, her chest tightening and her lungs no longer expanding to allow freshness to enter her airway. She felt light headed. With a gulp, she opened the door.

"Evan?" she asked; utterly confused.

Leilani wasn't sure how he found out the address to her unlisted home; he only knew of the penthouse she was previously renting. But, then again, enough money can buy any piece of information. Evan's eyes were bloodshot, his skin flushed and his nostrils flared. He was intensely disheveled and stumbled into her foyer, his steps uneasy, his hand gripping at the wall to secure his balance.

Leilani watched him as he made his way into her living room and his body fell on her sofa. She went to him and stood across the room, creating a safe distance between them. Leilani was not sure of his intention for being there uninvited and unexpected, but she knew that it was best if she didn't come near him. Evan was back with his ex-wife and soon to be a father.

"Evan, what—what are you doing here?" she asked, breaking the silence between them.

He didn't look at her, he shook his head repeatedly.

"I, I can't...I can't.." he shook his head, his eyes filling with tears.

Leilani saw the tears spill from his beautiful eyes. She stepped closer slowly, cautiously.

"Evan, breathe," she said.

He looked like he was on the verge of a nervous breakdown and it frightened Leilani. Evan inhaled sharply, his entire torso moving with the struggled inhale. He fought for air and was nearly Hyperventilating. *Shit*, she thought. *This is fucking serious.* Leilani covered the space between them and sat next to him on the sofa, resting her hand gently on his back.

"Evan, what happened?" She watched him. "What happened?"

He shook his head, crying harder.

Leilani's mind immediately went to his wife who would be about seven months pregnant with his child.

"Is it Sophie?" she asked.

Evan nodded, struggling to breathe again and gasping for breath.

"She's—she's, oh God, she's dead," he choked out, his voice breaking into a sob.

Leilani couldn't control her response. *Holy fuck,* she thought and quickly moved away from Evan.

"*What*?" she exclaimed, nearly yelling.

"She's dead," Evan said, sobbing.

"What –what..." Leilani paused in disbelief. "What about the baby? Is the baby okay?"

Evan shook his head again.

"She..." He paused and stared ahead as the scene replayed vividly in his mind. "We were—we were at a restaurant and she was going on and on about us having more children and..." He shook his head. "I told her...I told her that I couldn't stay with her. I told—I told her that once she had my baby that I'd be leaving her. That I'd be going for full custody for my son. She just...she flipped out. She completely lost it."

He paused, his thoughts racing.

"What did she do?" she asked.

"Sophie went storming out of the restaurant and was threatening me. She was—she was screaming that if she couldn't have me that I would never see my son and that—that I would regret the day that I left her for the rest of my life."

Evan stopped talking, his eyes filling with tears again.

"I tried to talk to her. I pleaded with her to just calm down and for us to go home and discuss it when she wasn't being so emotional. Then she just…she just ran out into the street. She—" He sobbed. "She jumped in front of a bus."

Leilani gasped and covered her mouth in shock.

"Oh my God!" she exclaimed. "*What*?! Oh my God, Evan… I'm—oh my God, I'm so sorry. I'm *so* sorry," she said reaching and pulling him into her embrace.

Evan sobbed harder, holding onto her for dear life.

"They couldn't save them. She—she had too much blood loss—her—her pelvis was completely crushed and she—she just bled out internally—she flat lined. She coded five times." He looked into Leilani's eyes, "She killed my son, Lei. She killed my son right in front of me," he said in between gut-wrenching tears. "How could someone be so evil? How could she be so cruel?"

"Shh," Leilani said softly. "Calm down, Evan," she comforted as she stroked his back. "Just breathe, Evan. It's going to be okay." Leilani closed her eyes, her heart aching for his loss. "It's all going to be okay. You couldn't stop her from hurting herself or your child. You couldn't stop her. It's not your fault."

Evan sobbed again.

"I shouldn't have told her I was leaving her. I should've just stayed with her," he said.

"Shh, just breathe. Just breathe," Leilani said softly. "Everything's going to be okay."

She held him until he calmed down and gently pulled away from his grip, looking at him.

"Hey," she said, reaching up to stroke his cheek.

They looked into each other's eyes and Evan gazed at her in silence.

"I'm better now that I'm here. With you," he said.

She stared at him and gulped.

"I'm glad you feel better. How did you get here? Are you well enough to drive?" she asked.

Evan gazed into her eyes.

"I'm glad you're here, Leilani," he said quietly, his hand touching her thigh.

Leilani casually pushed his hand away, stood and walked to her office. She went to the rolodex on her desk, flipping through it for a card. She heard his footsteps behind her.

"Evan, I'd still suggest you go see someone—a—a grief counselor to help you come to terms with this. Just one night isn't going to fix everything. It's going to—it's going to take much more than just a few minutes here with me," she explained.

She he pulled out the card and turned, gasping at how close he was to her. Leilani nervously cleared her throat, leaning backward; the desk's solidness stopping her from moving away.

"Um, here's a colleague of mine. He's a psychiatrist and—and specializes in grief counseling. He'd…"

She paused when she felt his hand touch her cheek. Leilani gently pushed his hand away.

"He'd be great for you to—to go see immediately," she continued, moving past him and walking back into the living room as he followed.

Leilani turned to look at Evan. He was hot on her tail and Leilani backed away, bumping into a wall. Evan gazed down at her, the redness of his eyes was beginning to fade and their vivid color was becoming more visible. She cleared her throat. The air was thick with awkward silence. Leilani could feel the heat between their bodies building as her pulse began to pick up its pace.

"Um, I hope that you're able to get through this. This is going to be very difficult and I'm so sorry for your loss, Evan. I can't…I can't even begin to fathom what you're feeling emotionally. But, I am truly sorry for what has happened and I wouldn't wish this on anyone," Leilani continued.

Evan sighed deeply.

"I'm glad you are still so wonderful," he said softly. "That's why I needed to see you. That's why you are the person I needed to be with right now. No one else could help me like you can. You have no idea how much you make a difference in my life."

Leilani watched him for a moment and inhaled deeply.

"Evan," she began.

"Leilani," he said softly. "Do you want to know why I told her I was leaving for good?"

Leilani raised a brow.

"No, I don't want to know." She paused. "And I pray that it wasn't because of me," she answered quickly, attempting to move her body forward so he'd back away.

Evan didn't move.

"You don't know how much I think about you. Even now— after—after all this happened, you're the first person I needed to get to—the person that I needed to see. I need you." He gazed at her for a moment. "I love you, Leilani."

Leilani looked away, searching for an easy escape. Her heart was pounding against her breastbone.

"Did you hear me? I love you," he repeated, stepping forward.

She closed her eyes and held her hands up, keeping him from moving closer.

"Evan, stop," she said firmly. "Just stop this."

He laughed nervously.

"Why are you being so...so cold?" he asked.

Leilani forcefully moved her body towards him, giving Evan no other option than to give her space. She walked away from him shaking her head as he watched her.

"You don't love me?" Evan asked.

"Evan, you just lost your wife and—and your child. You're talking irrationally. This—this is just your way of grieving and

I refuse to be a part of that process—in *that* way. I will be here for you for advice, for a shoulder to cry on, as a strictly platonic friend, but not..." She shook her head. "Definitely not like this."

He furrowed his eyebrows.

"Lei, I just told you that I'm in love with you."

She scoffed.

"You don't love me!" Leilani yelled. "So just stop saying that! You *don't* love me, Evan!"

He came towards her, pulling her to him and pressing his lips against hers. Leilani shoved him away and slapped him across the face.

"Don't you dare," she seethed.

He stared at her in disbelief.

"Why are you angry with me?" Evan asked, his lips trembling.

"Evan, why did you even come here? Huh? Why—why didn't you go to Sophie's family? You just disappeared? Have you even called them? Do they even know their daughter is dead? Have you done *any* of that? Or did you just come straight here thinking that I'd fuck your tears away?" Leilani snapped.

His eyes filled with tears again.

"Is that what you think this was about?" he asked. "I didn't come here for sex. I came here because I love you and—and I can't bear to lose another person in my life that means something to me. You mean so much to me, Leilani. I can't lose you too."

Leilani wiped her lips of his saliva, disgusted.

"Evan, just get out. Go back home, call Sophie's family, call your family, grieve with them, plan a lovely funeral, go see a counselor and move on with your life."

He stared at her and looked away, noticing the luggage scattered around her living room. His heart ached and his chest grew tight. He did not understand why she was behaving distant.

"Lei, why are you—why are you treating me like this? You're acting as if I never mattered to you."

She inhaled deeply.

"There isn't anything here for you anymore," she said.

"Where are you going?" he asked suddenly.

She furrowed her eyebrows. "Excuse me?"

"All of this luggage?" he asked, gesturing.

Leilani sighed.

"I'm leaving, Evan."

He looked at her, his eyes wide with fear.

"And going where?" He shook his head. "You can't leave! Where are you going?" he demanded.

"None of your goddamn business!" Leilani yelled in return.

He was quiet for a moment as he looked around, silently counting the pieces scattered about the hardwood floors.

Evan raised an eyebrow.

"Are you—are you coming back?" he asked.

"No," she lied, crossing her arms underneath her breasts. "I'm not."

He stared at her luggage and then nodded.

"So, what? This…this is it?" he asked.

"Evan," Leilani said and closed her eyes for a moment. "It's been it for a long while now."

He looked at her and Leilani could see the tears filling his eyes again. Evan cleared his throat, forcing them down and shifted his stance.

"Leilani," he gulped. "You can't leave. I can't lose you too."

She stared at him for a moment and felt pity for the hurt he was feeling. But, she had to tell the truth, no matter how heavy the weight of its harshness.

Leilani inhaled deeply.

"Evan, you never had me," she confessed.

Leilani watched his eyebrows twist in pain at her words and his nostrils flared as he attempted to hold down the tears. She couldn't allow herself to give in to comforting him in this manner. She knew he was hurting, but she knew it would also not be wise to mask over his pain with intimacy. Evan didn't need that—even though his brain was telling him that was the solution to his minimizing his anguish. He cleared his throat and wiped the tears from his eyes.

"Um…" Evan cleared his throat again. "I uh, I guess…" He inhaled deeply. "I'll uh—I'll be leaving now."

He walked towards her front door and Leilani followed him. Evan didn't stop; he continued walking and opened her door to freeze in his tracks. He and Darnell stared at each other. They both scanned one another from head to toe. Evan's heart sank farther and he realized why Leilani was being insensitive towards his plight for her love.

Evan turned, blocking Leilani's view of Darnell.

"One last request," Evan said.

Leilani stared into his eyes.

"Can I get at least get a goodbye kiss?" Evan asked, even though it was more of a plea.

Leilani gulped. "I don't think that's a good—"

Evan stopped her from speaking the moment his lips pressed against hers, seducing her to spread them and begin to dance her tongue with his. She moaned and felt her knees grow weak. *This man kisses like his life depended on it*, she thought. Evan felt his eyes sting with more tears. He was losing Leilani and he knew this would possibly be the last time that he would see her again, feel her close to him and enjoy her existence.

Evan felt his eyes fill with tears, so he pulled away sharply and stared down at Leilani's flushed face, her eyes still closed; her lips gaped and puckered from his kiss. She felt the breeze brush past her lips and opened her eyes, looking at Evan.

"I am really going to miss you, *Mrs.* Mathews," Evan said softly, stroking her cheek.

Leilani was speechless as Evan turned to exit, his eyes meeting Darnell's.

"Congrats, man. I wish you two the best," Evan said.

Leilani's eyes widened when she saw Darnell standing there. Darnell stepped inside and smirked.

"White boy's got some big balls," Darnell said grinning as he shut the door behind Evan. "You must've really did a number on him though cause I think I even saw his ass crying."

She rolled her eyes, coming down from her brief high.

"What is this? The soul train line?" Leilani complained.

She watched Darnell for a moment as he took off his jacket.

"What are you doing here, Darnell? In case you don't remember, this isn't *our* house anymore," she said.

Darnell raised his hands in surrender.

"Hey, I just came here to talk. I didn't expect to run into Meet Joe Black on my way out," he said.

Leilani rolled her eyes. "Don't start."

"For real though, is that the white dude you left me for?" Darnell asked.

"I didn't leave you for *any*one. I left you cause' you were a terrible husband, Darnell," she snapped, placing her hands on her hips.

Darnell raised an eyebrow and nodded.

"I guess I deserved that one," he said.

Leilani sighed and walked into her living room, sitting down. She watched Darnell as he entered the room and sat beside her.

"What do you want, Darnell? I have things to do," she asked.

"I'm just stopping by. I was out with a few co-workers and they got to talking about their spouses and families and it got me to thinking about you. A few of them even asked about you and about us," Darnell explained.

Leilani raised her eyebrows and smirked.

"I hope you told them there was no more *us*," she said.

"*Damn*, it's not even like that. I just came to see how you were doing," Darnell said.

They stared at each other for a moment and Leilani looked away, shaking her head.

"Darnell, you know you're not welcome here," she said.

"Trust me. I know where I stand with you. I know it's over," he replied.

"So why are you here?" she asked with raised brows.

Darnell shifted in his seated position.

"Believe it or not, just cause' you're divorced doesn't mean you completely forget the person you love. I still care about your well-being, Lei."

Leilani shook her head and laughed.

"Now *that's* comical cause' you never did when we were married unless it interfered with something you wanted to do," she snapped.

Darnell nodded.

"I see how this is gonna be. How long are you gonna hate me?" he asked.

She stood.

"I don't hate you, Darnell. I never hated you. I just got tired of your bullshit."

He stood with her.

"My bullshit?" he asked.

"Yes. Darnell, you…" Leilani paused for a moment and licked her lips. "You treated me like shit. Like you could care less if I was dead or alive. Every moment of our marriage, I second guessed if you even loved me in the first place. I never even knew why you married me. And honestly, I still don't know why."

"Lei, I never hurt you," Darnell said.

"Really? *Never*?" she asked. "You never made me feel like I didn't matter—like everything else meant more than me? You never abandoned me constantly – in times that I needed you the most? You never disregarded everything I felt—and everything that meant something to me in our relationship? Did you ever respect my wishes for you to act like my husband or did you constantly just criticize me and how you felt that I was *so* insecure?" she elaborated as her emotions welled.

Darnell stared at Leilani, seeing tears filling her eyes.

Leilani blinked the tears away and turned.

"Darnell, you're right. You never cheated on me as far as I could prove… You never hit on me, and you never physically mistreated me. But, *emotionally*, you really did a number and I don't know if I can ever forget that because I deserved *none* of it. I was a damn good wife to you. I gave you everything that you ever wanted – everything that you asked for, I did to the best of my ability. But, it was never good enough for you. I was never good enough for you. You always were looking for better and…" She shrugged. "I got tired of trying to compete with whatever image of a wife you felt you deserved."

Darnell shook his head. "It wasn't even like that."

Leilani smirked. "You sure fooled me," she said.

Darnell's eyes skimmed over her frame.

"Lei, you don't know how much I loved you and how much you meant to me."

She looked at him and glared, raising her finger at him.

"You're exactly right. I never knew because you *never* showed it," she said, roughly nudging his forehead.

Darnell gulped, their eyes locked with each other. He inhaled deeply and scratched his head, breaking the contact.

He cleared his throat.

"Well, so much for my visit," he said.

Leilani rolled her eyes.

"I don't know why you came by here in the first place. You should've kept driving," she retorted.

He looked at her, his eyes skimming over her frame again.

"You really have a way of shutting people down," Darnell said.

Leilani smirked. "Trust me, the feeling's mutual."

Awkward silence.

"Is that why you don't return my calls or my texts?" he asked.

Leilani inhaled deeply.

"We're divorced, Darnell. So, why should I keep in touch with you?"

He raised his eyebrows.

"Because at one point in our lives, we did mean a lot to each other," he said.

She exhaled.

"That doesn't mean I owe you anything. I gave a lot of myself to you and to be honest, you didn't know what to do with it at that point in our life when *you* meant a lot to me cause' I've never meant a lot to you. I was a convenience."

Darnell watched her for a moment.

"Did I really make you feel worthless?" he asked.

She raised her eyebrows and nodded.

"You were a pro at it. You don't know how uncomfortable I was around you. I had to build up the courage to even touch you or come near you," Leilani answered.

She smirked at herself in embarrassment of how she used to be with Darnell.

"I'm sorry. I didn't realize that I was that cold towards you," he said.

She shrugged.

"Darnell, we just needed to be apart. You weren't happy with who you married and I was trying too hard to get you to see how great of a woman I am. It took me all those years to realize that *you'd* have to realize that on your own. And…" Leilani sighed. "You just never did and I couldn't waste my life waiting for you to."

He stared at her.

"I did love you…I still do, Lei. But, I guess I just never learned how to show it. I really didn't mean to hurt you the way that I did. I never even realized how much I was even hurting you in the first place. You acted like you didn't need my attention or my reassurance. You were always *so* independent. You were such a strong woman that I never knew this meant that much to you."

"Strong? Yes. But, even the strongest person has their kryptonite and even though I never said anything, I did need you to be there for me, Darnell. I always did. I just never felt like I had to ask you for it. I felt that was something you should want to do out of love for me. I had a lot of adjusting to do when I was with you. I learned to be alone and to not *need* affection. It's become a blessing and a curse for me now," she explained.

Darnell was silent, he cleared his throat.

"Is that why you left him?" he asked.

"Left who?" she replied.

"Mr. European GQ model himself," Darnell said with a roll of his eyes.

Leilani sighed.

"His name is Evan, *thank you*. And I chose not to be with him. I'm too mixed up emotionally. I'd ruin any relationship that could be something before it even got started out of my own negative views of men… It just wouldn't have worked and to be honest, it won't work with anyone for a long time until I learn that men are actually capable of being genuinely loving and caring without wanting something in return," she said.

Darnell raised his eyebrows.

"Damn," he muttered and exhaled deeply. "I'm sorry Leilani." She shrugged.

"You didn't change me, Darnell. I changed me to be with you and I should never have done that in the first place. We just didn't belong together," she elaborated.

Darnell watched her as she paced in her satin pajamas. Leilani was always sexy to him, not only in her looks but in the way she carried herself. He didn't feel he had the need to remind her of how beautiful of a woman she was – because it was evident in all of her encounters with men and women.

"We should try to be friends, Lei," he suggested.

She stopped pacing and looked at him.

"Friends?" she asked.

Darnell nodded.

"At least if we can't be married anymore, no reason we can't learn to be friends. Maybe we'd be better at that with each other," he explained.

She laughed and put a hand on her hip.

"You're serious?"

He nodded again and smiled slightly.

"I am. We've known one another for over ten years, no reason we shouldn't be able to be cordial," he said.

Leilani inhaled deeply.

"Darnell, I don't know—"

"I'm not gonna try to be friends with benefits. Even though that's tempting as hell and I know I'd still want more than anything to be able to have that with you."

They both laughed.

"But, no. We're adults and I think with all that we've been through with our friends and in our lives that we should at least give it a shot," Darnell finished.

Leilani silently contemplated and Darnell could see the hesitation on her expression.

"What do we have to lose?" he asked.

She stared at him and nodded with a slight shrug.

"You're right about that one," she said.

Darnell glanced at his wristwatch.

"Well, tomorrow's Saturday. I don't have to work and I'm sure you don't either. Let's have a night cap and chit chat for a while. Catch up. I'd like to hear all about *Evan*," he said.

Leilani laughed.

"Evan can stay *my* business. Anyway, Mr. Workaholic is finally taking a day off? Say it ain't so," she teased.

Darnell held his hands up.

"What can I say? After you divorced me, it put some things into a much clearer perspective."

"Too bad it took a divorce to make that happen," Leilani muttered. "What's the *real* reason?"

Darnell chuckled.

"I fly out tomorrow afternoon for a conference," he admitted.

Leilani nodded. "I knew it…" she said.

They both laughed. Darnell followed her into the kitchen, watching Leilani turn on the Electrolux and place a teapot atop one of the burners.

"Care for some hot cocoa?" she asked.

"*Hot cocoa?*" Darnell furrowed his eyebrows. "I said a nightcap, not a PG thirteen sleepover!" he said.

Leilani raised an eyebrow.

"I've given up on the alcohol for a while and besides, I don't think it's wise for us to add the special juice to any of our one-on-one *unsupervised* interactions," she said.

Darnell shrugged.

"Alright then, I guess I'll settle for some hot chocolate then," he said.

"Good cause' if not, I was going to politely ask you to excuse yourself cause I don't know what type of party you thought this was gonna be," Leilani snapped.

They both laughed. Darnell watched her for a moment as Leilani tended to her activity of pulling out two mugs and spoons along with the container of Ghirardelli hot chocolate mix. Darnell went to Leilani and wrapped his arms around her from behind, causing Leilani to hold still for a moment and close her eyes in response to his warm embrace. Despite the failure of their relationship, she still loved Darnell and at times, she still did miss Darnell. She'd never admit it to him, but she knew deep in her heart that he'd always be her first love.

Darnell inhaled, taking in her sweet scent of lavender and peppermint.

"I'll always love you, Lei," he said. "You are one of a kind."

Leilani inhaled quickly. She briefly panicked with the thought that Darnell would attempt to rekindle their previous injurious courtship. She wanted to stop him in his tracks if that was his unspoken intention.

"Darnell, you don't have to..."

He interjected, not allowing her to continue.

"I want you to remember that. From the bottom of my heart, I never realized what I had until I lost you. But, I will always— *always* love you. You are an amazing woman and I just wish that I had seen that before you walked away," he finished. "You deserve a man that will cherish you."

Leilani felt tears sting her eyes, but she forced them away, taking in a deep breath and patting Darnell's hands for him to release her. She turned to look at him and cleared her throat, forcing down the tears. She noted the ones that were creeping into Darnell's eyes. She reached up and wiped the moisture from their corners, giving Darnell a warm smile.

"Thank you," she said quietly. "That means a lot to hear that from you."

He nodded, kissing her softly on the forehead and sniffed, clearing his throat and stepping away from her.

"So! Uh, what's on the agenda for the night since ole' boy is off limits?" Darnell asked.

"Well, I have a lot of packing to do," she said.

"That's right," Darnell said with a smile. "Your world trip, I forgot all about that."

Leilani looked at him and furrowed her eyebrows.

"How'd you know about that?" she asked.

"I called the office to speak to you the other day but you were in a surgery. Your assistant told me all the details."

Leilani shook her head, rolling her eyes in disgust.

"*That* woman!" she exclaimed. "I swear for Lord she's like the walking National Enquirer," she muttered with a smirk.

She turned and began to return to the living room as Darnell followed, forcing his eyes to not focus on the switch of her lower half against the satin fabric.

"So," she slapped her hands together. "You can start with this pile of clothes going in *that* suitcase," she said pointing.

Darnell's eyes opened wide.

"Hold up! You were serious about me helping you pack?" he asked with a laugh.

Leilani looked at him and raised her eyebrows.

"What did you think this was; a free sleepover? I don't even think so. Get to work, *friend.*" she replied.

About the Author

Kaya was born and raised in the Midwest, where she lives with her two young sons. She enjoys romantic movies and talking with her friends and family about God, life, and love. When she isn't busy being a mother and a daydreaming enthusiast, she spends her time working in the renewable energy industry to better our planet.